PRAISE FOR
THE LUCY HOWARD MYSTERY SERIES

"In her latest novel, Nichols takes readers on a wild ride with a charming protagonist who discovers honesty may not always be the best policy when it comes to murder. But when it comes to love, truth matters."

–Gaby Anderson, author of *South of Happily*

"Nichols creates a cast of funny eccentrics who are in way over their heads when it comes to star-crossed teen lovers and murderous family members."

–Kim Conrey, author of *Stealing Ares*

"I absolutely loved this book with its twists and turns. The characters are so well done and developed which makes the book come alive. The poignant message at the end was an eye-opening surprise that spoke to my heart personally."

–Amazon Review

"Be still when you have nothing to say; when genuine passion moves you, say what you've got to say, and say it hot."
–D. H. Lawrence

Thanks to my family, critique group, and all the people who believed I could say it hot.

A LUCY HOWARD MYSTERY

CANCELED POLICIES

LIES IN LOVE AND INSURANCE

KATHERINE NICHOLS

Black Rose Writing | Texas

ISBN: 978-1-68513-514-0
PUBLISHED BY BLACK ROSE WRITING
www.blackrosewriting.com

Printed in the United States of America
Suggested Retail Price (SRP) $21.95

Canceled Policies is printed in Calluna

*As a planet-friendly publisher, Black Rose Writing does its best to eliminate unnecessary waste to reduce paper usage and energy costs, while never compromising the reading experience. As a result, the final word count vs. page count may not meet common expectations.

ACKNOWLEDGEMENTS

Writing can be a lonely venture. That's why it's so important for writers to have a support system. As always, the Wild Women Who Write (Gaby Anderson, Kim Conrey, and Lizbeth Jones) were with me throughout the writing of this book. They supplied critiques and much needed encouragement.

Without the understanding of my husband, I most likely would never have finished this book. He handles most of the details of our busy life while I struggle with getting words on the page. My beautiful daughters, Laura and Kate, lift my spirits when they express pride in my work. And my grandchildren are the perfect distractions whenever I need to back away from the laptop.

Special thanks go to Reagan Roethe, head of Black Rose Writing, for continuing to support my writing. Cover designer David King's patience with me in finding the best way to convey the spirit of my writing has been essential in helping me find the right audience. I also want to thank Justin Weeks in sales for his advice on marketing and his quick responses to my questions.

Most important of all, I want to thank my readers.

CANCELED
POLICIES

CHAPTER 1

A gust of autumn wind dumped an avalanche of leaves directly onto my windshield. These dew-damp reminders of the end of summer fell in sticky clumps. I fought the temptation to turn on my wipers, aware of the snail trails of grit and grime they would leave behind. Later in the day, they would be dry and blow away on their own. All I had to do was wait.

But, as anyone who knows me will testify, Lucy Howard is not a waiting kind of girl. I tend to make decisions quickly, then just as quickly begin to question them. Everything from my choice of career to picking the right man has always been subject to this self-defeating process.

I'd almost quashed my doubts about abandoning my former dream of working as a curator of documents in a well-respected museum. Instead, I accepted the opportunity to become partner in an insurance investigation firm. Lured by the glamor of endless stakeouts and rummaging through suspects' garbage, I realized despite the drawbacks, I would never be bored in this line of work.

When it came to falling in love, my insistence on complete honesty hadn't exactly been an asset. From employing interrogation techniques to running background checks, nothing eased my mind about the trustworthiness of the men I dated. Until I met Mr. Perfect, a man so far out of my league I couldn't believe my luck. And I shouldn't have.

He not only humiliated me and broke my heart, but he also put my life in danger. Beneath his façade of perfection, he was a coward and a crook.

A strong breeze flurried around me, bringing with it an unseasonal chill. The image of the Wicked Witch carrying Toto away on her bicycle came to me. My cell phone startled me with its tinny rendition of "Who Are You." Normally, the song amused me. Today, it brought with it a different sort of chill.

"Don't answer it," I told myself. "Just let it go to voicemail."

For a moment I wondered if the ESP my favorite uncle insisted he possessed had rubbed off on me. Since he only mentioned his premonitions after they occurred, his record for accuracy was questionable, but I believed in him.

Still, ignoring a caller, even when it was designated unknown, wasn't my style. Like my insistence on transparency, the trait often caused trouble. From habit or ingrained pessimism, I automatically assumed it was the hospital notifying me of some terrible accident Mom or Dad or both were in. Or any number of other disasters.

Instead of a human response to my cautious hello, a recorded message began.

This is a collect call from—a click and pause before a familiar voice identified itself. The recording continued. *Select one to accept. If you do not wish to*—

I hung up before hearing my second choice because there were no options available when it came to the only prisoner who would want to contact me. It had to be Lance Crawford. The man who stomped on my dignity, destroyed my trust, and almost turned me into the worst kind of fool, a dead one.

· · ·

An irrational fear that simply thinking about him would conjure up my ex brought on a case of the shudders. I scanned my surroundings, then double-timed it into the building.

This morning, the reception desk was empty, giving the place an eerie vibe that matched my mood.

Elsie Erikson, once a con woman now an investigator and office manager for Farewell and Associates, usually arrived at least an hour earlier than anyone else. She filled in out front until our intern arrived.

In her late sixties, she radiated a tranquil strength, and I needed a heavy dose of it to shake my growing sense of doom. So, I turned down the hallway toward her office. My anxiety increased when I discovered her closed door. She was a strong proponent of creating a welcoming space with no physical barriers separating staff members. So, my grim imagination ran free and wild. Visions of her stroked out on the floor or being held captive by a hulking masked man flooded my brain.

"Paranoia is my enemy." I whispered the mantra given to me by the therapist my mother talked me into seeing after I was almost murdered. Other than remembering her smooth, round face and wire-rimmed glasses, the doctor became a blur to me. Most likely because I dropped out after my third visit. She was pleasant enough but only half right. Yes, paranoia often was an enemy. But if they were really out to get me, it could also be my best friend.

I reached into my purse for my phone and selected Elsie from my contacts. A muffled sound from inside the room stopped me from completing the call. My heart pulsed in my ears, and my mouth turned dry. In a ridiculous parody of an old detective movie, I pressed my ear against the heavy wooden panels and listened.

There was no mistaking the rich contralto of her voice, but I couldn't make out her words. The other person sounded female and from the erratic pattern of her speech, she seemed frightened or upset. A sudden burst of sobbing confirmed my assessment.

More confused than concerned, I started to knock, then decided to give my friend the privacy she obviously wanted. Although we met over a year ago, I'd only really gotten to know her over the past few months. Somehow, though, she filled a grandmother void I hadn't realized existed. My mother's parents died before I was born. My dad's father fell off a tractor, hit his head on a rock, and was dead before the next sunset. His wife had been a schoolteacher, stern but kind. After he passed, she lost interest in correcting our grammar and in just about everything else. She was gone long before her funeral.

Elsie became my go-to when I needed a different perspective or a pep-talk. She was my cheerleader and a source of comfort. And she had saved my life. If not for her quick response when she saw two masked women stuffing me into a van, it's doubtful I would be working at Farewell and Associates or anywhere else.

From the crescendo of sorrow coming from inside her office, I decided her plate was too full for me to pile on a little thing like my ex calling me from prison.

. . .

I didn't notice the splotches of printer ink on the sleeve of my brand-new cream-colored blazer until I extended my hand to greet Chuck Grover, one of my firm's top clients. Chuck's father owned a prosperous private investigation company in Atlanta. Unlike Farewell and Associates, his firm offered a wide spectrum of services. Suspect your husband is running around? Someone steal your copyright? Accused of sexual harassment in the workplace? Grover's got you covered.

Whether from an increasing lack of moral fiber or healthy cynicism in a competitive world, their business was booming. They focused on high-profile cases and trained a fleet of flashy private investigators who impressed clients with their expensive suits and shiny cars. Less well-dressed underlings got stuck with messy field work, like tailing and staking-out cheaters.

Because the Grovers liked the spotlight, low-level fraud held little interest for them. My boss Hugh Farewell thrived on these cases and appreciated referrals. For him, crooks were crooks regardless of the extent of the crime. The only time I'd known him to waver from his hardline approach was with Elsie. Instead of pushing for her to go to prison for a series of slip and fall jobs, he hired her as his assistant. With her help, we ferreted out badger games, where women trick men into compromising positions to blackmail them. She taught us about pigeon drops, a scheme that offers the mark an opportunity to share in "found" money for a small good-faith deposit as well as other complicated confidence schemes.

While not as thrilled as he was about nabbing petty criminals, setting things right for the victims satisfied my inherent need for justice. But days like this made me doubt my decision to turn down the position my family campaigned for me to take as a curator at the Atlanta History Center. I chose to join Hugh as his head of fieldwork. Although I was the only one in the department, he promised we would soon be expanding, and I could delegate the less glamorous aspects of the job, such as searching through trash, to the new hires. Six months later, I was still flying solo.

"It's a pleasure to meet you, Mr. Grover," I lied.

The only dealings I'd had with his agency were sitting in on contract negotiations with his father. My biggest concern had been stifling laughter when I first saw the man. With his protuberant eyes, pointed nose, and double chin, he resembled my uncle's overweight chihuahua Doris.

When Hugh roped me into taking the meeting with the son, I made some calls to get a feel for what working with him might involve.

I contacted the receptionist from my previous firm. Not one to hold back, she informed me Chuck Grover was the worst horn dog she'd ever encountered. "And believe me, I've seen more than my share."

Since she was well known for over-sharing salacious details about her love life, I believed her.

Next, I checked in with a friend who worked for another firm. She met Grover at an insurance conference and warned me to avoid being alone with him.

Finally, I called my best friend, Bethany.

"If it isn't Miss Lucy Howard, the most wonderful woman in the world." Her silky-smooth voice managed to be sensual and cool at the same time.

A natural redhead with an ivory complexion and full lips that curved upward even when she was angry, she commanded center stage in every room she entered. I became accustomed to fading into the background when the two of us went out together. The only occasion where she hadn't overshadowed me was when I met the former love of my life. Despite how badly that relationship ended—with him in jail for his role in an organ-selling operation and me almost getting killed by his girlfriend—the memory of that night still stroked my ego. He had chosen me over Bethany.

Jesus! Taking pride in being selected as a woman he could lie to and cheat on. How pathetic is that?

"I thought it was the entire universe. Is there a reason for my demotion?"

"Nothing that can't be fixed. Remember when we discussed how you were going to hostess a party for me?"

Although a prosperous real estate agent, she supplemented her income with a sideline gig, selling sex toys for Sensual Secrets. Last year, she talked me into ordering what was supposed to be a tasteful personal massager. I only agreed to the purchase because she promised to select one guaranteed not to do me any serious bodily harm. It turned out to be a gigantic glow-in-the-dark penis that promised an out-of-body experience. The only time I attempted to use it was when the lights went out and my flashlight was in the other room. Instead of shedding light, the stupid thing made a whirring sound and died.

When she asked me if I'd taken it for a test drive, I explained it had failed to deliver.

She gave me a shocked look. "Are you sure you pressed power? Because if you don't turn it on properly, it won't return the favor."

"Since when did you start talking like a sex robot? I may be sexually awkward, but I know how to press the on button."

"It's called the blast-off button."

"Whatever it's called, I pushed it, and it sputtered a second or two before dying out."

"I've known men like that. But fortunately for you, all our products come with a money-back guarantee. Wrap it up, and I'll return it for you."

I stuck it in my underwear drawer and forgot all about the thing.

Today, my friend explained that the sex toy enterprise had hit a slow phase. She attributed the decline to people getting out and about more after the end of the Covid epidemic. Because her products were so spot-on, repeat orders were dwindling. And so was her list of suckers willing to play hostess to gaggles of unfulfilled women.

I groaned inwardly while she extolled the benefits of the role and rattled off available dates.

"My schedule is crazy, but I'll email a date to you as soon as I can. Pinky-swear."

"I'm going to hold you to it. Oh, and I haven't forgotten about that faulty product. I want to check it out before I send it back. And we can apply the refund to future purchases."

I sighed my agreement, then asked if she'd heard anything about Chuck Grover.

"He's a self-entitled prick. Worse, he may be a rapist."

"Wait a second. He *may* be a rapist? Either he is or he isn't, right?"

She explained a friend of a friend dated him a few times. When she grew tired of him checking himself out in every mirror they passed, she broke it off.

"The rumor is he got rough with her. She didn't press charges, so there's no way to know for sure what happened, but I'd steer clear of the asshole."

Today, gripped in a firm handshake with said asshole, I decided he must have taken after his mother. His thick, sandy brown hair matched the color of his wide-set eyes. Below a straight thin nose, his lips formed an unexpected cupid bow that escaped looking too feminine because of the well-trimmed mustache above it. His only resemblance to his father was the beginning of a double chin.

"The pleasure is all mine." He lifted my hand, and for an awkward moment, I feared he planned to kiss it. Instead, he covered it with both of his. I wriggled out of his grasp and made a mental note to douse myself with the lilac sanitizer on my desk as soon as he left.

"I hope you won't think I'm being inappropriate, but you are a stunning woman."

My wavy brown hair is shoulder length with golden highlights, my eyes are greenish-gold, and the freckles sprinkled across my nose and cheeks aren't unappealing. But stunning was pushing it.

I pretended not to hear him and walked to the stairs. Although uncomfortable with him walking behind me, I had no choice but to lead him to my upstairs office. Remembering my friend's advice, I kept the door open.

"Nice view."

He leered and took a few steps toward me. Clearly, this was not a man impressed by the blazing colors of the maple tree reflected in the pond. Nor would he appreciate the simple beauty of the plump geese gliding on the surface of the still water. I wished those birds would pluck Chuck Grover up and fly north with him.

I ignored his cheesy line and slid behind my desk. "Yes, it is beautiful here. Please, have a seat."

Sunlight illuminated the brilliant oranges and pinks of the tree beside the pond below. The geese floating on the surface would be gone in a few weeks, and the water would be littered with leaves. But at this moment, all was painfully lovely.

I returned to the very unlovely scene playing out in front of me and watched as he settled onto the only other chair in the room.

"So, how can we assist you today?"

"Did you hear about the guy who fell from his office last week?"

If I hadn't read about it in the paper, I would have waited for the punchline his eager delivery promised. The article caught my eye because of the picture next to it. The dead man wore a tuxedo and a slender woman in an evening gown. He beamed at the camera in the way people do when they think they'll be young forever. Despite her plunging neckline and elaborate updo, she looked more like a sophomore at a senior prom. Sweet-faced with a shy smile and thick-lashed baby-doll eyes.

"He was an insurance salesman, right?"

"Ryan Miller was more than a salesman. He's the son of Edward Miller of the Miller Agency. The boy was heir to a fortune. More important, he was one of our own."

"So sorry for your loss."

He rearranged his perpetually self-satisfied expression into what I took as an attempt at something more appropriate, maybe sorrow or pain. "Thank you. We're all devastated, especially his poor father."

"I can't imagine how it must feel to lose a child. But I'm not sure exactly how we can help. Didn't the police say it was an accident?"

"That was the initial report. They're also considering the possibility he jumped."

"No," I said with irrational certainty. Nobody could fake a smile like the one on that young man's face. It etched his eyes with happy lines that would never have the chance to become permanent.

"Are you okay?" His voice startled me.

"I'm fine but still confused. Regardless of the final police report, his policy will provide for his wife, right?"

Our victim was an expert in the business. Even if I were wrong and he had killed himself, he would have taken care not to jeopardize a payout.

Grover narrowed his eyes.

"Providing for his beneficiary isn't the problem. You see, his father doesn't believe he jumped or fell. He's convinced someone pushed him and is certain the same person who stands to make millions from the boy's death is responsible. Miller wants you to prove that his daughter-in-law, Ashley, is a murderer."

CHAPTER 2

I stammered through the rest of my conversation with Chuck, promising I would discuss the matter with Hugh. His hand lingered on my back an uncomfortable extra second or two, but I managed to get him out of the office before it descended into the no-trespassing zone.

My first impulse was to run straight to Elsie for guidance on how to conduct a murder investigation. I doubted she had experience with this type of case, but she'd tracked down the crooked antiques dealer who swindled her nephew out of valuable family heirlooms after her sister died. And she faced down the women who wanted me and Lance dead. Her door was still closed, and I was in too much of a tizzy to eavesdrop again.

So, I called Hugh. As usual, my call went to voicemail, where I left a rambling message explaining the situation and my reluctance to be a part of it. Chuck's smarmy behavior would have been enough reason for me to beg off, but I could handle that. The prospect of delving into the death of a young man who might have been killed by the woman he loved, however, depressed the hell out of me. Plus, it was way over my pay grade.

My boss was working on a false injury case, and I had just closed the books on a babysitter who filed a claim against her employers. She said the loose carpet at the top of their steps caused her to fall and break her arm. We proved it had more to do with the pint of rum she consumed from their liquor cabinet. Other than taking care of some paperwork and updating our website, I had nothing going on, which meant my mind immediately turned to the call from Lance.

About a year and a half ago, my former boyfriend got involved with a hot colleague at his law firm. She talked him into teaming up with a local doctor and his nurse, who were part of an organ smuggling scheme. Hugh became suspicious about the number of appendectomy claims submitted by the doc's patients. We discovered he was offering money to desperate immigrants, mostly for kidneys, occasionally lungs. In turn, he sold his gruesome product for a profit. Lance created documents to make the process appear legal.

What my ex didn't know was the woman he was sleeping with had another lover, the doctor's nurse, a certifiable nut job who became dangerously jealous. Things were going well for the ghoulish team until my boss took on the case a few months after I caught my boyfriend in a compromising situation with his associate. There was no connection between the break-up and Hugh's discovery that Lance was a part of it, but I attributed the timing to karma.

The police found out the women had been responsible for the death of several elderly men. Because of their murderous past and our kidnapping, the judge gave them life with the possibility of parole in twenty. He went easier on my ex, sentencing him to five years. With good behavior, he could be on the streets in three.

I guessed that after hearing about Lance being strapped to a table while his female partners worked on their plan to kill me, then him—making it look like a murder-suicide—the judge had some sympathy for him. I made it clear I had none and never wanted to be in the same room with him ever again.

He knew this, so why did he think I would accept a collect call, or any other kind, from him?

Shouts from the direction of Elsie's office brought me to my feet.

I raced down the hallway and almost collided with a young girl wearing tight, dark jeans with a white, long-sleeved t-shirt. Her bluish black ponytail swung wildly as she shot past me.

"Honey, please come back." My co-worker joined me, but her visitor had already rounded the corner and disappeared.

I wrapped my arm around Elsie's shoulder. "Is there anything I can do?"

She shook her head. "I wish there were."

The tears spilling down her powdery cheek frightened me. We met when I entered her home under the pretense of getting her to sign a neighborhood safety petition. I was really there to find mitigating circumstances for the insurance fraud she committed. Elsie had me figured out from the second she saw me but played along like the cool crook she'd become.

That day her hands shook when she revealed the quilts her sister made over the years had been stolen by a deceptive antiques dealer. And she got a little misty-eyed when she told me how much her husband enjoyed a good bargain at the grocery store, but she recovered quickly. When it looked as if she might go to prison, she remained tearless and stoic. Seeing her cry now signaled how serious the problem was.

"Hey, did you forget who we are? I am Lucy Howard, protector of the innocent. And you are Elsie Erikson, the indomitable. Line-dancing queen and empress of your bowling team. Keeper of secrets and scourge of evil thieves. All we need is a plan. But first, tell me what's going on."

She straightened her shoulders and wiped her cheeks with her fingertips. "I guess our super-heroine status slipped my mind. Come on in and pull up a chair so we can get started righting some wrongs."

Once we settled in, she explained who the young visitor was and why she was so upset.

"The girl you saw hightailing out of here is my grandniece, Cody Rae. She's the daughter of my sister's only child, the one who got swindled out of our family treasures by that antiques-dealing crook."

Her tight-lipped smile suggested she was remembering how we'd helped the police catch that crook's killer and clear my uncle's name.

"I should have been mad at her daddy, but he can't help it if he's not playing with a full deck, at least not when it comes to business or picking wives. And we recovered the quilts and most of the Civil War relics. Anyway, he and Cody Rae's mom—she's a real piece of work—divorced a few years back. The poor kid didn't take it well. Not a surprise since her mother's been going from man to man, and her dad's always on the road with his job. I wanted to let her come stay with me, but the mother flipped out when I mentioned it. And her father had no idea what to do." She sighed and looked at her hands.

She was quiet for so long, I feared she might have completely lost her train of thought. "Is Cody Rae in some kind of trouble?"

"Not exactly, at least not right now."

The thundering sound of heavy boots echoed on the wood floor of the hallway. Within seconds, our boss bellowed, "Where the hell is everybody? Did I miss the email about this being a holiday?"

Elsie jumped up. "This is a terrible time to talk. Besides, it'd be good if you heard the story from her. Could you stop by after work?" She nodded in the direction of the footsteps. "For now, let's keep this between you and me, please."

"No worries. Hugh's the last person I'd go to for advice about a teenage girl."

She scurried to the front desk while I stopped Hugh before he could berate her for deserting her post.

"We were having a quiet, private discussion. Something you wouldn't understand. But I'm here now, and I need to discuss this Grover thing with you."

"What do you mean by *Grover thing*? Did that asshole make a move on you? I told his dad we'd only take a look at it if his shitbird son kept his hands to himself." His usual ruddy complexion flushed a dark red.

"Don't stroke out on me, Boss. I can handle that creep. It's the case itself that bothers me."

He turned and stomped away. I'd worked with him long enough to understand he expected me to follow. Inside his office, Hugh made his way past unpacked boxes of old files he would never need to a desk covered with yesterday's newspaper and coffee mug, half an unwrapped muffin, and an unknown substance I desperately wanted to believe was pipe tobacco. Somewhere underneath the rubble was an overflowing inbox. If there was an out one, I never saw it.

"Just toss that stuff over there." He motioned to a leather chair.

Throwing random paperwork was not my style. So, I arranged it into three neat stacks and placed them on an unopened cardboard box.

I caught a whiff of something other than my boss's unfinished breakfast. "Jeez, Hugh. This place stinks."

He pointed to the cluttered tarp lying on the floor behind his desk. Fast food wrappers, shredded paper, an empty soda can, and wadded tissues were scattered across it. "I sent the intern to collect the vic's trash. He was too late to get the garbage from his house, so all we have is this crap from his office."

I moved my chair as far from the smelly evidence as possible before sitting.

"If it's not worries about that pretentious jerk soiling your reputation, what *bothers* you about the Grover case?"

His sarcastic tone didn't surprise or annoy me. It was Hugh being his bad old self, which really wasn't all that bad or old. He had an image to maintain, and most of the time, I humored him. Not today.

"I'm concerned about the same thing you should be. The Miller agency has a lot of clout. They hired us to prove their daughter-in-law is responsible for their son's death. There's only one reason I can think of for the Grovers to do that, and it's to protect their firm from the possible blowback getting directly involved in police business might bring. We're the ones taking the risk. And what if we can't find evidence of her guilt? What if the woman is innocent, and we smear her reputation?"

"What if she isn't, and we assist the cops in catching the boy's killer? Either way, we make enough money to keep the lights on for a while. And I'm not without clout myself."

My face must have registered my continued objection.

"Hey, if it's that big a deal to you, how about I promise I won't ask you to do anything that puts you afoul of the law?"

"I've heard that one before. This time," I stood and glared at him, "I'm going to hold you to it."

He thwarted my dramatic exit.

"Wait a second, tough guy. I need you to put on your miniskirt and crop top tomorrow so you can pay a visit to Brookdale High."

I was momentarily stunned he knew the correct terminology for crop top although nobody referred to the tiny strips of cloth as miniskirts anymore. When I recovered, I asked, "Is that where the wife works?"

"Bingo!" He pumped his fist. "I've scheduled an appointment for you with Miss Tightass, the assistant principal."

I opened the folder he handed me. "And exactly why did Miss *Torrance* agree to see me, an insurance investigator, at 9:00 tomorrow morning?"

"I may have intimated you were working for the family on a tribute to their son and needed to speak to some of his wife's colleagues. Especially since his poor widow is too distraught to be coherent."

"You know, I wasn't all that crazy about high school the first time around. So, you owe me."

"Yeah, sure. Hey, wait. I almost forgot."

He rummaged through some of the papers on his desk and pulled out a plastic baggie.

"That useless intern managed to find something that might help us figure out what went on in the private lives of the young Millers."

I squinted at the contents, an unfolded matchbook. The words *Broadview Motel* were printed on the outside. Inside, someone had written in barely decipherable chicken scratch *room 213* and drawn a lopsided heart pierced by a very pointy arrow.

"What should I do with this?"

"Gee, I dunno. Maybe take up smoking? What do you think you're supposed to do with it? See if anybody we know spent quality time in the goddamn Broadview Motel."

I ignored the profanity and exited with the perfect amount of professional disdain. Unfortunately, it wasn't enough to make me feel the least bit better about looking for clues to pin a murder on a woman despised by her in-laws.

For the next hour and a half, I searched for potential reasons for their hatred. And found a big one.

A google search for *Ryan Miller newspaper photos* turned up several possibilities. The first and most interesting possibility was his engagement announcement. Handsome in an old money way—wavy blonde hair long enough to give him a youthful but not overly boyish appeal, pensive smile exposing straight white teeth, dress shirt unbuttoned at the top—the now-deceased insurance mogul stared at me. He stood behind a woman with locks that fell in curls over her bare shoulders. Her full lips stretched into a recklessly happy expression that lit her wide-set eyes and drew attention to her perfectly defined cheekbones. She exuded an energy the stiff about-to-be-married photo couldn't stifle.

The accompanying information was tastefully brief with only the when and where: three months from the date the picture was posted and Brookdale United Methodist Church. Other than the unusually attractive couple, there was nothing special about the article. Nothing except the bride-to-be wasn't Ashley Miller.

CHAPTER 3

If not for the ping of my phone announcing a text message, I'm not sure how long I would have kept digging for more information on the happy couple that wasn't.

It was Mateo Sullivan, the man my boss summoned to help find out if my sweet cross-dressing, narcoleptic Uncle Buddy had shot his rival in the antiques business.

He wore a tan cowboy hat that made him seem taller than his over six-foot frame. When he took it off, he revealed black wavy hair and dark brown eyes. But it was his voice that quickened my pulse. Smooth and slow, it flowed like thick hot fudge syrup.

Still reeling from my breakup with my cheating boyfriend, I was determined not to fall for him. We worked closely together to keep my uncle from being convicted of a murder he didn't commit, while sending my almost-fiancé to prison for crimes he did. Being with Mateo day and night, I learned to trust him as much as I was capable of.

The danger we encountered during the investigation heightened my senses. It intensified emotions and encouraged risky behavior, the type I had spent most of my adult life avoiding. With him, I found the courage to say *screw it* and ignore the possibility of heartbreak. Deep in my trembly soul, I faced down the fear that falling for him and losing him might break me. He became a quieting force during the wild ride our last year had been, and I realized he was the kind of man I could count on to be there to catch me. And he was.

Only sometimes, in the darkest hour of the night, I awoke from the fog of a troubling dream. Not frightening enough to be a nightmare, it swirled through my senses, leaving me twisting and turning with unidentified anxiety. I would reach out in a near panic to touch Mateo, comforted by his mumbling acknowledgement but unable to silence the raspy whisper of doubt wandering through the corridors of my mind.

As someone who had sacrificed herself on the altar of truth too many times to count, I knew he wasn't to blame for my doubts. He would never do anything to jeopardize what we had. No, that annoying itch in my brain was on me.

His text said he would be late getting home and not to hold dinner for him. I smiled for two reasons. When we began dating, he laughed at me for including emojis in my texts. When I explained those silly hearts or smiley faces brightened my day, he started adding them, ending today's message with a round yellow-faced character wearing a look of cartoon despair.

Not as touching but more amusing, was the idea of me holding dinner. We both knew my cooking sucked and that, at best, I'd be holding a takeout menu. That or a turkey sandwich with cheese.

As disappointed as I was about his late arrival, it would give me more time with Elsie and her grandniece and a chance to tell her about the case Hugh had thrust upon me. To deal with all the drama made me crave therapy, but not the mantra-creating kind. It demanded something hot and cheesy. So, I decided to pick up a pizza to share on my way to Elsie's.

After confirming Ryan Miller and the lovely Miss Fiona Adams hadn't gone through with their nuptials and later divorced, I checked to see if they had set up a website. While it was likely they had, it was also a good possibility she or one of her failed bridesmaids had removed it. I had to hope the wedding party had been too devastated or disorganized to revisit such a painful reminder of dreams denied.

If I hadn't been in such a hurry, I might have taken the time to wonder what it said about me that when I found them on The Love Knot, I gave myself a mental high five. As I read Fiona's version of their fairytale, I had the decency to experience a twinge of guilt at my original elation over hard evidence of their botched nuptials.

The couple started as friends in middle school, where Fiona described Ryan as shy but sweet. She quoted from her diary about their first kiss as freshmen.

"He tasted like a Baby Ruth."

And their first break-up that same year and how he turned away because he had tears in his eyes. They reunited after a week and vowed never to part.

By the time they graduated high school and decided to attend the same college, I began to worry I might go into a diabetic coma. But I never doubted her devotion to him, or maybe, like I had been, she was devoted to her idea of what the two of them should be.

Regardless, his much shorter account of their love story echoed its perfection. I suspected the bride-to-be was a co-author.

They were registered at Neiman, Nordstrom, Pottery Barn, and West Elm. And then they were over.

. . .

Elsie greeted me at the door and took the pizza from my hand.

"I didn't realize it would be so big."

"That's what she said. Oh my God. I'm turning into Hugh."

"Impossible. There's beer and soda in the fridge. Cody Rae's already got hers." She cut her eyes to the Coke Zero on a placemat in front of an empty seat. Elsie leaned closer and whispered, "She's washing up. I should warn you—"

The appearance of a petite creature with delicate features on her heart-shaped face interrupted her warning. I recognized the large tabby she held as Dr. Jekyll, Elsie's temperamental feline. I met the little doctor the day I tried to con my way into his owner's life to find out if she had committed insurance fraud. With her usual sharpness, she'd seen through my feeble attempt at outwitting her. Today, the cat narrowed his eyes in what could only be kitty suspicion, jumped from the young girl's arms, and shot down the hallway.

The overhead light cast a sheen over Cody Rae's long locks, creating a blue-black gloss, like a crow after a visit to the salon. The startling contrast with her flawless, pale complexion emphasized heavy-lashed emerald eyes.

She wore an oversized flannel shirt in baby-blanket shades of pink and lavender. Unbuttoned to expose the swell of her surprisingly well-endowed breasts, it evoked a very different image. I imagined her waking up one morning to discover not only had her assets developed overnight, but so had her influence over the opposite sex. The question became would she use her newfound power for good or evil, and, at her age, would she know the difference?

"Hey, honey," Elsie scurried to her side. "This is Miss Howard, the woman I told you about." She nudged the girl toward me. "And this is Cody Rae, my sister's granddaughter."

She tilted her chin upward and gazed at me with a challenging directness that made her seem older than she was. Her squared shoulders and straight-lipped expression gave off a defensive air, but the dark circles under those green eyes and the deep hollows below her sharp cheekbones told another story. My problem would be determining which version was the real deal.

"It's nice to meet you, Cody Rae. Please, call me Lucy." I reconsidered offering her my hand for fear the formal gesture might make her uncomfortable.

She remained stone-faced but surprised me by extending a stiff arm, turning me into the awkward one.

Elsie rescued me from the teenager's overly firm grip. "Let's eat first and talk after if that's okay." She turned to her grandniece, who shrugged and sat down. "Anyone need something to drink? I'm going to grab a beer."

"Make that two." I needed liquid courage to face this tiny teenager.

I gulped a third of the bottle before making a lame attempt to engage her in the conversation.

"How do you like school?" I tried.

She took off a piece of pepperoni and stuffed it in her mouth.

"Do you have a favorite subject? I always enjoyed my English classes." *Could I sound anymore nerdy?*

I expected a sneer or some other sign of scorn. But her dismissive shake of the head, accompanied by a request for more soda was somehow more humiliating. I didn't even warrant ridicule.

Elsie answered, "Maybe it's a little late for caffeine?"

I held my breath and waited for an eruption of sarcasm. But Cody Rae surprised me again.

"Okay, water it is." She pushed back from the table. "You sit. I'll get it. You don't need to wait on me, you know."

Her gentle tone and soft smile struck me as sincere. She filled her glass with ice, while I picked at the label of my almost empty bottle and scolded myself for being too quick to judge her as sullen and difficult.

"How about you, Miss Howard? I mean Lucy." She grinned and narrowed her eyes before turning them in the direction of my Corona Light. "I bet you could use another drink. I'm sure Aunt Elsie has something stronger if you need it."

That sounded great to me, but I wasn't going to reward her snarkiness, so I declined her offer and asked for a soda I didn't want.

A sigh of exhaustion escaped from me. If this is what parenting felt like, I would opt out, thank you.

Elsie patted my hand. "How did the meeting with Chuck Grover go? I hated that you had to deal with him yourself."

"It wasn't all that bad. Pretty boring stuff."

She arched an eyebrow. "Right. Dull insurance talk. You can fill me in later."

"She means after I leave the room." Cody Rae had been so quietly intent on the pizza—the kid ate like a dockworker—I'd almost forgotten she was there.

"That's not it, honey."

"It is exactly what you meant."

An unexpected laugh erupted from her lips. It sounded genuine, as if it was the result of real amusement.

"It's okay. I have homework and insurance talk is totally boring." She rose from the table and cleared her plate. "Anybody else in the mood for a brownie? I made them myself. From a box but still."

Her sudden shifts in tone and personality caused my head to spin, but I accepted the offer and waited as she removed the pan from a cooling rack and began cutting them into pieces with a butter knife.

"Are you sure you're all right with telling Lucy how you ended up at your crazy old great-aunt's house?"

Cody Rae broke off a piece of brownie, chewed, and swallowed before answering. "You can tell her."

"Of course, I could, but..."

"It's always better to hear a story as close to the source as possible. You know, for investigative purposes."

She squinted her eyes at me, and I waited for her to ask exactly what I meant by *investigative purposes?* Thankfully, she didn't because I had no clue how I would answer. It just sounded professional and objective enough that it might not spook a troubled kid.

"It's pretty simple. Mom's dated a long line of losers since she and Dad split up. Shirtless jerks who take up the whole sofa drinking beer and scratching themselves. One nerd from the bank where she works, but I think he was married. They were all mostly harmless. Until now. This time she's *in love*."

Scorn bordering on bitter hostility accompanied the two words that should have signified happy times were on the way.

The girl stabbed her brownie and shoved the plate away, then examined her cuticles for so long I decided I must have missed the official end of the story.

When she slapped her palms on the table, I jolted upright, slopping soda onto the embroidered placemat. "Anyway. Two's company and I'm the crowd. So, here I am."

"And I couldn't be happier about it." Elsie leaned forward and smoothed her grandniece's hair.

"Your mother's all right with your being here?" As soon as I heard myself, I cringed at how tone deaf the words were.

"Believe me, she's chill with it. According to Mommy dearest, she doesn't give a fuck where I go as long as I get my sneaky ass out of her house and stop trying to come between her and the only man she ever truly loved. To make sure I got the point, as I was leaving, she threw the asshole's tennis shoe at me."

Before I could decide if she was exaggerating the story for effect, she carried her plate to the sink and popped the remaining bite of brownie into her mouth. "Well, that homework isn't going to half-ass do itself. Is it okay if I grab a glass of milk?"

"Absolutely, dear. Didn't I tell you to help yourself to anything you want?"

When she faced the refrigerator, I noticed a red-clay smear on the back of her shirt. It wasn't until I stepped away that the smudge morphed into a familiar shape. It was the smeared sole of a tennis shoe.

CHAPTER 4

Elsie filled two glasses with Makers Mark and ice, then suggested we take them into the living room. I sat on one end of her floral sofa, surrounded by matching pillows. She took the other.

"I hate talking about this behind her back, but the child is bad about shutting down. It's hard to get her to speak about much of anything, especially anything concerning her home situation. That's the most I've heard her say since she showed up this morning."

"Is there any chance she could be making things sound worse than they are?"

"Her mother's been a mess for as long as I can remember. My sister was not at all thrilled with her son's choice. I don't doubt for a minute there's been a parade of trashy men marching through that house. But this one, *the only man she's ever truly loved?* Something's off about him."

I suspected the same thing when Cody Rae repeated what her mother said about her coming between the two of them. The words set off my creep alarm.

"I agree. It sounded as if he might have made a move on the girl."

Elsie gulped the rest of her drink and poured another. "If that son of a bitch hurt my baby, I'll cut his balls off."

Her threat startled me. Not because of her capacity for violence. She hadn't shied away from a little gunplay in her rescue of me from Lance's crazy co-conspirators. Her actions had been so perfectly timed it was months before I thought to ask how she knew where I was. In her soft, unassuming manner, she tried to say it was luck. When pressed, she explained she came to my office about her stolen quilts and had seen me being abducted. Without thinking, she followed the van, calling the police as she drove.

So, I wasn't shocked by her ferocity toward anyone who hurt someone she loved. Her referral to the male genitalia was, however, out of character for her. It signified there were no limits to what she would do to protect those people.

"She doesn't strike me as the type of person who would take any crap. Did she mention anything at all about the new boyfriend before I got here?"

"Only that he's a total douche, and they hate each other."

I threw back the rest of my bourbon and tried to imagine a scene where Mom tossed me to the curb. I couldn't.

"Good God. What about the father?"

"Gerald is in some podunk town where the cell service is terrible. But he won't have a problem with her staying here. And I want her with me. Art and I wanted children. We charted my cycle and tried all sorts of positions. Talk about taking the romance out of it. One doctor insisted all I needed to do was relax. Another suggested adoption as a cure since lots of women got pregnant after adopting a baby. We considered it, but by the time we were on the waiting list, we were too old. So, we gave up and decided we were enough, just the two of us."

She stared into the amber liquid in her glass as if searching for answers in tea leaves. In the year-and-a-half I'd known her, she'd shared snippets of her life with Art. I knew he loved BOGOs at the grocery store and rescuing starfish at the beach. And he was an excellent dancer. Now I had a hint of all the lost possibilities and longings his death left behind.

Tears welled in her eyes whenever she talked about him, which made me reluctant to ask questions. A rookie mistake for helping people you love deal with loss.

I had stumbled into friendship's no-woman's land. It was gratifying that she thought of me as someone she could trust. But I was helpless against the pain etched on her face. I imagined all the "what ifs" associated with that past. I had no words of comfort for the loss of a child that never was.

The only sound was the ticking of the mantle clock. Finally, she broke the silence.

"I'm afraid I won't be up to the challenge of dealing with a sixteen-year-old, especially one as beautiful and smart as she is."

The image of my friend tackling an armed woman who was at least fifty pounds heavier than she was crossed my mind. I remembered her fearlessness and wondered if I would be sitting here with her now had she hesitated.

But she didn't need another pep talk about how we were bad asses. She wasn't wrong to question her ability to handle a kid like Cody Rae, a girl whose mother put lowlife lovers above her daughter. And a father who chose his work over his child. She had a right to be a handful.

Despite her age, I had no doubt Elsie had the physical stamina to be there for her sister's granddaughter. It was more about having the emotional reserves and patience to handle the problems today's teenagers faced. I also suspected that for her it was partially about proving to her childless self that deep within she had what it took to be a mother.

"Elsie, I can't think of anyone better than you to take on someone who needs unconditional love and support. I know firsthand how good you are at that. And I seem to remember a gun-toting wild woman leaping from the supply closet to rescue me and Lance."

"Too bad I had to save that jackass, too. But facing down two crazy-assed armed women is a piece of cake compared to keeping up with my grandniece."

We spent the rest of the evening discussing the practical aspects of her situation. She lived in the same school district as Cody Rae, and the girl was doing well academically and socially. I almost spit out the sip of my second drink when Elsie told me the kid was on the cheerleading squad. After trying to picture her prancing around with a peppy grin, I decided she must be a different kind of cheerleader. More of a cheer boss who towered from the top of a human pyramid and shouted, "I said smile, goddammit," and everyone grimaced in response.

I assured my friend she had everything under control. "And I'll do anything I can to help."

I immediately regretted my hollow offer. It's what people say to make themselves feel better when they end up doing nothing at all.

"There is something you could do. Cody Rae's fall break is coming up next week. I'm worried about her sitting here moping or worse, hanging out with the wrong crowd. What if we asked Hugh to hire her to fill in for the intern? If it's a money problem, we can take it out of my salary."

"Thanks to our boss being a bit of a cheap ass, Farewell and Associates has plenty of cash. The issue will be how to get him to think it was his idea."

I finished my drink and got a bourbon induced inspiration. My plan was too nebulous to share, so I decided to tell her about it later.

After my foolish promise, we talked about the Miller case. She agreed we were overstepping the unspoken rules of insurance investigation, the most important being not to stick our noses into police business.

"I'm sure Hugh's got one of his guys working on finding out what the cops know." Elsie was referring to the army of men our boss relied on for inside information. Hugh had contacts everywhere, from auto repair shops to the State Department.

"He does but hasn't come up with anything yet. According to Chuck Grover, they're considering accidental death or suicide. Ryan Miller's dad is the one who's certain it's a murder."

"What makes him think that? I mean, lots of people have in-law trouble, but believing your son's wife is a stone-cold killer is extreme. Does he have any proof?"

"Hard evidence? I doubt it or he wouldn't need us. And the Millers are high society types. It'll be like pulling back molars to get him to drag family skeletons out of the closet. I'm going to insist Hugh handle him. I prefer digging up my buried bodies online."

I filled her in on what I discovered about Ryan and his childhood sweetheart.

"The challenge will be finding out why they broke up. The obvious answer is Ashley was involved. I've only seen pictures of the two women, but if we're going strictly by looks, Fiona is the hands-down winner."

"Photographs don't capture the essence of a person. Ryan's widow could be the type who sends out signals only specific men can hear. Like a specialized dog whistle. Too bad you can't take a red-blooded American man with you when you talk to her."

"Well, Hugh's losing his hearing, and if she does emit male-seducing sound waves, I sure as hell won't be taking Mateo."

"Don't be silly. Remember when Odysseus plugged his men's ears so they wouldn't be lured to their deaths by the sirens?"

She waved off my blank look and continued. "What I'm trying to say is that man is so smitten with you, he's immune to anything Ashley's got. But back to your dilemma. You didn't want to interfere with a murder investigation. Technically, there isn't one, so there you go."

I agreed with her premise, and although I knew we were splitting hairs, I felt a tiny bit better about my upcoming visit to the high school where our suspect was probably doing nothing more than murdering her students' love of the English language.

CHAPTER 5

Elsie's notion about it being impossible to interfere in a wrongful death investigation which never existed was logical. But I was uneasy about getting involved in what might be a futile attempt to make sense of their son's last moments. My limited experience with suicide came in high school when a classmate's older brother hanged himself. He left no note or clues as to why he considered his life unlivable. Like most egocentric adolescents, the concept of ending my own eluded me. No way the world could go on without me in it. Now, I understood there are people who can't imagine it going on with them in it. At the time, I pushed the tragedy aside with little effort.

My classmate and her family weren't so lucky. After their divorce, the father moved to Colorado. The sister dropped out of school and fell into a drug-infused spiral. The mother slipped into a shadow state and refused to leave the house. An old friend told me the poor lady currently resided in a memory care facility. I hoped she stayed in a pleasant, hazy condition. An alternate reality that allowed her to believe the boy—all grown up, maybe with children of his own—would be stopping by to take her out to lunch or bringing roses for her birthday.

The contrast between that image and the life Mateo and I were building frightened me. By acknowledging my happiness, I worried I might catch the attention of some jealous goddess who would rain down disaster just to teach me a lesson. Each time he left my sight, I feared he would be gone forever. My therapist said these kinds of thoughts were examples of catastrophic thinking. She explained they were part of a general anxiety disorder when a person imagines the worst outcome for any situation.

I smiled and nodded at her diagnosis, then wondered if a brain tumor might be the basis for my gloomy outlook. Regardless, the possibility of losing Mateo scared the hell out of me.

When I saw his SUV in the garage, a sharp pang of longing began in a spot near my heart and traveled south. It wasn't exactly sexual desire although that was a big part of it. It was more a combination of the relief of coming home and the joy of knowing he would be there. I wanted nothing more than to curl up next to him on the sofa and zone out on mindless TV before heading to bed.

He met me at the kitchen door and wrapped his arms around me. When he stepped away, I protested.

"Not yet. Hold me just a little longer."

"Tough day, babe?"

"You could say that." I sighed and stepped back.

He kissed my lips. "Somebody tastes like bourbon. Good thing I'm a whiskey kind of guy. Can I pour another one for you?"

I shook my head and took his hand. "Sit with me for a while."

We snuggled under the quilt Elsie gave me from her sister's collection. Blocks of pale pink, baby blue, and soft yellow enclosed a wide-brimmed bonnet in navy and white. I traced the profile of the little girl beneath the hat.

After a few minutes of blissful silence, I recapped my day, beginning with my visit with Elsie and her grandniece. When I reached the part about Cody Rae's mother throwing her out of the house, he interrupted.

"Wait a minute. Are you telling me her own mother threw her out over some loser?"

"That's right. And I bet that loser might have gotten too friendly, and the mom got jealous."

"When you say too friendly..."

"I'm not sure. The girl is tiny but smart. I'd guess it's not the first time she's been in close quarters with a sleazebag. For some reason, though, this must be different."

The shoulder I leaned against tensed, and his voice deepened. "If by different, you're saying this *gilipollas* did something to her, we need to find out and take care of him."

Despite the rush of savage adrenaline that shot through me as I pictured exactly how Mateo might do that and how I would help, I couldn't keep from smiling. Prick sounded so much more insulting in Spanish.

"We're on it. But she's a teenage girl with the usual distrust of adults. Not that she doesn't trust Elsie, but talking to someone who's like a grandmother to you about being sexually abused can't be easy. Don't worry. We'll figure it out, and when we do, you'll be the first to know."

I continued the saga of my crappy day with an explanation of the Miller case and why it bothered me.

"I'm sure Hugh's in touch with the police. He's too savvy to screw around with an open murder investigation. Still, tread lightly, and if you get a bad vibe from anyone, call me. Not that I doubt you can handle it. Just so you have backup."

We had multiple discussions about how I had no intention of becoming some kind of damsel in distress who constantly needed rescuing. It was in his nature to want to be the knight in shining armor, so it was especially hard for him to step down from his trusty steed. But he was trying, which made me love him even more.

I don't know why, but I considered not telling him about Lance's call. It had nothing to do with worrying Mateo might be jealous. He knew my only holdovers from the relationship were contempt for the man and regret I hadn't ended it sooner. It was more an irrational sense of shame connected with getting a collect recording from prison.

Complete transparency turned out to be a good decision because after I explained my ex had called and admitted how much it unsettled me, the phone rang.

Once again, the caller showed up as unknown but not the same number as this morning.

"I better take this. It might be about the Miller case."

Mateo groaned and nodded.

"Is this Ms. Howard? Lucy Howard?"

"That depends on who's calling."

"This is Simon Elliott. You don't know me, but I represent your former fiancé, Lance Crawford."

"I wouldn't exactly say fiancé, but marriage was on the table. Of course, that's all over." Why did I feel the need to explain myself to this stranger? "Ms. Howard is no longer at this number." I silently vowed to have it changed.

Before I could disconnect, he shouted, "Wait a second, please. If you'll hear me out, I promise not to bother you again."

Setting up a new phone would be inconvenient, so I sighed and said, "I'm taking you at your word on that. But make it quick. I have something very important to do." I wiggled my eyebrows at Mateo and put the caller on speaker.

"Mr. Crawford suggested you would be more comfortable speaking with me."

"Was it because I hung up on his jailhouse call, the way I should hang up on you now?"

"Please, hear me out. I have some important information for you."

"What kind of information?"

"It involves some paperwork my client needs access to. It would be better if we met in person, but I promise it will be quick. Perhaps I could stop by your office Monday morning?"

I looked to Mateo, who shrugged and mouthed, "Why not?"

Off the top of my head, I could think of at least ten reasons why it wasn't a good idea for me to have anything to do with my ex or his smooth-talking lawyer. But his shift in tone from conciliatory to self-assured, as well as the nature of the content of whatever the paperwork was piqued my curiosity.

"My morning is tied up. How about three o'clock?" I expected him to quibble, but he immediately agreed and was still thanking me when I ended the call.

"So, how do you feel about talking to this guy?"

"Any time I spend connected to my loser ex-boyfriend is a waste. And I can't imagine why he thinks I would do anything to help him. But Lance won't stop until he gets his point across. A few minutes with an attorney beats the hell out of dodging jailhouse calls."

"Want me to be there when the lawyer shows up?"

The idea was appealing. But it also went against the strong, independent image I'd been working on.

"I'll be fine."

After a night of fitful sleep filled with dream snippets of men falling from building tops and women laughing when they landed, I woke to find a note on my pillow. Mateo had gone in early but promised to be home for dinner.

The last line of his message warmed me almost as much as his body had.

If you change your mind and need me to be with you when you meet with the lawyer, text me and I'll be there.

And he meant it. No matter how important his business was, he would drop it for me and be by my side as fast as possible. One of the many things I loved about him, his devotion strengthened me. More empowering was the knowledge I didn't need him to intervene.

In the beginning, Mateo feared he was a rebound. But he never gave up. He helped me realize I was more humiliated by Lance dumping me than wounded by his loss. Even after that, I refused to be the kind of woman who jumps into a new relationship before making sure she burns any leftover clothing or memories from a bad one. We vowed to take things slow and easy. Two months later, he had more clothes at the cottage I rented in Grant Park than he had at his place. And we were discussing adopting a rescue dog. So much for slow and easy.

Only sometimes, in the darkest hour of the night, I awoke from the fog of a troubling dream. Not frightening enough to be a nightmare, it swirled through my senses, leaving me twisting and turning with unidentified anxiety. I would reach out in a near panic to touch Mateo, comforted by his mumbling acknowledgement but unable to silence the raspy whisper of doubt wandering through the corridors of my mind.

As someone who had sacrificed herself on the altar of truth too many times to count, I knew the man beside me would never do anything to break us apart. I accepted that I was the author of my fears. And wasn't admitting you had a problem the first step in solving it? Or something like that.

CHAPTER 6

Students ignored the third bell ringing from the intercom system and continued sauntering into Brookdale High School with no obvious sense of urgency. From my vantage point behind plexiglass windows in the reception area, I observed a clump of girls move as if they were a single unit and marveled at the way they kept pace with each other in outfits so similar they became uniforms—crop tops underneath plaid shirts like the one Cody Rae wore, leggings disguised as jeans, heavy boots in varying shades of brown and black.

Styles had changed since my high school days, but the attitudes they projected hadn't. They proclaimed a sense of invincibility, a pronouncement of independence despite their obvious insistence on conformity. This we're-going-to-live forever vibe made me wish I could be as confident in a future that promised endless possibilities.

The clear backpacks were a reminder of how easy it would be to take away those possibilities and how futile it was to rely on transparent plastic material to stop an unhinged shooter on a bloody mission. Traffic slowed as students slogged through metal detectors, another simulation of security.

Instead of reassuring me, this lame attempt to keep them safe was annoying. Because no amount of youthful self-assurance or well-meaning policies would save them if some crazy-ass killer was determined to gun them down.

Two boys in black hoodies slouched by. Had they chosen their attire to reflect dark moods, or was I reacting to a stereotype perpetrated by conservative media and film makers? In less than ten minutes on the property, paranoia had me judging kids by how they dressed and the way they walked.

"Miss Howard." The secretary at the check-in counter stopped me. She wore a hot pink sweater set with an enormous orange and yellow leaf pin over her heart. I suspected she had thematic jewelry for every season and occasion. "Mrs. Torrance will see you now. Show her the way, Kanisha." She inclined her head toward a desk near the back of the room.

The girl sitting there looked up through a curtain of brown braids threaded with gold. For a second, I thought she was going to ignore the woman, but she pushed herself to a surprising height. Her pale-yellow t-shirt complemented the streaks in her hair as she focused dark eyes on me. With her slim but athletic build and high cheek bones, she reminded me of one of the West African goddesses I studied in my college comparative mythology course.

This young deity nodded to me and grabbed her backpack.

As we left, the desk dragon issued a last warning. "Please keep in mind, Miss Howard, Mrs. Torrance is a busy woman."

Something about the way she kept saying *Miss* Howard rubbed me the wrong way, as if she were judging me but for what? Being single? Loitering in the lobby?

"We're all busy women," I replied, matching my tone to hers. "I certainly wouldn't want to keep you from offering friendly greetings to all the visitors."

I was surprised at how easily I regressed to my snarky teen years. Less surprising was my lack of remorse over it. When Kanisha rewarded me with a slight smile, I experienced a rush of satisfaction.

"Mrs. T is past the library and to the right. Stay close to the lockers, and you won't get run over."

"Thanks for the tip. I can take it from here if you need to go back to the office."

"Are you kidding? I can't stand her. She's always giving me the stink eye, like she thinks I'm a thief. As if there's anything there I'd want. Follow me, and walk slow, okay?"

Walking slowly wasn't a problem, especially after a baritone voice blasted over the intercom, commanding students to get to class immediately. The crowd made up for its earlier lack of urgency by stampeding through the hallways, scrambling and shoving in both directions.

Kanisha was a pro at navigation, cutting a path as we passed the glass-enclosed media center. Despite the arrangements of chairs and tables in convivial small groups and the colorful book displays on the walls, to me it simulated a video game shooting gallery, one that could quickly convert from virtual to reality.

A woman in a maroon pantsuit stood beside a door with a plaque above it labeled Torrance, Assistant Principal. She exuded an air of authority that made me want to confess all the times I cut school and got away with it. I remembered my status as a grown-up and straightened my spine.

"Have a seat while I herd stragglers to class. Kanisha, perhaps Ms. Howard would like something to drink."

I started to decline the offer, but the girl mouthed "Please," so I asked for tea, thinking it would take longer to make. She grinned and meandered down another hallway, leaving me wondering when or if she would return.

Mrs. Torrance ended her guard duty.

"We have an open-door policy. You don't have to worry about any of the students listening in. They have zero interest in what adults have to say. But if you're concerned over privacy issues, we can relocate to a conference room."

Another small group scurried by without giving us a second glance. I tried to mimic their disinterest by pretending not to see them but did a double take when the last girl passed. Her movements were languid, almost liquid. Despite the heavy bag on her back, her arms floated, her hips barely swayed. Other girls looked to the left and right, checking their reflections, playing for reactions from their peers. She kept her eyes forward and her head held high, as if daring somebody to hurry her along. Set apart from the gaggle of females directly in front of her, being solitary didn't seem to bother her. She could have been any pretty, petite teenager. But when she tossed her long dark hair and sent it rippling across her shoulders, there was no question who she was.

I turned to the hallway in case she broke form and looked into the office. Then I shielded my face with a folder and watched as she disappeared into a classroom on the right.

Mateo's favorite old movie, *Casablanca*, came to mind.

Of all the schools, in all the towns, in all the world, Cody Rae Frazier walked into Brookdale High School.

"Ms. Howard, is everything okay?"

"Oh, yes. Everything's good."

"I believe you wanted some information on Ashley Miller. There's not much I can tell you about her on a professional level. And we had so few personal exchanges. She came onboard first semester as a long-term sub for a teacher on maternity leave. When she decided not to return, we offered Ashley a contract for the rest of the year. Confidentiality policies dictate I'm not allowed to comment on her classroom performance."

"I understand completely. The family isn't interested in that. They're hoping some of their daughter-in-law's colleagues might provide insights into Ryan's frame of mind since poor Ashley has been too distraught to discuss much of anything."

Other than a slight raise of her left eyebrow, Mrs. Torrance gave no indication of how she felt about my portrayal of her employee as a devastated widow.

"I spoke with the head of the English department. She shares my concerns about your conversations with Ashley's fellow teachers turning into gossip sessions."

"I promise it won't be anything like that. Honestly, I'm only interested in what they can tell me about Ryan." Damn. I'd broken a cardinal rule of investigative deception. Never use the word honestly to emphasize your trustworthiness. If you have to say it, obviously, it doesn't apply to you.

From her frown, I suspected she had conducted multiple interrogations where students' vigorous protests of their innocence included language similar to mine. Her desk phone lit up before she could continue questioning me.

"Excuse me. I have to take this." She answered, then put the caller on hold. "The English department is on the other wing of the school." She tore a note from the pad and began jotting down directions.

Kanisha magically appeared before she finished.

"Even better, our aide can escort you there."

I noticed she wasn't carrying a cup.

"I trust you'll respect the policies we discussed." Whether she didn't expect one or believed my answer would be less than truthful, she waved us out and returned to her call.

"Mrs. T is big on policy, but she's okay for an administrator. Sorry about the tea. They were out."

The hallway seemed smaller without students. The unnatural silence reminded me of horror movies set in empty high school buildings, which were filled with zombies or chainsaw wielding maniacs. The greasy smell of french fries wafted from the cafeteria and blended with the essence of cheap aftershave and stale body odor. Another aspect that hadn't changed all that much. I suppressed a shudder.

She cleared her throat. "Are you here about Mrs. Miller?"

I gave myself a mental smack. I'd been hanging out with a girl who, on a daily basis, moved in and out between teachers and students. And I hadn't asked her a single question.

"More about her husband, really. His family is planning a memorial and hoped his wife's friends might have some nice things to add. You know, sweet stuff she said about him or pictures she kept at work." There was no need to mention anything about suicide or murder.

"Why don't you ask her?"

"She's crazy out of her head with grief."

"She's crazy all right." She mumbled. "That's the English department. I should check back in the front office before the bell rings." She turned to walk away, but I grabbed her by the backpack.

"Just another minute or so, please. I need to learn as much about the Millers as possible. And I can tell you're the kind of girl who knows what's going on in the whole school."

My attempt at flattery seemed to have had little effect on her, but she didn't pull away.

"Look, all I know is Mrs. Miller had her own special way of teaching. She was always staying late to help students with their writing." She put air quotes around her words.

"I'm sorry, but I don't get it. Isn't helping kids improve their grades a good thing?"

"Sure. But she was real picky about who she helped." More air quotes.

"What do you mean?"

She bit her thumb, then looked away.

"Please, Kanisha. It could really be important."

"Not if you're looking for *sweet stuff* about Mr. Miller."

I must have been totally off my game if I couldn't fool a high school girl.

"What if I was after more than that? Let's say anything that might help his parents understand exactly what happened to him. Maybe the names of the students she tutored?"

"I was never in her class, so I can only tell you what I heard from other people. The rumor is that she didn't just tutor anyone. She's mostly into jocks. You know, big muscles and tiny brains. Usually, football players or wrestlers, the type who go with cheerleaders and homecoming queens. But sometimes she went after musicians."

The bell rang, and Kanisha disappeared into the hordes of teenagers pouring out of classrooms, leaving me to question her use of the phrase *went after.*

CHAPTER 7

I took a deep breath and stepped inside a space large enough to be a classroom. Teacher desks lined the walls in a hodgepodge of arrangements. Some faced the wall, others the open area, and a few clustered together in tight pairs or triplets. A psychologist would have a field day analyzing what the choices of positions said about the inhabitants. At a rectangular table in the middle of the room, four women and two men chatted as they ate their lunches. A busty woman waved her hand in the air for emphasis, but everyone kept talking and chewing as if she weren't there.

She tapped the water bottle in front of her with a plastic fork, cleared her throat, and half-shouted, "Excuse me. But this is an important matter. That refrigerator hasn't been cleaned in over a month. I've been working on a cleaning schedule, and I need—"

"Now is not a good time to air our dirty laundry." I jumped and turned to face a sturdy woman in a low-cut orange blouse with flowing sleeves. A large gold locket dangling from the chain around her neck nestled between the crevice of exposed cleavage.

"I hope I didn't startle you. I'm Sue Ann Porter, chairperson of the English Department. And you must be the lady from the memorial service."

Her heavy drawl suggested she came from somewhere more rural than suburban Atlanta. Possibly South Georgia or Alabama, could have been Mississippi.

"We need privacy." She inclined her head to the silent group. Stiff reddish gold curls that framed her square face barely moved.

"Let's go to my room."

She led me down the hallway, hips bound in a straight skirt, its seams stretched close to the breaking point. Along the way, I introduced myself and repeated my lame-ass cover story about collecting happy things to say at Ryan's funeral.

Unlike Kanisha, Sue Ann seemed to buy it although I might have been the one buying the tale she spun once we were seated— she, behind her desk; me, in a chair beside her.

"As I told the police, I'm pretty sure I was the last person to speak to the poor guy. He'd been hounding me about taking out a policy on the kennel out back of our house. Total waste of money, but my husband Ron is flat out crazy when it comes to his huntin' dogs. This is my big baby. We chaperoned the prom."

She reached for a photograph of her and a heavy-set, flushed-face man. His boyish buzz cut did nothing to hide his receding hairline. Dressed in a blue-plaid suit pulled tight across his barrel chest, my grandmother on my mom's side would have said he looked like ten pounds of mud poured into a five-pound sack. My mother would have pegged him as due for a stroke any minute.

Sue Ann wore a mint-green chiffon number with flowy sleeves. She held the picture closer and traced her outline before setting it down.

"I never got to go to my own prom with Big Ron. We broke up a few months before the dance, and I went to the prom with the captain of the football team. He's some hot shot lawyer in Montgomery."

She set the photo down a bit harder than necessary and continued. "Ryan said there were structural issues with the building that might cause flooding or something awful like that. Anyway, he convinced Ron to get the insurance but not before we rebuilt the whole damn thing. The man's an idiot, but what are you going to do?"

She looked at me from behind red-framed reading glasses that magnified her pale blue eyes. I realized she expected a response from me, but I had nothing. So, I put on a sorrowful face and shook my head as if I, too, suffered from having a moronic husband. It must have been enough.

"I was explaining the situation to Ryan when his phone interrupted us. The polite thing would have been to let it go to voicemail but no. He had to answer it. I can't stand it when people do that, as if I'm not just as important as whoever the hell is calling. He walked out to the hallway, acting like he had some big secret I wasn't supposed to hear. I had a good mind to tell him to forget it. That we'd find another insurance agent who had some manners."

Her sudden pause made me worry she'd begun to doubt my motive for talking to her, and I was relieved when she continued with her story.

"But he didn't give me time. Said he had an emergency and would be in touch. I guess he took care of it. Or it took care of him. Poor Ron is all torn up about who to call about insuring that oversized doghouse."

Sue Ann signaled the end of her rant by fanning her cheeks with a manilla folder. Then she opened a drawer and took out a lipstick and compact. While she retouched her makeup, I speculated about the level of rage in her narrative. She was clearly furious at a dead man because he found something more pressing than making sure her dogs stayed warm and dry.

Twice in less than ten minutes, she had rendered me speechless. Luckily, she took great care applying a bright shade of red to her thin lips, giving me time to regroup. One last glance in the mirror and she turned to me, her expression appropriately solemn with all traces of fury gone.

I recovered from my confusion and picked up where she left off. "That is a problem, but you'll find someone. Back to Ryan's memorial. Would it be accurate to say he was hard working?"

A dark look flashed over her face. It passed so quickly I wasn't sure it had been there in the first place. "Hard working?" Her lips tilted upward. "Yes, please quote me as saying when it came to hard work, Ryan Miller took the cake."

The bell rang, and she rose to walk me to the door.

I followed Kanisha's advice about hugging the locker walls as I maneuvered past students to the front office, where I checked out. My guide had fled as soon as possible or had never returned to her post. Either way, she was gone before I had the chance to thank her for her help.

Sitting in my car, I realized I'd gotten so enthralled in the kennel insurance saga I hadn't asked Sue Ann how the young widow seemed to be managing her grief. However, the narrator of the dog drama provided me with some interesting insights into her nature. There was more to the story about a woman so angry about being put on hold that she acted as if she'd forgotten the man who pissed her off had fallen or been pushed to his death.

And Kanisha's comment about the students Ashley tutored gave me a whole new area to pursue.

But approaching the widow to discuss her after-school remediation sessions would be tricky.

Although it was past 12:30 and the last thing I'd eaten was a protein bar, the idea of investigating what went on between Ashley and all those hormonal teenagers took away my appetite.

When Dad was their age, boys given the chance to do more than fanaticize about their sexy teachers were considered lucky. He had been foolish enough to express this opinion after meeting my senior high school English teacher at an open house. We stopped for milkshakes on the way home, and my poor father made the unfortunate observation that it must be hard for the guys to concentrate.

"What exactly do you mean, dear?" My mother tapped her straw against her cup.

Whether from the sugar rush or a brain freeze, he failed to notice the temperature at the table had fallen below that of his chocolate shake. Worse, he missed the change in atmosphere and the subtle warning dropped with Mom's saccharine *dear.*

"You know, that whole hot for the teacher Van Halen thing." He began a fractured rendition of the song, gradually fading out when he registered the look on my mother's face.

We finished our milkshakes in silence.

Mom was ahead of the times in her belief that no adult, male or female, should take advantage of a minor, even an extremely willing seventeen-year-old. Then, people had no understanding of the problems that could result from these unequal relationships. Later in life, these men often suffered from alcohol or drug abuse, along with emotional attachment issues.

If asked how they felt about the special attention, most would have said to hell with long-term consequences.

But teenage boys can be sensitive. It's easy for them to equate sex with love. And sometimes easier to let their emotions take control, turning what they mistakenly see as a true connection into an obsession.

If one of those kids had fallen hard for teacher, would it be too farfetched to believe what should have been a harmless schoolboy crush had turned deadly?

· · ·

Sitting in the school lot, this line of thought did nothing to bolster my resolve about talking to Ashley. While she might not be a cold-blooded murderer—possibly wasn't even aware one of her sex-drugged lovers, or whatever they were—who had killed her husband, she was responsible for creating a dangerous situation. It was also possible she had manipulated some poor sucker into doing away with Ryan. If she was that clever, she might not fall for my cover story about gathering material for a memorial. Since there were no others available, I had to chance it.

It occurred to me I still didn't understand exactly how her unlucky spouse had met his end. I checked for messages from Hugh and found none.

The first person I wanted to call was Mateo, not so much for help in how to convince Ashley to talk to me, though. I loved to imagine the smile on his face when he saw my name on caller id and hear the lift in his voice when he answered. Those unconscious things people do when they love each other.

The exact opposite of whatever happened between Ashley and those besotted boys or in her now defunct marriage.

"You've been on my mind all morning." He gave me his Saturday night DJ impression, husky yet smooth.

"I have?" I tried to match his sexy tone, but my heart wasn't in it.

"Aren't you going to ask what I was thinking?"

He sounded a little let down I hadn't responded with more enthusiasm.

"I bet I can guess," I purred, joining the game. For a moment, images of his body next to mine cleared my mind of the morning's debris.

"How about we compare notes later tonight? Let's say after dinner? Or before might even be better. But I'm guessing you didn't call to proposition me. What's up?"

I summarized Kanisha's account of the rumors circulating about Ashley's after-school activities and the department head's preoccupation with Ryan's rude dismissal of her kennel concerns. Then I told him about my plan to interview her as soon as I came up with a plausible reason.

"Any chance we can meet for lunch?"

"Sorry, babe, but I have back-to-back meetings."

I hid my disappointment and asked him to check with one of his police contacts to see if there'd been a ruling on cause of death.

"I will, but don't expect too much. The lab is extra careful in ruling a questionable death a suicide. I can be available after two. If you change your mind about having back-up when you talk to Lance's attorney, let me know."

His presence would make it easier to get both lawyer and ex out of the way. But it would expose him to a part of my life I preferred to keep as separate as possible. So, I told him I had everything under control, said goodbye, and turned into Wendy's for a Frosty.

. . .

When I reached the office, Elsie sat at the reception desk, talking on the phone. I waited until she hung up to ask where the intern was.

"He pulled another no-show. I think he got tired of going through other people's trash. When Hugh found out, he yelled for me to cut him a check and explain we'd no longer be needing his services."

"Hugh's exact words, huh?"

Her grin affirmed my guess our boss had been much more direct and colorful in his firing of the boy. "No, but the poor kid was about as useful as teats on a bull."

"Still, you shouldn't have to handle two jobs. This could be the perfect time to hit him with adding Cody Rae to the staff."

"You might want to wait. He's been cursing at the phone all morning."

Before I had the chance to ask for details, the buzzer announced an incoming call.

"I'll check in later," I said and headed to my office to type up my notes and catch up on some paperwork.

At 2:30, my cell phone rang. I recognized the number as Elliot's. The first thought that came into my mind was that he was calling to cancel our meeting. Rather than being irritated at the disruption of my schedule, I experienced a rush of relief. It was, however, short lived.

"There have been some, uh, developments in the case, making it more urgent. Is there any possibility we could meet sooner, now if possible?"

Despite my belief the urgency had more to do with his timeline than a serious issue, I dismissed my childish desire to make him wait and agreed to see him as soon as he arrived.

"I'm in my car across the street from your building."

His halting speech caused my right eye to twitch. I couldn't tell if it was an act or if there was something real behind his weirdly immediate need to talk to me.

"I guess you can come in now, then."

"Thank you, but would it work for you to meet away from your office? Say, the coffee shop around the corner?"

"Is that really necessary? My day is packed." Not true, but the idea of sitting down with someone who knew more of my former boyfriend's secrets than I did held no appeal for me.

"It would be safer for you and me."

I started to demand an explanation for his dramatic word choice. But I didn't want to encourage him. "How will I know who you are?"

"Don't worry. I'll recognize you."

Less than ten minutes later, a man in the kind of suit Lance used to wear before he swapped his pricey clothes for an orange jumpsuit stood and waved to me from a table near the back of the shop. I grinned at the image of my sexy ex wearing the only color he couldn't pull off. It turned his tanned face into the yellowish hue of a lemon shoved in a refrigerator drawer and forgotten.

When I approached, his attorney rose and extended his hand. At what I surmised was well over six feet with a chest and biceps that strained at the fabric of the expensive suit, he looked more like a linebacker than a lawyer. I hesitated a second before accepting his beefy paw. Not because I was uncomfortable with the relatively masculine greeting, more because he might take it as pre-acquiescence to whatever request he planned to make.

Although his attire was similar to my ex's, he failed to project Lance's brand of self-confidence. When he greeted me, he tugged at the sleeves and struggled to button the jacket. I reminded myself his discomfort wasn't a bad thing. After all, my former boyfriend's demeanor hid his deceptive nature. Rather than leave the man's hand hanging, I accepted the gesture with a firm, quick grip.

He waited until I got settled before sitting. "I appreciate you meeting me like this. Better no one sees me coming and going from your office. Can I get you something? Coffee? Tea?" He pointed to his cup and pushed his chair back.

I shook my head. "I'm good. Aren't you being a little paranoid? It's not as if someone's staking out Farewell's. Or are you afraid you're being followed?" My intention was to lessen his drama with what I meant as humor. His serious expression demonstrated my attempt failed.

"I wasn't personally involved in Mr. Crawford's trial, so I doubt anyone is interested in me. I'm more concerned with your welfare, Ms. Howard."

His tone projected sincerity, but I didn't go for it. My brief experience with the legal system taught me criminals weren't the only ones who couldn't be trusted.

"Why in the world would you be worried about me?" I forced a half-laugh.

"Because they found Roberta Garrison this morning, hanging in her cell."

"You mean hanging as in, like, dead?" He nodded. "Dear God."

I trembled at the memory of the nurse involved in the organ-smuggling ring. True, the woman was a first-class bitch, including everything from screeching obscenities on the phone to holding me at gunpoint while deciding the best way to position my lifeless body. Despite those memories, I didn't celebrate her death. From what I learned about Lance's girlfriend Janelle Ragsdale, not her real name, Roberta was a victim of deceit and manipulation. Yes, she had the potential for being a stone-cold killer, but Janelle seduced her, then nurtured her inner monster.

"I can't say I'm surprised. She was extremely unstable. Locked up and separated from her homicidal love, taking her own life wouldn't be that big of a reach."

"If it was a suicide."

"What else could it be? Weren't they keeping her secluded from the other prisoners?"

"Internal prison security's not as tight as the public likes to believe. The psych ward is notoriously understaffed, and workers have been known to suffer from their own issues, which could include greed. It wouldn't be shocking if one of them was hired to take care of a troublesome inmate. Roberta's death is worrisome, but it isn't the biggest issue at hand."

He took a sip of coffee while I tapped my fingernails on the table. "So? What is more important than a possible murder, and how does it concern me?"

"Around the same time guards were cutting Ms. Garrison down, a riot broke out over a hundred miles south in the prison housing her accomplice. Two inmates were involved. One's in critical condition; the other's in the morgue."

"Wait. Are you saying both Janelle and Roberta are dead?" The impossible coincidence rippled the hair on my arms.

"No. Janelle wasn't the one killed. Video footage of the incident shows her stabbing the deceased woman."

I had no problem picturing Lance's ex-girlfriend filing a toothbrush into a homemade shiv and jabbing it into another human but doubted she would do so for a purely recreational motive. "Was there bad blood between her and the victim?" I winced at my accidental insensitivity before deciding it didn't matter. Whether Janelle acted to up her prison rep by getting rid of a rival or work out her anger issues, why should I care?

Then I realized Elliott wouldn't be here unless the deaths concerned me.

"Hold on a second. Do they suspect a connection? And even if they do, Janelle's already serving multiple life sentences for killing her ex-husband as well as the doctor. And they're looking at her for at least two other unsolved murders. It's not like she'll be getting out and showing up at my door anytime soon. And won't she be under tighter security?"

"Normally, she would be. The problem is that after Ragsdale stabbed her fellow inmate, she disappeared into the crowd of rioters. And now, it seems, she's disappeared completely."

CHAPTER 8

After several seconds of stunned silence, I regained the power to speak.

"Way to bury the lead."

He shrugged. "I didn't mean to. Everything happened so fast, and this isn't the kind of case I usually handle."

"Thanks for looping me in, I guess. But you weren't aware of this when you asked to meet with me."

He admitted his original request was for a very different reason and spent the next half hour explaining that Lance was working on a deal with federal prosecutors. Big surprise, he hadn't been completely honest concerning the extent of his knowledge regarding the organ dealing ring. On the advice of his previous attorney, he remained quiet about how the enterprise crossed multiple state lines. Had he revealed this information, no judge would have considered house arrest, the sentence he'd hoped for. Plus, he would have been culpable in the ongoing case.

Since no one believed his story about being coerced into committing the crimes, he hired another firm to work on cutting a deal in the upcoming trial.

Without giving away confidential information, Elliott shared that in addition to a computer file, Lance kept hard copies as well. As an attorney, he was aware of the value of presenting originals as evidence in a courtroom. His records included names, dates, transactions, and other highly sensitive material he claimed he couldn't discuss.

"As additional insurance against retribution from the associates he never met, he stored the hard copies in a security box at one of the banks he did business with. He gave the computer files to the Feds. They're unaware of the hard copies."

"So, what's the problem? Hold on a second. If you're expecting me to organize a going away party for Lance, you've come to the wrong place."

"That's completely understandable. But the issue at hand involves the person who does know about the hard copies. When he hid the evidence, he was still, um, involved with Ms. Ragsdale. As proof of his devotion, she insisted he give her the key. Obviously, this was before she tried to kill him."

I had no trouble accepting that aspect of the story. With his unfaltering love for himself, he couldn't imagine any woman he wanted would ever be disloyal to him. Paired with a staunch belief in his own cleverness, he made for an easy mark.

"What's the worst that could happen? Even if Janelle takes the contents of the box, there's no way the FBI would arrange a deal for her."

"True. But if the files came into the wrong hands, not only would it create some ambiguity about their value in Crawford's deal, but it could also put him in danger."

"I assume you're referring to the higher-ups he worked for."

"Exactly."

Something about this part of the story bothered me, but I couldn't figure out what it was. Lance had been savvy enough to know Janelle might be a knock-out in a flashy, low-cut blouse, but she played better behind the scenes than on his arm at a company dinner. He needed me out front, someone he considered easy to manipulate and respectable, to climb up the ladder at his firm. It wouldn't have made sense for him to put her in my place.

It wasn't until after the doctor's murder that he realized how dangerous Janelle was. She might be smarter in a cutthroat sort of way, but even with his ridiculous ego, he knew not to place his future in the hands of a woman like her. I doubted he would entrust anything of importance to her.

"Same question as before. How does this involve me?"

"Crawford started to worry about Janelle and tried to talk her into returning the key. That's when she told him she'd hidden it where no one would ever look. He's certain it's somewhere in your apartment."

"Are you kidding me? Why the hell would he think that?"

"He says that's exactly the sort of thing Ms. Ragsdale would do."

I recalled the evening he stopped by after I caught him literally with his pants down in his office. He begged me to take him back, and for a moment I considered it. The idea of a life as the wife of a prominent attorney had been appealing. But I came to my senses, threw him out, and changed the locks.

A few days later, he showed up at my door and forced his way in, screaming we weren't over until he said so. I chased him out with an umbrella and flung an unopened soda bottle at him with enough velocity to do some serious damage if my aim had been more accurate.

Not long after that, Janelle and Roberta kidnapped us. The authorities sent Lance to the hospital for injuries suffered during his time with the deadly duo and then directly to prison. He never got the opportunity to pass go or recover his get-out-of-jail-free backup.

"I don't know how he came up with the idea. Janelle's not crazy. She's more of a sociopath, which means she'd never put herself in danger. And that's exactly where she would be if we found incriminating evidence."

There was no reason to mention that Mateo and I had done some serious reorganizing after he moved in. I cleared out a bunch of my stuff to make room for his. I poured through every keepsake and old jewelry box before donating or pitching the contents. Not coming across a mysterious key didn't mean it wasn't there, but those were the logical choices for hiding it. The same held true for inside my collectible pig cannisters or my CD holders. We had no loose bricks around the fireplace nor trees on the property with deep knot holes like Boo Radley's in *To Kill a Mockingbird.*

"Perhaps you're correct, but where Janelle's concerned anything is possible, which is why we're here. We hoped you would allow me access to your home."

"Let's see if I have this straight. Lance has already given the information to the Feds. They don't know about the original documents. Only Janelle knows where the key is hidden. So, wouldn't she be the one the bad guys would go after?"

"That's right. But if the wrong people get the evidence first, Mr. Crawford's deal could be jeopardized. And he is worried about your safety and reputation if the Feds discover anything in your apartment."

"That man is a lying bastard who isn't capable of considering anyone but himself. Besides, not only did I have nothing to do with the doctor's organ stealing scheme, but I also took part in exposing it."

"That is the accepted version of the story. Unfortunately, the authorities might begin to question your involvement."

"Are you kidding me?"

"Of course, it's highly unlikely they would suspect you of being anything but an unwitting accomplice."

"Hold on there, buddy. Maybe I should get a lawyer myself because this conversation is starting to feel as if you're trying to intimidate me into letting you search my home. I may have been lacking in the wits department when it came to trusting a slick-talking attorney who said he loved me. But I'm not stupid enough to let you rummage through my private property, especially since you haven't been totally forthcoming with me."

The bland expression he maintained throughout our conversation darkened for a second before returning to its original one. He leaned forward and raised his hands in what I took to be a *who, me* gesture.

"Please, don't try to tell me Lance Crawford would have thrown away the chance to avoid prison time for any reason other than he was scared shitless about testifying against what must be some serious-level criminals. After being locked up for a while, my guess is he's more afraid of those inside."

To his credit, Elliott didn't deny it. He finished the last swallow of his coffee, handed me a business card, and asked me to take more time to consider giving him access to my home. I took it without promising anything.

· · ·

No one was at the reception desk when I returned, but voices sounded from down the hallway. I considered sharing the news of the death of Nasty Nurse and the escape of her counterpart with Hugh but wanted to run the story by Mateo before I told anyone else. That left hiding in my office or checking in with my boss. The first option gave me too much time to worry about how to avoid any involvement with my ex. At least the second would take my mind off a situation I had very little control over.

Elsie sat in front of Hugh, taking notes while he talked. I tapped on the open door.

"Just wanted to see if you have anything new on the Miller case. I can come back if you're busy."

"Nothing we can't get to later. That okay with you, Elsie?"

His civility surprised me. When I first met the man, his idea of good manners included not trimming his toenails while sitting at his desk. He frequently joked about his favorite topics—boobs and booze—and refused to embrace the concept of a human resource department. Since starting his own company and hiring Elsie, he morphed from not caring about anyone else's opinions to only being a little rough around the edges. His occasional slip-ups in crudity kept him from being boring.

She stood. "Absolutely. I'll type this up before I leave."

"No hurry. You put in two full days handling your work and that idiot intern's. Go home. On your way out, contact that temp agency and get someone in here to answer the phones for tomorrow."

She wasted no time with goodbyes, and I didn't blame her. Despite his personal growth, this display of congeniality was so out of character, I'm sure she was afraid he'd return to his senses and retract the offer.

I sat in the chair she vacated, wondering who had stolen the real Hugh Farewell and replaced him with this much nicer clone.

"Nothing new on my end with the Miller case, other than half a dozen emails from Grover. How did your trip back in time go? Did you pick up a hot jock?"

"Dear God, no," I shuddered. Images of Ashley naked on the lap of an underage football player filled me with disgust, not desire.

His puzzled expression reminded me he was in the dark about her extra-curriculars. I spent the next thirty minutes filling him in on what I learned. When I finished, he removed a bottle of bourbon from his drawer.

"Hand me a glass and get one for yourself."

Unlike my boss, I preferred to keep my day drinking to a minimum. Today qualified as an exception.

"What's your gut telling you about the wife?"

Although I'd explained to him multiple times my gut and I seldom communicated, he refused to believe me.

"I got nothing. She could be slutty without being a murderer or the victim of a hateful rumor campaign. It wouldn't be the first time people spread lies about someone whose only crime was being young and attractive." Sue Ann Porter's plain, middle-aged face came to mind. "What interests me is why she was working at all.

Ryan's family probably wasn't thrilled about having a lowly teacher marry their son. I'm guessing they expected her to join the garden club and volunteer with some charity like emotionally distant cats when she became a Miller.

"I gotta say, mean girls and high school scare the unholy shit out of me. So, what's your next step?"

"Guess I'll go interrogate the widow. Definitely not looking forward to it."

"Can't blame you. Why don't you take that hot friend of yours with you? The one at your birthday party. She had red hair down to there and giant knockers. Is it Barb? Betsy?"

"I believe you're talking about Bethany."

"That's right. Bethany." He stared into his bourbon so long I thought he'd forgotten I was there.

"Hey, stop undressing my best friend in your mind. I should be pissed at you for objectifying her, but you've given me a good idea. We'll say she's writing an article about Ryan for the paper, and the family hired me to make sure it reflected well on them. She'll love it."

"Will she enjoy going to the funeral, too? Haven't heard when it is, but you need to be there."

"Bethany refuses to go to funerals. She says it's because they're so sad, which is a load of horse hockey. It's really because black washes her out. But shouldn't the head of the firm be there to represent us?"

"No way. All those people eating little sandwiches a few feet from a corpse everybody pretends looks so natural. The whole thing is fucking unnatural. The viewing's bad enough, but at least there'll be alcohol."

I sighed. "All right. But I need you to clue in Grover the Sleaze about my cover story in case the family wonders who the hell I am."

"No problem." He titled his head and frowned in my direction. "What's with you and the shit-eating grin?"

I wasn't about to tell him he was mixing up wet Catholic wakes with dry Baptist send-offs. Sharing that information would most likely get me assigned to attend the viewing and the funeral.

"Just remembered something Mateo said this morning." I felt my smile stretch as I pictured Hugh searching frantically for a non-existent bar.

He reached for the bottle and poured himself another. When he held it over my half empty glass, I shook my head.

"Suit yourself." He took a gulp and sighed. "Good stuff. You got anything else?"

"There is, but it's not related to this case." By now, I was no longer certain there was an actual key, which meant Simon Elliott wanted in my house for another reason.

That idea created more urgency, enough that I decided not to wait to bring Hugh in. It was always tricky knowing how much to share with my boss. He hated Lance the whole time we were dating and had been happy we broke up. He enjoyed helping put together a case against my ex and his accomplices and had thrown an in-office party when they all went to jail.

I was afraid he would fly into a rage if I told him about Janelle's escape and Lance's possible deal with the Feds. But there was no way he wouldn't eventually find out. He'd be more enraged to discover I kept it from him.

"What is it related to then?"

"It's about Lance and Janelle. Roberta, too, but she's not really part of the problem. Not directly, anyway."

He set down his glass. "What the hell are you talking about?"

I took a breath and began my story. At the end of it, I stopped and waited for the explosion, but he surprised me. Instead of roaring, he sat there for a few seconds, then tossed back the rest of his drink.

"That miserable sonofabitch," he whispered so softly I had to lean forward in my chair. "No way in hell I'm going to let him weasel out of what he did to you." His whisper turned into a hiss, and his jaw tightened. "Does Mateo know that crazy bitch is on the loose?"

"You're the only one I've told. And it won't matter if they already caught her. I can't think of a good reason for her to come here." Unless she really had hidden something in my apartment and wanted it back.

He reached for the phone on his desk and scrolled until he found what he was looking for. I rose from my chair, but he motioned for me to sit. His normal ruddy complexion had paled and hardened into a frightening mask of fury.

"Sullivan, we've got an emergency. The Ragsdale woman broke out of prison, and I'm afraid she's coming for Lucy."

CHAPTER 9

By the time Mateo arrived, I had recovered from the impact of Hugh's announcement. The frantic look on my handsome boyfriend's face when he rushed into the office made it clear he hadn't.

"Jesus Christ, Lucy." He scooped me from my seat and held me tight, almost too tight.

"Hugh shouldn't have blurted out that Janelle stuff." I pushed against his chest. "Except for having trouble breathing, I'm perfectly fine."

He seemed doubtful but released me, and I provided a replay of my conversation with Elliott.

"So, you see, there's no reason to worry about her wanting to hurt me. If there really is a key at my house, which I seriously doubt, all she wants it for is to make sure her boss knows Lance is the one who ratted them out to save himself."

"If I believed that, I'd help the crazy bitch find it. But Ragsdale's not your normal, run-of-the-mill psychopath. Unfortunately, she's a special case, which means there's no way to predict what she'll do." Hugh leaned back in his chair and stared at the ceiling. His total calm unnerved me.

"True, but one thing that woman always puts before anything else is her own interest. I bet she's long gone." I looked to Mateo for affirmation, but he shook his head.

"Remember when someone trashed your apartment last year? We thought it was Lance, but the way the place was all torn up seemed like whoever did it had major anger issues. What if the break-in had nothing to do with theft? What if Janelle came in to hide something instead and left a mess because she was pissed?"

I was surprised to have forgotten an incident that made me feel so violated.

I conceded it was a possibility and joined them at the conference table to devise a plan for keeping me safe. I didn't share their concern about Janelle. Although she had been frighteningly cheerful about executing Lance and me, rather than malice, she had simply been cleaning up a compromising situation. It was more about business than glee.

If it had been Roberta—whose fury drove her straight to crazy town—on the loose, I would have welcomed an armed guard to accompany me throughout the day. But Janelle had no reason to stick around. When I repeated this theory, Hugh's composure disappeared and his voice rose at least two octaves.

"Goddammit, Lucy. The woman is dangerous."

"Come on. She's not stupid, and she never struck me as the kind of person who'd be out for revenge. Slowing down to deal with me doesn't make sense. She's probably three or four states away by now."

I turned to Mateo. "Go ahead. Explain I'm right."

Before he responded, Hugh slammed his thick palms on the wooden surface. "Good God. Just because she didn't have lunatic stamped on her forehead doesn't mean she's not as demented as her dead girlfriend. And please don't tell me it's a coincidence that insane woman strung herself up hours before Janelle escaped."

"Are you saying she had something to do with Roberta's death? What possible reason would she have for wanting to have her killed?"

Mateo took my trembling hand and brought it to his lips. The warmth from his kiss turned cold when I saw the fearfulness in his dark brown eyes. His words made me shiver.

"We suspect another one or more are involved. Someone who not only wanted Roberta permanently out of the way but is coming for Janelle, too. That kind of escape requires inside help. Somebody must have been planning her getaway all along. Roberta's death must have spooked them into stepping up the timeline. That or the same person who helped Janelle get out also assisted in the hanging of her sidekick."

"If we're right," Hugh said, "that asshole Johnston had national, possibly international, connections."

The asshole in question was Dr. Andrew Johnston, the quack scamming insurance companies with fake appendectomies. In addition to the money he made for surgeries he didn't perform, he collected cash for the kidneys or lungs from those he did. Although he hadn't struck anyone as masterminding the scheme, Janelle and Roberta murdered him before the authorities got the chance to find out what his role was.

"Let me get this straight. You guys believe the doctor had a boss who's behind Roberta's death, and he killed her because he was afraid she'd talk? And now he wants Janelle dead for the same reason?"

This whole thing was beginning to sound like a game of Clue, only with real candlesticks and knives. And not fun at all.

"That's what I would do if it were me and I was a ruthless killer," Hugh said. "I'd eliminate anyone remotely involved in the ring because it's a solid business decision and the only way to make the operation secure."

"If you're right, Lance is on that list."

He nodded. "He'll be on the top of it when word gets out he made a deal."

"Let's say there are international criminals behind all this. Why would they want to kill me? I already testified at Lance's trial."

Both men exchanged glances before Hugh said, "These aren't the kind of people who can afford to leave any loose ends."

"Are you saying that's what I am? A loose end."

"Probably not, but we can't sit around waiting to find out. I've got a friend who's an expert in locating stuff. He agreed to come over tomorrow and toss your place. If there's a key, he'll find it."

"Hold on a minute. I don't want my apartment tossed by anyone." I stood for emphasis.

"Sorry. Poor choice of words. I invited a lovely gentleman over for a scavenger hunt on the grounds. Afterwards, the two of you can drink tea and eat crumpets. Better?"

Mateo came to my side. "I'll be there to make sure the search is thorough but nondestructive." He put his arm around me and whispered, "And no one but me will touch your unmentionables."

His attempt to lighten the situation failed.

"Hey," Hugh said. "I'll join the party. You're welcome to supervise if you want, but Grover's getting antsy. If he suspects we're taking time away from him to work on another case, he's likely to stick his nose in our business. Hell, who knows? He might even try to insert himself into our investigation to help close it faster, so we can devote all our effort to finding out who killed the Miller kid."

I knew he was yanking my chain but couldn't stop myself from reacting. "No way is that ever going to happen. Go ahead. Search my place. I trust Mateo to see that you don't mess it up beyond recognition. Just keep that creep far away from my apartment."

"Lucy," Hugh spoke in a softer tone. "I understand why you wouldn't want a stranger messing with your stuff. But this could turn ugly fast. People willing to steal and sell organs can't afford to take chances when it comes to liability. And that's what you are to them. They won't hesitate to squash you like a bug."

His colorful choice of words sent a wave of nausea over me. I pictured myself as a spider crawling up the wall, minding her own business, when *wham*—out of nowhere, a rolled-up magazine smashes me into oblivion.

. . .

The idea I might be splattered like an unfortunate insect took away my appetite. But Mateo insisted I had to keep up my strength.

When we reached home, he poured a glass of wine for me and set about whipping up chicken enchiladas. The onions and garlic sizzling in the skillet reminded me of our first meal together at his aunt's restaurant, El Encanto. He greeted the hostess, his beautiful cousin Sofia, with an enthusiastic hug before she seated us at his regular table. They teased each other as we ate, making me wish I had a better relationship with my own extended family. His gentle smile when he spoke of how the young girl had chosen a school close by so she could help with the business had warmed me more than the tequila.

Since then, he had invited me several times to accompany him to his parents' home for dinner, promising there would be no inquisition about our plans for the future or my fertility. And each time, *yes* was on the tip of my tongue. But *not yet* tumbled out instead.

Today, his cooking filled the air with the aroma of comfort and security. For him, preparing a meal for someone he loved was part of the language of love. He was equally fluent in other ways of expressing his feelings.

We took our plates to the glassed-in sunroom my landlords added to what had originally been a carriage house. The older couple converted the space into an apartment for their pothead grandson. When he threw one too many parties, they tossed him, fumigated the unit, and rented it to me. They spent most of their time in Florida. The kid headed out west, where he could puff himself into oblivion.

The bright blue and green tiles on the wrought-iron table, a gift from Uncle Buddy's antique shop, gave the room an air of festivity. Although well into my second glass of chardonnay, I was not in a festive mood. Not even the golden glow of the weeping willow outside the window lifted my spirits.

It did, however, remind me of the poor Barbie doll hanging by her slender neck from a branch of that tree. An ominous warning for me to stop investigating the organ smuggling ring. I ignored it and almost got killed. Not only had I survived, but I helped end the ghoulish enterprise. Or so I thought.

"Are you going to keep pushing those black beans around your plate without taking a bite and praising me for my culinary skills?"

"I'm sorry. We just worked so hard to lock up Lance and Janelle, and now they both might get away with stealing organs from desperate migrant workers."

"Mi amor." He lifted my chin. "I give you my word that will not happen."

Much later, I lay in his arms, moving with the gentle rhythm of his breathing. I remembered his face when he burst into the exam room where Lance's ladies had planned to kill us. Greeted by the chaotic scene of bodies strewn on the floor, he hadn't known if I was dead or alive. Our tearful embrace when he discovered I wasn't hurt was the moment I knew we were meant to be together. And every day, our love had grown stronger.

But was it strong enough to make an impossible promise possible?

• • •

"Seems like you got your appetite back." Mateo smiled as I scooped scrambled eggs over my left-over beans and enchiladas.

"Sorry to start without you."

Still damp from the shower, he kissed the top of my head and joined me.

"You're okay not being here for the search, aren't you?"

"Not really, but like I said, I trust you. And while you were lounging around this morning, I got this great idea. Bethany's all about going with me to talk to the widow, but she won't be back in town from some real estate convention until tomorrow. I called Ashley and her mother picked up. I gave her the story about setting up an appointment with the reporter."

I noticed a few bites of rice left. "Are you going to eat that?"

"Help yourself." I emptied the bowl onto my plate and stuffed a forkful in my mouth. I washed it down with a glass of orange juice and continued.

"At first, her mom got huffy with me, but I insisted we would tell the story from Ashley's point of view and wouldn't print it without their approval. I felt shitty about lying, especially after how happy she sounded when I assured her the truth about her daughter would come out. Then I thought about the possibility her little girl was screwing around with underaged boys and didn't feel so bad."

When I stopped for a breath, he asked, "How many cups of coffee have you had?"

"Only two, no, possibly two and a half. Okay, three. But I'm more excited than over-caffeinated. Go ahead. Ask me why?"

"Why are you so excited, Lucy?"

"Because of Fiona Adams."

His total lack of expression reminded me I hadn't told him about Ryan's former fiancé. I gave him a quick rundown of the little I discovered about her, including new information gleaned from an early morning internet search.

"She opens the St. Ann's food pantry on Wednesdays, which means she's there today. I'll give her the gathering-comments-for-the-memorial story, pretend I got her name from a Classmates page, and act like I don't know anything about them being a couple."

"You think she'll go for it?"

"It doesn't really matter. The way she reacts is the important thing."

"What if she has a bad reaction, as in get the hell out of here before I brain you with this giant can of sweet potatoes?"

"Unless she put on a lot of post-break-up weight, I can take her, sweet potatoes and all."

"I don't doubt it, but it would be better if someone went with you."

"Bethany's not exactly a soup-kitchen kind of girl. And Hugh doesn't do well getting classy women to spill their guts for him. I promise to stay in a public place and not let her lock me up with boxes of dried pasta."

He sighed and rinsed his plate. "I'm not worried about Fiona. "

"I understand, but it's to Lance's advantage not to tell any of his gangster-style partners about me. Besides, I have my pepper spray, rape whistle, and the cool whacking thingy you got for me."

"You mean the collapsible baton you refused to clip to your belt?"

"It makes me look fat, but I'll attach it to my purse."

"Fine. But if you don't text me every two hours, I'm siccing Hugh on you."

"Every two hours, sir. Yes, sir." I saluted and stood on tiptoe to kiss him goodbye.

CHAPTER 10

I wasn't concerned about being taken out in the food pantry of a church, but Mateo's suggestion about bringing someone with me gave me an idea.

Cody Rae greeted me from the reception desk. "Good morning, Ms. Howard. I'm your temp girl, Ms. Saunders." She pointed to the name tag on her blouse. The teen had pulled her hair into a bun that sat low on the back of her neck. Instead of heavy eyeliner and dark lipstick, she wore a dusting of blush and a light coating of lip gloss.

Elsie rounded the corner with a soda and Danish. "I see you've met our temporary receptionist." She winked, and Cody Rae broke character with a giggle.

"Have you introduced her to Hugh?"

"Briefly. He was in a hurry, so there wasn't time to chat."

I had trouble picturing my surly boss chatting with this bright-eyed version of Elsie's great niece, but then I couldn't picture him having a chat with anyone. "So, Miss Saunders. Would you hold you down the fort while Ms. Erickson and I go on a secret mission?"

. . .

A thin woman with steely gray hair twisted into tight curls stood on the other side of the counter in the basement of St. Ann's

Church. Behind her, stacked canned goods were arranged in orderly rows. She nodded toward a sign taped to the wall: *Drop-off to Your Left.* Then she narrowed her eyes and looked me up and down.

"Can I provide assistance with bringing in your donations?"

Shit! Why hadn't I grabbed some creamed corn or pinto beans on my way?

"I'm sorry. I don't have any."

The church lady removed a pair of silver-rimmed glasses previously hidden in her wiry perm, slipped them on, and gave me another once-over before announcing in a cool, clipped voice, "St. Ann's never turns away anyone in need."

"Oh, no. I didn't come here for groceries."

"Coats and sweaters are in the annex with the rest of the clothing." She stepped back from the counter. Apparently, Christian charity had its limits.

"Thank you so much, but I only came to see Ms. Fiona Adams. She runs the morning shift, right?"

"Ms. Adams is busy in the receiving dock. I'm afraid she'll be tied up for the next hour or longer, depending on how many people *did* bring donations."

I ignored the not-so-subtle dig and said I wanted to help with the unloading. "Can you point me in her direction?"

"Only registered volunteers are allowed in that area." She executed a military turn of dismissal.

A pear-shaped man in a tight clerical collar approached from behind the guardian of the pantry. I braced myself for getting tossed out of church the way my youth leader bounced me and my teenage boyfriend for making out in the vestibule.

From the corner of my eye, I saw Elsie peeking around a barrel full of stuffed bears. We agreed to arrive separately. While I talked to Fiona, she would pretend to sign up as a volunteer to get to know our target's co-workers and milk them for gossip.

I shook my head, and she stepped out of sight. If I got thrown out, she still might be able to dig up something.

"There, there." Instead of asking me to leave, the man draped an arm around the grumpy guard dog's shoulders. "Remember, dear, we never refuse any help the Lord sends. Please provide her with a nametag and accompany her to the dock."

Her silent eyebrow raise suggested she questioned the source of this particular aid, but she kept quiet.

"I'm headed to a staff meeting, or I'd stay and get better acquainted. You ladies have a lovely day."

She winced when he patted her on the back, and I wondered if the gesture felt as condescending as his referring to her as *dear.*

She grabbed a stack of Visitor labels and shoved one across to me.

"Thank you, so much." My bright smile did nothing to melt her icy hostility.

She strode from behind her protective barrier and stood in front of me, tapping her foot as I printed my name.

"I don't have all day."

"Sorry. Let's go."

We stopped at an oversized walk-in closet with a wide shuttered window that took up the back wall.

"You have a volunteer, Ms. Adams," she announced before heading toward her post.

Her emphasis on the word *volunteer* made me sound more of a suspected serial killer than one of the Lord's handy women.

The lady kneeling among bags and boxes scattered across the floor stood and squinted at me.

"I didn't see anyone signed up for the morning shift." Although there was no hint of antagonism in her response, she wasn't exactly welcoming.

I introduced myself and explained I was more of a spur of the moment do-gooder, then confessed, "I really came to talk to you."

Fiona stood, dodging loose cans and dislodged diapers, as she moved closer to me. If not for my unpleasant guide's confirmation, I wouldn't have recognized this frail creature as the woman in the engagement photo. Her hair was no longer artfully arranged to accent her fair complexion. She had restrained it in a tight, no-nonsense ponytail. The high cheekbones that once accentuated her loveliness had sharpened into a caricature of themselves. The light in her eyes that brought life to the engagement picture had disappeared.

She still buzzed with energy, just not the joyful kind. Before, her expression transformed what would normally have been a stiffly posed announcement of upcoming bliss into a portrait of a woman deeply and happily in love. Today, there was a frenetic quality to her movements, as if giving way to stillness would bring dire consequences.

I had seen this behavior in my mother when Grandma Tucker died.

For the first time, a rush of guilt came over me as I spun my story about gathering material for a memorial. I watched Fiona's stoic expression crumble as tears pooled in her eyes. Her lips quivered and her pale cheeks became almost translucent. I vowed to make Hugh handle his own dirty work from now on.

At the end of my explanation, she stared past me for so long I turned to see what had stolen her attention. I saw nothing, but that didn't mean she hadn't. I imagined it was some ghostly reminder of what she had lost—twice, I suppose—or the dismal image of her life without the hope of reclaiming Ryan.

"I'm sorry if this is too much for you. I can come back another time."

She remained silent long enough that I debated waiting her out versus leaving the poor woman alone. She decided for me.

"This isn't a good place to talk. There's a sandwich shop around the corner."

Her distracted look disappeared, replaced by one of unsettling composure. Perhaps what I took for grief had been something else—an emotion I couldn't identify.

Within ten minutes, we were seated in a booth waiting for the server to bring our drinks. Coffee for me, tea with a fancy flower name for her.

"If I understand you correctly, you want me to provide material for Ryan Miller's memorial service. The same man who promised to love me forever only a few weeks before he deserted me. Is that right?"

Her words should have sounded angry or at least bitter. Instead, her delivery was robotic. Clearly, she was no longer the girl who thought her high school sweetheart tasted like a Baby Ruth. If she ever had been that girl.

A middle-aged woman carrying a tray with our order arrived. As she set the steaming mugs on the table, I considered my response. I expected a negative reaction from Fiona and had planned to pretend I didn't know about Ryan's deceit. Her tone suggested she was too sharp to fall for my story. So why had she agreed to talk to me?

"I hoped giving you a chance to share your feelings would shed more light on what he was really like. If you were able to say anything positive about him, it would say more about his character than praise from his family and friends. I didn't realize how hurtful it would be for you."

My last statement was partially true. I hadn't expected her to answer my request with some inane comment about her fiancé's excellent hygiene or luminous smile or with "Get the hell away from me." But the way our meeting played out in my mind had been so different from reality, I was at a loss and almost told her the truth. And I might have. Only she said it first.

"Ms. Howard," she began.

"Please, it's Lucy."

"As I was saying, Ms. Howard. I seriously doubt you came here expecting me to express my undying affection for my ex-fiancé. The Millers would never be tacky enough to solicit random comments about their only son. They were and still are completely devoted to him and blind to his shortcomings. Like many parents, they refused to acknowledge his role in our breakup. Instead, they put all the blame on her, especially after the unfortunate *miscarriage*."

She poured hot water from the ceramic teapot and daintily stirred the darkening liquid. I added cream and fake sugar to my coffee and blew on it to keep myself from grinning in triumph. Not only had she confirmed the rumor of Ashley's pregnancy, but she also chose her words in a way that indicated she accepted the part about it being a convenient means of dragging Ryan to the altar.

But I wasn't ready to go along with the theory that the only reason he married her was because he thought she was carrying his child. I couldn't ignore the possibility Ashley had been pregnant. Or that he was happy about it and totally captivated by his bride. Only an examination of her gynecological records would reveal the truth, which didn't matter anyway.

What mattered was the family saw their son's new wife as a seductress who lied to steal him from the right woman for him and for them. I understood why they considered her capable of murder. I wasn't certain Fiona agreed with their assessment.

"It sounds like you have some doubts about your ex's role in breaking off the engagement."

"Doubts?" She snorted. "You forget how long we were together. I knew exactly what kind of man he was. I accepted his lies and occasional infidelities and never expected him to change. You look shocked."

"More surprised, I guess." I recalled the newspaper photo and wondered if she was really that good of an actress. Rather than bring that up, I improvised. "You certainly convinced the Millers you were the perfect pair."

"That's because we were. I come from a solid stock—as Mr. Miller would say. We weren't as well off as they are but were quite respectable. The one flaw they recognized in their son was his lack of intelligence. The expectation was I would be the woman behind the man. They were relying on me to guide him in his career and beyond. His father wanted him to go into politics and knew he wasn't up for the challenge. I was."

Once again, I had to sit on my hands to keep from celebrating. In the Millers' eyes, Ashley had killed their son and their own ambitions. While it was possible they were right, it was impossible they were able to see the situation for what it was.

"And you were okay with all of this?" I immediately regretted my judgmental assessment. Fiona didn't seem to mind.

"There are worse things than being the wife of a powerful man. And God help me, I loved him. Still do if I'm being honest. But my shrink and I are working on that." She smiled for the first time. "I imagine it will be easier now that he's dead."

. . .

Fiona's words echoed like footsteps behind me as I hurried to my car, where Elsie waited.

"You look a little pale, dear," she said as I slid into the driver's seat.

I cranked the engine but didn't pull out of my parking spot. "That woman was cool, calm, and scary as hell." I reviewed our conversation, ending with her pronouncement that recovering from the loss of her ex would be easier now that he was no longer living.

"That is cold, but who would blame her? Getting displaced by a woman, a girl almost, you consider inferior in every way. This could prove to be as simple as *if I can't have him, nobody can.*"

"True, and if he'd been poisoned or electrocuted by a rigged toaster, I'd have no problem believing Fiona was behind it. Those methods require careful calculation and the desire to escape punishment. As for pushing someone out of a window, that's a crime of passion, a heat of the moment action. Like throwing noodles in someone's face. No one has the energy to fan the flames on that kind of fury for months. It's been almost two years since Ryan dumped her."

Elsie smiled at the reminder of my reaction to catching Lance with Janelle and flinging Chinese food at him. "I suppose you're right. Still, living with the humiliation of everyone in your circle knowing your sad story might ignite a slow burn, the type that explodes when you least expect it."

"Instead of narrowing our list of suspects, it's growing faster than I can keep up with it. Please tell me we don't have to add any of the church lady volunteers or condescending pastors."

"The person in charge of interviewing volunteer applications is on vacation. According to the lady over the processing of clothing donations, Fiona hadn't joined the crew until after the break-up, so no one knew him. I did manage to loosen up the dragon behind the counter. Surprise, surprise, she doesn't hold Fiona in high regard. Insists she only works at the church to show everyone that she's a kind and generous person instead of a selfish socialite. Other than demonstrating a poor example of Christian charity, her only other contribution was a comment about Fiona not spending much time between men. She seemed to think our girl got involved with some secret lover shortly before Ryan's death. When I pressed her, she didn't have anything more specific than that Fiona started getting her roots done regularly and had that certain spring in her step."

I closed my eyes in frustration. What began as a quest to confirm or reject the Millers' accusations had developed into an Agatha Christie style mystery, complete with a complicated list of characters.

Desperate to create order where there was none, I shot out of the lot. "This case or non-case or whatever it is, is driving me crazy."

"I think we both know what you need."

"Not a bad idea, but Mateo's tied up, and my head's not in the right place."

"Honey, I'm not talking about sex. What you need is some quality time with your spreadsheet."

She knew me too well.

In the parking lot, Elsie said she wanted to run by her house to check on Cody Rae. I told her not to come back to the office since she could easily work from home.

The darkened reception area gave me second thoughts. So quiet I heard the refrigerator humming from down the hall, the room seemed muffled in cotton. I wondered if there was such a thing as too much serenity.

"Don't be silly." The sound of my voice startled me as it echoed down the hallway, but I was determined to tough it out. My cozy office with its cheerful view eased my nerves. When I clicked on the new workbook tab, my anxiety dissolved.

The phone stopped me before I started. I tried hard to ignore it, but I had too much rule follower left in me.

"Farewell and Associates, Lucy Howard speaking."

"You've got that sexy receptionist thing going on."

Whether it was from the frustrating day I had, or from being sick and tired of dealing with annoying males, I snapped.

"I don't know who this is, but you have reached a place of business. You have two seconds to identify yourself before I hang up."

"Sorry, sweetheart. I hoped you'd recognize my voice. It's Chuck." His words slurred together, and I wondered if he'd been drinking. His next statement made me certain he had. "And you're even hotter when you get pissed off."

"Mr. Grover, the office is officially closed. What's a good time for me to reach you tomorrow?"

"How about half past kiss my ass?" He chuckled at his sparkling wit. "Just kidding, darlin'. Mr. Miller's been crawling all over me to find out about developments in the case against his daughter-in-law. I promised to get right on it. Let's meet for a drink and discuss your progress."

"That won't be necessary. I'll provide a full report to you within the next few days. Until then, please tell your client we've uncovered some very interesting facts that may or may not point to Ashley."

"Yeah, yeah. I'm sure you have, but the wife's always the best bet. Much more likely than any piece on the side."

"I can assure you we're on it. Now I have to go."

He sputtered a few expletives before I slammed the phone onto the receiver.

I refused to let that asshole ruin a date with my spreadsheet. I returned to the program and titled my work "Suspects in the Miller Case," then double checked to make sure autosave was on. My column designations were no-brainers: Suspect, Motive, Location at Time of Murder, Probability of Guilt, Notes.

Although Ashley made the top of the list, she wasn't really my first pick. For motive, I typed in money and added love with a question mark. I couldn't wrap my head around the possibility she would kill her husband to be with one of her boy toys. But I didn't understand the appeal of bedding young boys, either. I put fifty/fifty in Probability of Guilt, then decided not to make any guesses until more of the columns were filled and deleted it.

Fiona came in at number two because of her closing statement about her mental health improving with Ryan dead. I logged revenge as her motive but had trouble picturing her pushing him over a railing. Hers would be a dish served colder than a little over a year.

My third column was Unknown Boy. Flying into a hormonal rage and tossing your rival off a building fit the profile of a teenager in love.

Sue Ann Porter came in as number four with Disgruntled/Jealous colleague from work in parentheses. Since I only spoke with the department head, I filled in her motive with Kennel Insurance and laughed at the absurdity.

Then I remembered what Kanisha said about Ashley's choice of boy toys. Mostly jocks, the kind who went with cheerleaders and homecoming queens. What if one of those girls got mad over losing her boyfriend to Ashley and killed Ryan as revenge? Wait, that didn't make sense. If that were the case, she should have taken out the teacher, not the husband, unless that teenager tried to seduce him and totally lost it when he rejected her. I couldn't imagine a scenario where a horn dog like him would say no to an offer from a hot teenage girl but added another column for Jealous Girlfriend.

All the blank columns and rows started to get on my nerves, so I closed my laptop.

With so many suspects running around in my brain, I had forgotten about the men tearing up my apartment.

CHAPTER 11

I sent Mateo a text asking for an update on the search at the place that served as my refuge from the rest of the world's craziness. He replied they were about halfway through and not to worry because they were being careful to put everything back where it belonged.

His reassurance was doubly sweet. Like most couples who lived independent lives much longer than they'd been together, we had our pet peeves. Or I did, anyway. One was people not returning my things to their proper places.

His was my tendency to throw myself into my work.

I had scoffed at Hugh's suggestion I get back to the Miller case. How the hell would I be able to concentrate on anything but the pile of rubble I imagined awaiting me at home?

It seemed the two men I spent the most time with knew me better than I did. Once I accepted the challenge to discover the truth, I forgot about everything else. From what I learned so far about the Millers, I'd need more than my super-power of concentration.

And there was something bothering me about Chuck's call. I needed someone to bounce ideas around with and called Elsie. She answered on the first ring.

"Thank God, it's you. About that promise."

. . .

She opened the door before I rang the bell. With lips set in a tight, thin line and eyes darting from me to the kitchen, her demeanor projected the same urgency I heard earlier in her voice.

In a parody of cheerfulness, she half-shouted, "Lucy! What a wonderful surprise. We were just about to have a piece of chocolate pie."

The scene at the table dampened my enthusiasm about dessert.

Cody Rae leaned over a sandy-haired boy in an Army surplus-style jacket. He stared ahead while trailing his fork through meringue. Neither appeared to have heard Elsie's exuberant announcement of my arrival.

"Honey, would you introduce your friend to Lucy while I get her a plate?"

The fog of misery covering the teens must have been too thick to penetrate because they seemed not to notice we were there.

I said, "That's okay. We can do that later."

She sat upright and snapped her head toward me, then blinked. "Oh. You."

Not exactly an endorsement but not a *get-the-hell-out-of-here reaction* either. I took it as a small victory and slid into the chair across from them.

"Yes, me. Lucy Howard."

The boy's eyes were deeply shadowed, making him look haggard and tired, way beyond his years.

"Nice to meet you, Ms. Howard. I'm Danny Braden." He extended his hand, startling me with the simple gesture. I accepted his firm, dry grip, impressed by whoever was in charge of teaching manners at his house.

"Ms. Erickson explained you're afraid the authorities want to question you about Mrs. Miller's husband."

On my way to Elsie's, she filled me in on her niece's version of events. Cody Rae said there was nothing going on between the teacher and the troubled boy beside her. But when he'd gone home, he found the police parked at his house after. His mother was in Ohio taking care of a sick sister, so he sped past, straight to where he knew she was staying. Her theory was Ashley was trying to frame Danny.

She insisted to Elsie that the only thing between them was friendship. Their body language and the way he turned toward her before responding suggested otherwise.

"It's okay. She works with my aunt investigating Mr. Miller's murder, which means she knows what a bitch Mrs. Miller is. So, go ahead; tell her what happened."

I detected a slight twitch in his right eye seconds before he looked away.

"Danny, you can trust her."

Her use of that word heightened my growing discomfort. Should I stop him before he admitted to something incriminating? It occurred to me I shouldn't be concerned. A sixteen-year-old boy wasn't about to confide his secrets to a grown woman, no matter how much his *friend* wanted him to. Especially not if they wouldn't line up with what he already shared and could endanger whatever their relationship was.

"It's not that," he stammered. "I just don't like talking about it."

The poor kid looked as if he were about to cry, and that's when I felt certain he had not resisted Ashley's attempts to seduce him if only on an emotional level. A boy his age would be no match for a grown woman who had the hots for him.

A burst of anger shot through me and not just at Ashley. I was also angry with my father and all the men who secretly high-fived boys like Danny for being lucky. His luck landed him in a situation he wasn't prepared for. Even worse, his teacher might have manipulated him into doing something he'd regret for the rest of his life.

Despite his unwillingness to talk, he provided the same basic account as Cody Rae's. In his version, however, Ashley came across as less of a seductress. Instead of predatory, she sounded more like an overly affectionate adult who unintentionally involved him in her personal business. It had all been a giant mix-up, according to the boy. She mistook his appreciation for all the extra help she'd given for feelings he didn't have. She must have gotten confused when she mentioned him to the police.

Throughout his recitation, Cody Rae maintained a blank expression. When he finished, the only sound in the room was the tapping of her nails on the table until Elsie suggested we go to the den to let the kids have some privacy.

"Wow," I said as I sank into the sofa. "What a mess."

"That's putting it mildly. The poor thing can't catch a break. First, her mother betrays her. And now that foolish boy stomps on her already broken heart."

Compared to Ryan Miller, Cody Rae's luck wasn't all that bad. But I understood. Ashley's husband was beyond help. The sad girl in the kitchen still needed ours.

"So, you didn't buy all that misunderstanding crap?"

"No, and neither did Cody Rae. If it weren't for him hurting my niece, I'd feel sorry for the boy."

"It's obvious he has a thing for Ashley but doesn't want her to know. I guess he gets points for not rubbing her nose in it."

"Unless the kid's covering for somebody, maybe for himself."

It took a second for me to get her meaning. "Jesus, Elsie. Do you think he could be capable of shoving a man out the window? I bet he doesn't have to shave more than twice a week."

"I'm not sure what to believe, except that my niece is crazy about him, and young people in love can be dangerous."

Her words stayed with me as I considered my spreadsheet. Adding a column for Danny was a no-brainer. Not as clear was whether to include Cody Rae.

•   •   •

I sighed in relief that the only vehicle in my driveway was Mateo's black Bronco. The search party had ended. I unlocked the door and stepped inside, bracing myself for the possible chaos awaiting me.

Instead of looking as if a police team had tossed the place, the small living room to my left appeared untouched. I walked past a tidy den, where a TV newscaster announced the weather report was up next.

Mateo called out from the kitchen. "Beer, wine, or margarita?"

"Yes, please." I found him standing in front of the refrigerator.

"Rough day?" He wrapped his arms around me and held me close. I nodded into his chest.

"I suspected it might be. That's why there's a pitcher of margs in the fridge with our names on it. Curl up on the sofa while I pour you one."

I stood on tiptoe and kissed his cheek. "I'm going to love you forever and ever."

"You better. Now go."

The first drink went down easy as I listened to Mateo explain the search was a bust.

"What does Hugh think about not finding the key?"

"He didn't seem surprised. He never believed it would be there. Said anything coming from that scumbag had to be taken with an entire shaker of salt. He added a few more creative insults."

It warmed my heart that my boss hated my ex almost more than I did.

"Lance isn't known for telling the truth. But technically, he never told me about the key. That came from his attorney. Funny how he hasn't gotten back to me."

"It wasn't a total lost cause. We did find those wedding pictures of Buddy and Norm you've been looking for."

My uncle married the love of his life a few months after being removed from the list of suspects in the murder of his rival antique dealer. I printed photos from my phone of the ceremony, planning to compile them in an album.

"Oh, my God." I snuggled closer to him. "Where were they?"

"In the box of sweaters under the bed. They're on the kitchen counter now."

I closed my eyes at the memory of Buddy's sweet, round face glowing as he walked his husband down the aisle of the Lutheran church. Growing up in a small Tennessee town in the early fifties with three burly brothers hadn't been easy for him. He spent much of his time pretending to like girls when it was really their outfits he coveted.

His status as an undiagnosed narcoleptic who frequently dozed off at the most inconvenient times—singing in the choir at church, waiting to be summoned to kick an extra point during high school football games, and later, behind the wheel—didn't help. People called him lazy or simple-minded or both.

An observant ER doctor who recognized his symptoms during an examination after one of his driving accidents saved him from a life of misery, and he became the incredible Lady Lola, the most popular performer at Belle's Bountiful Beauties. A spat with the owner before the place shut down helped him get serious about his second passion, antiques, and he opened his own business. He met Norm at an estate sale, and the two had become inseparable.

The first real conversation Mateo and I had was when he interviewed me about the uncle I adored. If he'd been the least bit put off by Buddy's theatrical experiences, we would have ended before we began. I didn't realize it at the time, but his casual acceptance of the only adult in my life who never shied away from the truth was the moment I fell in love with him.

After a second drink, I told him about the sour-faced church lady and my conversation with Fiona and continued with my encounter with Cody Rae and Danny.

"Except for adding a cast of thousands to my list of characters in the case, I'm no closer to finding out what happened to Ryan Miller than when I started. Bethany's picking me up at nine, but I doubt we'll learn much from Ashley." My friend always insisted on driving because she said I drove as slow as her grandpa.

"Are you kidding me? The two of you will crack that poor woman like a walnut."

"I sure hope so because this whole hot for teacher situation makes me queasy."

"We can't have you off your game." He traced my jawline with his fingertip and trailed kisses from my neck to my collarbone. "Turns out, I've got the perfect cure for what ails you."

And he did.

CHAPTER 12

Mateo left a sticky note on the dresser saying Sofia had invited him to lunch and he had several meetings with clients, so he would be home late.

Wincing at the sight of my tangled hair and swollen lips, I stepped into the shower and lathered up with the sweet smell of jasmine. Only after the faucet ran tepid did I turn it off, wrap myself in towels, and head to the bedroom to dress.

The bitter-rich aroma of coffee lured me to the kitchen where I found another message underneath a banana muffin covered in plastic.

Heat for fifteen seconds in the microwave. Heart, M.

With a Mexican mother and a second-generation Irish dad, Mateo measured love with equal parts food and drink. Sometimes, it was difficult to remember this was the same man who had been prepared to take down my kidnappers with deadly force if necessary.

I followed his instructions, then took muffin and coffee upstairs, where I dried my hair and put on makeup.

The doorbell rang at precisely 8:55. Bethany's real estate career transformed her into a model of punctuality. It did nothing to tame her wild side, but she'd become an expert at projecting an aura of professionalism. In a bright green and navy floral midi-dress, she looked like a society gal who'd gotten bored with her perfect life and taken a job as a feature writer, strictly for the hell of it. Her auburn hair lay in a sleek low bun on the back of her neck. Small pearl earrings and matching necklace completed the picture.

As usual, she made me question my choice of outfit, but it was too late to change out of my standard investigative uniform: black jeans, oversized white shirt, and light-weight leather jacket.

"I haven't been this excited since Robby Pendergast broke up with that slutty cheerleader and asked me to the prom. Scoot over before I pee my pants." She brushed past me.

"Since who did what?" By the time she reappeared, I remembered Robby was the school quarterback Bethany shamelessly pursued until he dumped his girlfriend. "I remember you going to prom with that tennis player?"

"I didn't say I went with Robby. Just that he asked me. But who cares? We've got a suspect to interrogate."

On the way, I reminded her we wouldn't be grilling a career criminal. "All we know for sure is her husband's death is suspicious."

"And that she's a sexual predator."

"An alleged sexual predator. As far as Ashley's concerned, we're there to help memorialize her husband, not portray her as a murderer. If we come across as threatening, we won't learn anything useful."

Ashley and Ryan bought a house in an established subdivision. The homes were mostly ranch-style, heavy on brick fronts and wrought-iron railings with postage-stamp-sized porches. Theirs had a side entrance garage and a neatly kept stepping-stone walkway.

Some of the paint on the white shutters was peeling, and a giant spider's web dangled from the awning above us. But lush flowering ferns swung from under the gutters. A jaunty sunbonnet wreath with fake blue roses adorned the bright red door.

Ashley Miller opened it before we rang the bell. In her arms, an apricot poodle wriggled and let out a series of high-pitched howls. She cradled the dog like a baby.

"Hush, Taffy. These nice ladies are here to help us. Please, come in." Her hair hung limp against pale skin, and dark smudges below long-lashed blue eyes gave her a haunted look. Yet she maintained a girl-next-door prettiness. Although she probably weighed less than a hundred pounds, her hips swayed seductively beneath tight, ragged-at-the-knees jeans as we followed her inside. I could almost hear a murmur of adolescent boys sighing as she wrote grammar rules on the board.

Still holding the squirming dog, she ushered us into what my grandmother would have called the parlor. To regular folk like me, it was the living room. The contrast between cluttered arrangements of seashells and baskets against the periwinkle walls and the fluffy, stark white rug made my eyes hurt. And an ancient upright piano near the entrance to the adjoining area reminded me of afternoons in the stuffy home of my frustrated teacher.

"I'll just be a minute." She motioned toward an overstuffed loveseat of bright yellow and lavender flowers. "Have a seat while I get Taffy settled in the bedroom."

As soon as she was gone, Bethany wrinkled her delicate nose and said, "This room looks like a Laura Ashley store exploded."

I shushed her but didn't disagree.

"Shush yourself," she replied, then added, "There's no way she heard me over that yowling mutt."

She raised an eyebrow, then walked to the mantle and ran her fingers across the ornately patterned white wood. I squeezed between color coordinated pillows and cleared space for her to join me.

"Do you know how much these houses are going for? If she'd let me give this place a serious makeover, we'd make a fortune."

A blur of motion outside the old-fashioned picture window sent me back to my childhood. The blackbird hurling itself toward us veered away at the last minute, unlike the poor birds who battered themselves against what my mother referred to as our view of the world. She took great pride in the gleaming glass surface until tiny bodies streaked it with gore and forced her to put up curtains.

"*We?* Even if Ashley wants to sell, you can't be her realtor because you are a feature writer for the *Marietta Neighbor.*"

"Nobody can live off that measly salary. I consider my newspaper work as a creative outlet. My regular job is in real estate. The first step is to establish a rapport with my client. Plant a little seed, then come back later to seal the deal. Don't worry. She won't suspect a thing. For now, it's all about painting a flattering picture of the grieving widow and her deceased husband."

When Bethany told me not to worry, I felt a tremble of terror and seriously questioned bringing her. She flashed her killer smile and continued strolling around the room, checking out baseboards and peeking behind framed family photos clustered on the walls.

I focused on those tableaus of relatives and loved ones. Throughout my brief career snooping through people's lives, I'd gotten pretty good at reading the frozen smiles captured by the camera's lens. Thin-lipped mommies with hands squeezing the shoulders of grimacing children. Stoic daddies with fingers stiffly splayed at their sides. And the kiddies with sullen eyes.

Even the best photographers couldn't tamp down all those swirling emotions, at least not in every shot. Often, it was nothing more than the pressure of trying to simulate perfection. But sometimes it was more. Suppressed anger over suspected infidelities, fear of a stinging reprimand, worry about a failing business.

This couple's photographer had been very good. Other than a slight tightness in Ryan's lips and a faraway look in his wife's eyes, both of which could be the result of wedding jitters, the Millers could have been the standard bearers for wedded bliss. If not for the possibility she murdered him, I wouldn't have bothered to take a deeper dive. Ashley's return put my swim on hold.

"Taffy has been a complete wreck since we lost Ryan. Of course, everyone has." Her wide eyes glistened with tears that pooled without spilling over.

She sat in a brilliant yellow chair across from us and crossed her legs at the ankles, the way my mother insisted ladies did. The slight swell of free-range breasts under her oversized t-shirt didn't quite fit that image.

"We are so sorry for your loss," I began.

"Such a tragedy," Bethany added and patted our hostess's shoulder before sliding into the seat beside me.

The young widow pulled a tissue from her pocket and dabbed it over dry cheeks. "It's been a nightmare. Not just my husband's death." She leaned forward and spoke in a softer voice. "People are saying I had something to do with it."

Bethany exhaled a lengthy *No*, and I elbowed her exaggerated performance. Our hostess seemed not to notice.

"I didn't believe it myself at first. Not until *she* came right out and accused me."

We followed the direction of her shaking pointer finger and landed on a five by seven photo perched on the top shelf of the bookshelf. Ryan stood behind a seated older woman with his same high forehead and cheekbones. The *she* in question had to be her dead husband's mother.

"She has always hated me." As she stared at her nemesis, her eyes lost their liquid innocence. A flash of bottomless dark in them reminded me of a shark I once saw in a tank at Sea World. I blinked, and the grieving widow was back.

"Believe me, I tried everything to win her over. But I just wasn't good enough."

"Mothers can be difficult when it comes to their baby boys." Bethany shook her head with convincing sympathy. I remembered her line about establishing rapport and experienced newfound respect for my friend's acting ability.

"I suppose so, but she's not the only one spreading hateful rumors about me. That's why I was so glad when you called to set things straight."

My heartbeat quickened with excitement and a little pride at how easily we'd manipulated her into spilling her secrets.

Bethany interrupted my internal celebration. "Exactly. So, why don't you tell us about you and Ryan? How devoted you were to one another. And how happy he made you."

Ashley's eyelids fluttered rapidly as she tossed her wavy blonde hair over her shoulders. As if on cue, sunlight played across her heart-shaped face, illuminating the freckles on her perfect little upturned nose. What teenage boy could resist a woman-child like her? Especially if she didn't want to be resisted. She gave my friend a Mona Lisa smile and sighed.

"We were so happy. Or at least I was."

My spine stiffened, and Bethany grabbed hold of the pillow that had fallen onto her lap.

I cleared my throat, then said, "I'm sorry, but I'm confused. You *were* happy?"

Ashley covered her face and peeked through her fingers, looking even more childlike. "Oh, please, please don't put that in your article."

"This is completely off the record. I'd never publish anything that would make things worse for you."

"Absolutely not," I added to the first genuinely honest statement Bethany or I had made since arriving. Of course, we wouldn't be publishing anything because we were big fat liars, but I pushed that aside.

"It's just so hard to know who to trust."

"Pinky swear, your story is safe with us." Bethany held up her little finger, and Ashley curled hers around it.

I squelched the bubble of laughter threatening to burst to the surface and blow our cover. When they turned to me, I nodded solemnly. "Pinky swear." But I didn't offer my own digit.

Ashley sat quiet for so long I thought she noticed my failure to cement the oath and had decided not to continue. Bethany tensed beside me, and I willed her to wait out the silence. A series of angry yelps shattered the stillness.

"I'm coming, baby." She bolted from the room.

"What the hell?" Bethany whispered. "She'll be back, right? Because no way am I leaving without hearing the end of that story."

The click of toenails against hardwood floors answered my question as Taffy plummeted through the doorway directly onto my friend's lap. Ashley scurried to retrieve the dog but not before the pup removed most of Bethany's carefully applied blush with her slurpy kisses.

"Oh my God. My sweet girl never does that." She hugged the animal to her chest. "She usually hates everybody but me. She must be telling me you're someone I can trust."

CHAPTER 13

After listening to Ashley's account of her deteriorating marriage, we promised to get back to her before we published the memorial piece. Almost as shocking as what she said was the effect it had on Bethany, who seemed to have been rendered speechless. At least until we pulled out of the driveway.

"Well, that was a surprise."

"More a seismic shift in the atmosphere." I leaned against the headrest and closed my eyes, replaying the last hour in my head.

Ashley insisted we have iced tea and homemade sugar cookies before she picked up her story. We relocated to the kitchen with its pale peach floor tiles and cream-colored cabinets. She poured our drinks into crystal glasses and placed the cookies on a blue and white platter before sitting. Taffy hopped up and snuggled onto her lap.

"As I said, Ryan changed. He was so quiet, like if he spoke, secrets might come pouring out. I started to wonder if he'd found somebody else and was trying to find the best time to break the news to me."

Bethany, although never married, had been close several times. And she knew quite a bit about men.

"Oh, honey. That's not unusual. All guys change after the honeymoon phase is over. But that doesn't mean they don't love you. And it certainly doesn't mean they're cheating on you."

I dug my nails into my palm to keep from blurting out my take on infidelity. Lance continued lavishing me with attention while seeing Janelle on the side. Since he was a sociopath, I supposed his behavior might not count. So, I stayed quiet and nodded in agreement.

"I convinced myself it was my imagination. He seemed sort of, you know..." She stroked the little dog's silky hair and stared into the distance, either searching for the right word or taking care not to say something that could incriminate her.

"You mean distant?" I offered.

"Yeah, that's it. Distant. Real distant. I would be talking to him, and he wasn't all there. I guessed he might be worrying about not selling enough policies. Or he had another argument with his father. That man kept demanding more and more."

From the information Hugh gave me, Edward Miller provided his son with office space, a part-time secretary, and a client list most agents would have killed for. How much pressure could Ryan have been under?

"But it got worse." Her emphasis on the word *worse* made me fidget.

My friend, however, leaned closer to Ashley and patted her knee. "Exactly how bad did it get?"

"He, uh, well. He stopped wanting to, you know." Her voice was so low, I barely heard her. Then she took a deep breath and spoke a bit louder. "He almost never wanted to do *it.*"

Usually, I'm mildly curious about other people's sex lives. Are they having more fun than me? Do they do kinky stuff? But when a person can't even say the word "sex," my interest wavers.

Not Bethany. "You mean you stopped having intercourse?"

"We didn't completely stop. But it was hardly ever—three, sometimes four times a week."

I choked and sent a spurt of tea out of my nose. Bethany slapped me on the back a little harder than necessary. Taffy whined, and Ashley appeared to be concerned. I wiped my chin with a cloth napkin.

"Went down the wrong way. Please, go on."

"It was the phone calls that convinced me it had to be another woman. Late at night, I heard him whispering in the bathroom. I couldn't make out what he was saying, but he was using his sexy voice."

I had my doubts about her ability to discern sexiness without being in the room. From the frown on Bethany's face, I guessed she was skeptical, too.

"There could be an innocent explanation," I said.

"That's not all." She popped up fast enough to elicit a yap of protest from Taffy. The three of us watched as she opened a drawer and removed an envelope.

"The week before Ryan passed, I found this in the glove compartment of his car." She thrust a folded piece of white paper in front of me. Unfolding it carefully, I recognized it as a cocktail napkin. Someone had drawn an oversized heart with a message inscribed in it. *I'll never forget last night.*

The logo had been torn off, and the handwriting was cramped and sloppy. Ashley dissolved into harsh sobs. Bethany gently patted her shoulder while I pocketed the scrap of paper and eased out of the room.

· · ·

"Did you buy that sob sister act?"

I braked hard on the passenger floorboard as she sailed into the far-left lane, cutting off a rental truck pulling a camper.

"Jesus. That was close."

She ignored my outburst and turned up the radio. Pat Benatar demanded to be hit with a best shot, and I prayed not to be hit period.

"So, what's your take on the weeping widow?"

"Honestly, I'm not sure." Yes, it had crossed my mind Ryan might be fooling around. And if Ashley knew about it, that made her a stronger candidate for being his killer.

"You're kidding, right? That woman is such a phony. Homemade cookies, my ass."

"I suppose. But telling us she suspected her husband was cheating on her doesn't make sense. And they were definitely store bought."

"And way beyond the best-buy date, just like that little girl act. Which reminds me, I'm starving. Let's get lunch, and you can tell me why you stole that ratty napkin."

I gritted my teeth as she soared across three lanes of traffic to the next exit.

Over a much-needed glass of wine, we continued our discussion about Ashley's veracity and my petty theft.

"I kept expecting you to ask about her private tutoring." She put air-quotes around *tutoring*, then bit down on a slab of buttered French bread.

"Should I have brought that up before or after she told us how happy she'd been before discovering her husband wasn't? And exactly how would that question fit into the fake memorial article?"

Bethany took another swallow of wine. "You've got a point. I doubt she would tell the truth anyway. So, what's with the napkin?"

During the harrowing ride to the restaurant, I forgot about the barely legible message scrawled on the crumpled paper. I removed it from my pocket and smoothed it out as much as possible.

She stared at it before asking, "Wonder what was so *unforgettable* about it?" Holding up the breadbasket, she waved to our server. Her smile had its usual effect, and the young man rushed to the table as if we'd set it on fire. If she noticed his flushed face and trembling hands, she gave no indication, most likely because she was used to such reactions from members of the opposite gender.

I retrieved the baggy containing the matchbook Hugh had given me.

"Our intern found this in Ryan's trash. Well, he's not ours anymore because he got fired. Anyway, check it out." I pressed it flat, logo side up.

Bethany squinted. "The Broadview Motel on Scenic Highway? Never heard of it."

The waiter returned with our bread and mumbled our salads would be out soon. He had to use both hands to steady himself enough to pour additional water into our glasses. I thanked him, and he scurried away.

"Me, neither. But that's not the point. Check out the handwriting."

She lined the napkin and matchbook side by side and underlined the words with her finger as she silently read. "Could the same person have written them?"

"Are you kidding? See how all the letters slant to the right except the o's. They are perfectly vertical. And the hearts? The hearts are a dead giveaway. The left side is round. The other is all scrunched up."

"True, but only one has a spear chunked through it."

"That's an arrow, and there's not much room for it with the words. Besides, the matchbook probably came before that unforgettable crap. What happened in 213 must have been good enough to warrant a little something extra."

Our salads arrived before we had the chance to speculate on the sort of activities that deserved special mention on a sexual performance chart. I preferred not to mix food and sex. Bethany had no such compunctions but always gave her full attention to whatever meal she was eating. As usual, she asked for the dessert menu and selected creampuffs covered in chocolate sauce.

"How do you eat all that and never gain weight?"

"It's been scientifically proven that a deviant lifestyle burns more calories. If you and Mateo turned up your freak, you could skip Zumba for a month."

"We are plenty freaky. And I like Zumba."

"Right. So, what's next Nancy Drew?"

"Let's see if we can find out exactly who's been getting their freak on at the Broadview Motel and who'll never forget it."

She grinned and licked a dollop of cream off her lip.

Only minutes ago, I'd been patting myself on the back over how easily we'd gotten Ashley to spill family secrets. A flash of her dead-eyed shark stare came to me, darkening my mood and leaving me to wonder who had out-maneuvered whom.

CHAPTER 14

We drove straight to the address on the matchbook and pulled into the parking lot of a mustard-yellow building. The paint on the unit doors had once been brown before being covered with an insufficient coat of red. Uneven black numbers like the ones taped on cheap mailboxes proclaimed there were fourteen units and a Manger's Office. The ghost outline of the missing 'a' indicated it had disappeared long ago.

Bethany wrinkled her nose. "All I can say is I hope they brought their own sheets and plenty of disinfectant."

"There's not enough bleach in the world." I shook my head. "Let's get this over with. Just sitting here makes me want to take a shower."

We stumbled over broken patches of concrete on our way to either the manager's office or a year-round nativity scene. Neither Mother Mary nor angels stood guard in a lobby smelling of mildew and onions. Only a pear-shaped man in a graying wife-beater t-shirt sat at the register with his back to us, revealing an intricate comb-over frighteningly similar to the rear end of some kind of marsupial. A Hank Williams, Jr. song I recognized as one of his ballads to white supremacy played in the background. The buzzer signaled our entrance, and the guy at the counter turned around but didn't glance up from the bare-breasted beauty gracing the pages of his magazine.

"Good afternoon." He finally glanced up at me, and I gave him my best imitation of Bethany's killer smile.

Instead of melting with desire, our host removed the cigarette stuck behind his ear, taking strands of greasy black hair along with it. He placed it in the space between his front teeth and tapped his dirty nails on the sign-in sheet.

Bethany leaned over the peeling linoleum countertop and squinted at the plastic nametag half-buried in exposed chest fuzz. It read *Assistant Manager Earl.*

"Is that good ole' Hank, Jr. on the radio? We absolutely love him. Were you at that concert in Lakewood? Oh, my God." She quivered with excitement over meeting a fellow fan although she detested both the artist and his music.

I waited for the heat to blossom on his oily neck, but he only scratched the side of his nose and said, "It's $30.00 an hour, cash in advance, no checks, no credit cards."

It was my turn to stare. I didn't know whether to be more shocked at the price—reasonable or extravagant?—or from Earl's immunity to my friend's allure or from his assumption we were lovers.

I recovered my ability to speak before Bethany did. "Oh, no. We're not, not that there's anything wrong with it. My best friend from high school is married to a lovely woman. We haven't seen them recently because they bought an alpaca farm in the mountains. I love alpacas, and the countryside is beautiful. But I'm more of a city girl."

"Lady, you can be a wolverine for all I care. In case you hadn't noticed, this is a motel. So, if you're not here for a room, what the hell *do* you want?"

I shrugged and looked at Bethany. She scowled at the first man who had resisted her charm since her breasts developed. Then she transformed her annoyance into aggression. "Okay, Earl. We're working in cooperation with the Dekalb County Family Court and need some information."

I bobbed my head in agreement and admiration.

"If that's what you're after, try the library. Nobody under twenty-one is allowed to check in without an adult. We don't deal with no juveniles. All our paperwork is up to date, including the health inspection."

I was too relieved he hadn't asked for identification to comment on his defensive stance on the cleanliness of the place.

Bethany pressed on. "Go ahead, Miss Thomas. Show him the photo."

It took a second or two for me to realize I was Miss Thomas and to remember the folder in my purse with Ashley and Ryan's engagement picture from the newspaper.

"Have either of these people been guests of your establishment in the past year?"

He hesitated, and I stepped it up with a little assertiveness of my own. "Look, sir. We didn't come here to cause you or your business any trouble, but if you don't cooperate, we'll have to resort to *other measures.*"

I sounded like my high school principal when he terrorized us with the prospect that our latest indiscretion could end up on our permanent records. I swelled with pride when Earl turned pale. No doubt he already had quite a *permanent record.*

"Never seen the blonde, but the guy used to come in here about once a week up until a few months ago. Now, I've got some paperwork to catch up on." Obviously, he considered the interrogation at an end.

Bethany didn't.

"You recognize the man but not the woman?" Her high pitch indicated a lapse in cool, but she recovered fast. "What I mean to say is if she wasn't the one who checked in with him, who did? We need a description of whoever accompanied him."

She impressed me with her ability to react so quickly on her feet, a crossover skill from being in the real estate business. She removed a small notepad from her purse and flipped it open as if this were one of her many daily interrogations.

"Come on, lady. I don't give a damn who goes into the room as long as it's paid for."

"Shouldn't both names be on the register?" I asked.

He rolled his eyes.

Unless Ryan registered as *Mr. and Mrs. Smith*, there might be a clue in whatever fake name he used. "Show us where he signed in." I had to fight back adding please to my demand. People with authority do not beg.

"You think I memorize the guest list? Since you asked so nice and I'd do anything to get you two out of here, I'll try to find your guy."

He flipped through several weeks of pages, then stopped and jabbed a fat finger at the neatly penned signature: *Lord and Lady Chatterley* next to what appeared to be some sort of taco sauce stain.

"That's them. The Chatterleys. Cash in advance, never caused any trouble. Not like some of the people who come in here." He focused his narrow eyes on me and frowned.

Another time and I might have been intimidated by his confrontational glare. But I was stunned by their choice of pseudonyms.

Bethany didn't skip a beat. "What about her car?"

He cut her off. "What the hell? I'd like to see some identification or screw the Dekalb court. I'm calling the cops myself."

I abandoned trying to captivate him with my smile and went with a little flattery and a lot of double-talk. "That won't be necessary. You've been very helpful, and we plan to mention it to our friends at the Georgia Hotel and Motel Association Review Committee. There's one more thing."

I pulled my phone from my pocket and tapped on camera. "I need a quick photo in case we have to match signatures." I snapped a few shots before he had time to protest.

"Come along, Ms. Lawrence. We're late for our appointment with the commissioner."

I was on a roll and we were out the door and in the car before Earl finished scratching his crotch.

. . .

Ten miles down the road, we were still laughing and congratulating ourselves on our award-winning performances.

"I can't get over the two of them calling themselves Lord and Lady Chatterly?"

Bethany's blank expression reminded me she majored in business.

"Sorry. *Lady Chatterley's Lover* is this hot British novel that was really ahead of its time. It came out in the late 1920s and was about this aristocratic lady who's sexually frustrated because her husband's in a wheelchair. English was my major, and I didn't study it until my junior year in college. There's no way Ryan Miller ever read that book."

"He could have seen it on Ashley's bookshelf, and the title stuck with him. Or he thought it was funny to reference one of his wife's books while he was cheating on her."

I shook my head. "That's way too sophisticated for an insurance salesman. And I don't want to sound bitchy, but Ashley hasn't taught anything more advanced than grammar and comp. There's no way she read that on her own. They made some old movies from the book but nothing the Millers would have liked."

"What if the idea came from his lover? And before you get all literary analysis on me, she probably saw the title of the movie on Netflix and took it for an episode of *Gossip Girls*."

The driver behind us blasted his horn when Bethany swerved into the exit lane without using her blinker. "When you asked me to go with you to talk to Miss Slutty Teacher, I had no idea how much fun we'd have."

"The paper announced the funeral will be day after tomorrow. At least reconsider going with me. Nothing says you have to wear black."

"I wish I could. But I scheduled an open house. Why don't you take your Irish-Latino lover?"

"He has to go to a conference in D.C. I considered asking Mom, but she and Dad are on a cruise to the Bahamas. Besides, she wouldn't approve of me intruding on people who are grieving. In her defense, it is a pretty shitty thing to do."

"Sounds like the perfect event for your charming boss."

I shook my head. "He won't admit it, but I get the impression funerals scare him. Nope. It's little ole me poking around a bunch of mourners. Not exactly something to be proud of."

"Don't feel bad. You're just doing your job. Honestly, I can't wait to hear all about it."

"Well, I'm not looking forward to going by myself."

She stopped at the main entrance to my building and shut off the engine before slapping her hand on the steering wheel. "I've got it. The perfect companion to snoop around with at a funeral."

The light in the back of my brain flickered on. "Oh, my God! Why didn't it come to me sooner?"

We grinned at each other and shouted at the same time. "Uncle Buddy!"

I was still beaming as I waved goodbye to Bethany and started up the office steps, expecting the place to be empty since mine was the only car in the lot. I discovered I wasn't alone when the intruder stepped from the shadows.

CHAPTER 15

I fumbled in my purse for the pepper spray Mateo insisted I attach to my key chain and shouted, "Stop where you are. I've got a gun."

A familiar voice responded. "Please, Miss Howard. Don't shoot." Instead of the army jacket, Danny wore a dark gray sweatshirt with the hood pulled over his head.

"You scared the bejesus out of me. Never, ever sneak up on me like that. What if I really had a weapon? Where would you be then?"

"Sorry, I didn't want anyone to see me. Wait, you don't have a gun? 'Cause that freaked me out."

"That doesn't make us even. But who are you afraid of? What's happened?"

I pictured him going to Ashley's house, expecting her to run off with him or at least welcome him into her bed. If she rejected him, who knows what he might have done? I regretted telling him about not having a gun. A closer look at his face erased any doubts I had about the boy being dangerous.

Heavy-lidded eyes, hollow cheeks, and slumped shoulders made him seem both younger and older. I had nothing to fear from this tired kid, who carried a burden far beyond his years.

"Never mind. Let's get you inside."

He followed me up the stairs to my office and wrangled out of his backpack before sitting in the chair next to my desk.

"How about something to eat or drink? We have juice, soda, and coffee. The doughnuts are a little stale, but there are peanut butter crackers."

"Just water, please."

When I gave it to him, he gulped it down in two long swallows. He swiped his hand across his lips, then crumpled and uncrumpled the empty bottle without looking at me.

After popping the tab on a can of Coke Zero, I asked, "Who are you hiding from, and what do you want from me?"

"Last night, Cody Rae dropped me off at home. I snuck through the back in case the cops sent someone to watch the place."

I remembered his mother was visiting her sick sister. The idea of Danny alone in a darkened house, fearful that any minute the police would come crashing through his door, saddened me.

"It must be hard for you to deal with this without your mom."

He shook his head. "After Dad died, she got real depressed. The doctor prescribed her something she can't drink with. The past few months, she's been getting better. I want to keep her out of all of this for as long as possible."

From his expression and choice of words, I gathered he understood the severity of his predicament.

He pushed the hood back and ran his fingers through his hair. I resisted the urge to smooth it in place. Danny Braden had suffered enough from the attention of an older woman. Because, despite his denials to Cody Rae, I was certain there had been more between the boy and his teacher than academics.

"I'm sure the police only want to ask you a few questions about Mrs. Miller."

"That's just it. Anything I say is going to come out all twisted." He sniffed and turned his head away from me.

I patted his shoulder. "The authorities are pretty good at finding out stuff. Shouldn't they learn the truth from you instead of second hand?"

"What difference does it make? Nothing I do will help. She warned me about this."

"Warned you about what?" I suspected the *who* was Ashley. I hoped the *what* wasn't a confession of murder.

"She said if I talk about any of it, people won't understand. And if the cops find out, I'll need a good attorney. Miss Howard, we can't even afford a lousy lawyer. And public defenders will want me to take a plea."

I put my hands in my lap, so he wouldn't see them trembling. Ashley had to be the one who threw in the line about public defenders. I wished we'd been nastier to her during our fake interview. Now, I needed to say something to keep Danny from blurting out his role in Ryan Miller's death. But I had nothing.

"A plea? Did she tell you to do that?"

"No. It just seemed like the best way to stop all the craziness. But if I accepted one, it would be a lie. And I suck at lying." He smacked himself hard on the forehead. "I'm such an idiot."

When I realized he was lining up for another shot, I grabbed his arm and held on tight. "You're not an idiot, but you will be if you keep knocking yourself on the head. I can help you find a good lawyer who'll take your case pro bono. Why would you need to lie? Before we go any further, tell me what the police suspect you've done and what you really did."

"Mrs. Miller said they would accuse me of killing her husband because of our, uh, our, you know."

"Please, be more specific about exactly what went on between you two."

His face and neck became dark scarlet before fading to a deathly white. "At first, it was all about helping me be a better writer. She said I was good enough to get a scholarship someplace with a journalism department. She worked with me on a story about the impact mass murders have on students. I submitted it to the school paper. They published it. She told me to use it as part of my application to college next year. Called it brilliant and said I should come to her house for dinner to celebrate."

I imagined my idea of celebrating with a minor was nothing like Ashley's. His miserable expression confirmed that supposition.

"I wish I'd never gone. She's so sweet and pretty. I never dreamed somebody so great would care about me. I didn't plan it; it just happened."

"You do realize Ashley Miller is a grown woman, and you are under seventeen? None of this is your fault, not legally or morally."

"She said that's what people would say. That everyone would blame her, and it would ruin her life if her husband found out. So, we had to stop meeting outside of school."

"Did that upset you?" Stupid question, but better than the one I really wanted to ask, which was did it make you want to kill Ryan Miller.

"I hated it. But I got where she was coming from. She's great and all that, but it was a lot. Cody Rae calls her too needy. But she hates her. Sometimes Mrs. Miller talked about how she wished we were together like a real couple. Then she'd start crying. I tried to come up with something to say to stop her from feeling so crappy, but all I could do was think about what would happen if I brought her to the prom? Weird, right?"

Although I wanted to explore that image, I shook my head. "The weirdest. So, weren't you angry when Mrs. Miller dumped you?"

"She didn't dump me. She let me go because I was ready to fly on my own. I was sad, but I had Cody Rae. We've been best friends since middle school. She knew something was wrong and stuck by me."

"You're lucky to have her." I doubted his luck would hold now that his good buddy, who probably thought she was much more than that, figured out the truth. "To be clear, though, you had nothing to do with Ryan Miller's murder."

"Murder? Ashley—I mean Mrs. Miller—she said I shouldn't call her Ashley anymore—told me the cops said it was suicide. She was really upset about that because she doesn't believe he killed himself, that it must have been a terrible accident. Whatever. But I didn't have anything to do with it."

I believed him but needed to push a little harder. "It happened last Tuesday sometime in the late afternoon or early evening. Where were you then?"

He closed his eyes for a second before answering. "I was supposed to go to work at the Golden Rooster after school. But Mrs. Miller asked if I could meet her in the Target parking lot at 5:00. She said it was important, so I called in sick. I waited for her until 6:30, but she never showed up. I walked around the park to figure out what to do next. I didn't get home until after 7:30."

"Did you see anybody? Someone who could vouch for you?"

"You mean an alibi?" His head dropped to his chest before whispering, "No."

"Sometimes that's not a bad thing. Innocent people rarely concern themselves with stuff like that. But it does make talking to the police trickier." I wondered if Ashley hadn't set it up so he wouldn't have anyone to corroborate where he was. Was she capable of such cold-blooded calculation?

He leaped to his feet, and I jumped up with him, as if we both expected the homicide department to barrel through the door in response to my mentioning them.

"The cops might be watching, which means I've gotten you in trouble, too." He made a grab for his bag, but I got to it first.

"Did you forget you're dealing with a professional claims investigator?" I pasted a smile on my face, hoping he would buy my make-believe confidence. In case he didn't, I followed up with fast talk.

"Most likely, the police are only at the gathering information stage of the investigation. Avoiding them was smart. With your break coming up in a few days, no one should be suspicious if you don't show up for classes. It'll look as if you left early for a vacation. Now, we need a place for you to stay. It's only a matter of time before somebody connects you and Cody Rae, so Elsie's is out."

He groaned, and I was glad I hadn't expressed my growing fear that the authorities might consider the girl a person of interest and come to question her.

"Is there someone you could visit, preferably in a different state? A relative or friend?"

He shook his head. "Other than Mom, my aunt's all I've got."

"That's not true. You have me and Elsie and Cody Rae. And if you're up for it, I have additional candidates for your extended family."

CHAPTER 16

I tapped my fingers on the steering wheel as we waited for the light to change. He'd taken the news he would be staying with my uncle and his husband in the back of their shop better than I expected. Whether from exhaustion or resignation, the idea didn't seem to bother him at all.

My conversation with Buddy hadn't gone as smoothly. His familiar greeting, "Past Perfect Antiques," had been followed with a squeal of delight when I said hello.

"Lucybird! It has been forever. I hope you're calling to tell me you and that delicious boyfriend of yours are available for dinner. Norm, it's Lucy. She's coming for supper."

I laughed. Family can be a huge pain in the ass. But there's nothing like the joy of being adored by the same people who drive you nuts.

"You saved me from granola and yogurt. Mateo's working late, but I have a friend I want you to meet."

"Please don't tell me you and Mr. Hot Stuff broke up."

"No, not that. Before I explain, though, I need your help with something."

On the list of things my uncle loved, helping with an investigation was near the top. Tying it to attending the funeral of a stranger sent it soaring off the chart. Both allowed him to flex what he called his "acting chops." Although quite talented, his tendency to throw himself into the role could create more problems than he solved. For instance, the time I asked him to check out a pain clinic as part of an insurance scam. This included pretending to have a serious back issue. His purpose was to discover how easily the doctor would provide a prescription for heavy-duty drugs supplied by their onsite pharmacy.

Within an hour, they fixed him up with three separate prescriptions, two of which were opioids. The plan was for him to get the meds and leave, but as a method actor, he couldn't resist character development. So, instead of exiting stage right, he added a bout of back spasms, frightening the patients in the waiting room and agitating the staff. He hollered and moaned until the doctor ordered his assistant to call for an ambulance.

I imagine they're still marveling at his miraculous recovery. Buddy's only regret was not getting to take a bow.

Despite his willingness to tackle other parts, we hadn't involved him in anything else. Until now.

"What is it this time? A stake out? Because my new meds are great."

The poor man had a cabinet filled with drugs that failed to deliver on their promises of miraculous relief from his narcolepsy. I feared this was another of those.

"Or is it medical fraud? I love those. My hip displacement routine is so good I almost convinced myself I needed surgery."

"Not as dramatic. More subtle and complicated."

"Nobody does subtle like your complicated uncle."

I gave him a brief description of the Miller investigation and explained I wanted him to accompany me to the funeral to scope out the crowd.

"You mean in case the killer shows up to gloat? Who should I be? A distant relative of the deceased?"

"How about you go as my uncle accompanying me to help gather more complimentary material for the victim's memorial piece?"

He sighed. "Well, I suppose that's an okay starting point. Count me in."

After promising to work on his script over dinner, I shifted to my more delicate request.

"There's one more thing I need."

I summarized Danny's situation, glossing over his relationship with Ashley as a schoolboy crush because it didn't seem right to share something so devastatingly intimate. Then I played to Buddy's anti-establishment sentiments. Both he and Norm had been social activists, starting as frustrated young men denied basic rights and continuing into their middle years. If I presented Danny as a victim of police persecution, a scapegoat for the fat cats, they would lead the charge to keep him out of the hands of the Man.

His response surprised me and not in a good way.

"I want to say yes, but I have to talk it over with Norm since it could be dangerous for him, too."

"I may have exaggerated a little. It's not like he's on the FBI Most Wanted List. We're not even sure if the police are looking for him."

"I didn't mean that kind of danger. Honey, not everyone is as open-minded as you. Two gay men hosting a sleepover with an adolescent boy? You're talking about the possibility of a shitload of trouble."

"Oh, Buddy. I'm so sorry. That thought never crossed my mind. I'll come up with something else."

"Don't apologize for being a loving human being. And I didn't say no. Have dinner with us. We need to discuss plans for the Halloween party. And we'll see how it goes with your young friend."

. . .

During the short drive, I tried to provide my passenger with an explanation of narcolepsy that would stop him from freaking out if

Buddy drifted off mid-sentence without completely overwhelming the boy.

I almost told him Buddy's official diagnosis included cataplexy, then realized the scientific classification of his disorder wouldn't do justice to the misery it caused. So, I ran through the basics and said the condition was relatively rare and explained usually its victims suffered from one or two symptoms. They might stay awake most of the night and drop into a sound sleep at random times during the day. Some experienced terrifying visual or auditory hallucinations that left them disoriented and frightened. I wrapped it up by saying my sweet uncle was plagued by all three.

During my lecture on How Narcolepsy Destroys Lives and Reputations, Danny stared at me so intently I worried he'd slipped into a hypnotic trance or had been bored into a coma. When I stopped, though, he reanimated and asked when the symptoms began.

"Good question. Typically, it manifests from about seven to mid-twenties. My mother says she doesn't remember a time he didn't fall asleep without warning and wake up screaming from nightmares he couldn't describe."

"Poor guy must have had it rough."

"Lucky for him, he's always been able to make people laugh. But you're right. Kids made fun of him, and adults insisted he was plain lazy."

"Is he better now?"

Although the question wasn't unexpected, I stumbled with the answer. "Yes and no. They keep trying new medications, but so far, nothing has completely controlled his symptoms. But he won't give up."

"I'm really sorry he has to go through that stuff."

Impressed with what I interpreted as quiet sincerity, I agreed. We rode the rest of the way without talking. By the time I pulled into the store lot, Danny was slumped down, snoring softly. Rather than wake him, I cut the engine and lowered the window. A tinny rendition of a familiar tune I couldn't place drifted from the speaker in front of the shop.

A series of thunderstorms with heavy winds had damaged the original sign. The new one proudly proclaimed *Past Perfect* in flowing old-fashioned script. The name was a tribute to Grandma Taylor, Buddy and Mom's mother, who taught English for over three decades. Her ability to diagram a sentence in under ten seconds, regardless of its complexity, stunned onlookers and set her apart from her peers. Sadly, she was rarely asked to perform this intellectual parlor trick.

My uncle loves holidays—big one, little ones, and practically obscure ones. He practices a strict code concerning the amount of time that should be devoted to each and is especially fastidious when it comes to his favorite, Halloween. Because he adores everything about it, he refuses to rush the season of ghosts and ghouls. After proclaiming any presentation of pumpkins, witches, evil dolls, and vampires before September 10th tacky and disrespectful, he began researching unusual occasions to fill the days before he allowed himself to release the spirits.

A streamer above a granite table announced today was both Wonderful Weirdos and Teddy Bear Day. The guests were an assortment of bears in fancy clothes. When I saw the Bettlejuice doll peeking out from behind a gold and black urn on a Victorian pedestal, I recognized the background music. It was "The Banana Boat Song." Clad in his trademark striped suit with his wild reddish-gray hair sticking out from a receding hairline, the mannikin's dark-lined eyes focused on the terrifying centerpiece. Uncle Buddy had captured the moment the shrimp cocktail turned into bloody fingers reaching for the dancing diners.

He combined whimsy with a foreshadowing of All Saints Eve, and I remembered why he was my favorite relative. A snort from the passenger seat reminded me why I was visiting him.

"Guess I conked out on you. Did I make us late?" A lock of light brown hair fell across his right eye, and he pushed it aside.

"Not at all. I was checking out the window."

He leaned forward. "I recognize that song. Cody Rae and I used to watch that movie all the time. She likes to dance around and sing *day-o* at least a hundred times."

The image of Elsie's serious grandniece belting out the Harry Bellafonte tune made me pause. "That would be quite the sight."

"She sings it really good."

"I bet. So, let's go introduce you to the guys."

I led the way down the path to the backyard, stopping at the wrought-iron gate, complete with leering gargoyles.

"It's been a while since I visited, so I can't prepare you for what's back here. You ready?"

He nodded. I stepped into the yard. Danny stopped beside me.

"Wow," he whispered.

The green toilet with a tank full of ferns and a bowl overflowing with rubber ducks was gone. In its place, a three-foot-tall white wizard gnome, cigar dangling from his lips, gave us the middle finger salute. Four smaller gnomes, each clutching a bottle of whiskey, sprawled in various stages of intoxication in a semi-circle in front of their leader.

A grinning caricature of Venus still rose from her pink faux marble clamshell, but the flock of flamingoes that had once greeted her had flown the coop and been replaced by rainbow-colored chickens perched on a sheet of plywood.

"Looks like he's just getting started." I pointed to the corner of the yard where a leafless tree with spindly branches and a fat trunk stood. "Get a little closer and check out the knothole."

He walked a few feet from me and stopped. "Wait. Is that a face?"

"Yep. And look at the skinny arms ready to lob apples at you. It's a nightmare return to Oz."

"The prison?"

"Dear God, I'm old. Please don't tell me you never saw *The Wizard of Oz*."

"Oh, that one. This place is cool, except for the naked lady. Is it me, or do her eyes follow you around, too?"

I laughed. "You're not the first person to say that. There's more on the back porch."

The screen was unlocked. As soon as I stepped in, a life-size raven with a sharp, oversized beak blocked my way. I shrieked at the same time Danny bumped into me.

"That damned old thing has a mind of his own." Buddy's partner Norm rushed from inside to keep me from being attacked by the escapee from a Poe poem. He scooted the bird out of the way, then motioned toward the kitchen. "Come on in, so I can get a good look at my beautiful girl."

Over a foot taller than me, his hugs were enthusiastic without being overwhelming. He let me go and grinned at me. It traveled to his eyes and created a spiderweb of crinkles. His hair had transitioned from salt and pepper when we first met to a brilliant white. He kept it long for fans of the country rock band he played in from time to time. He wore his usual attire, a concert t-shirt and a pair of well-seasoned jeans.

"You are a real stunner, kiddo." Other than Mateo, Norm was the only man who made me feel as pretty as he insisted I was.

The dense aroma of spicy tomato sauce misted the air. "Is that your mama's beef and sausage recipe?" He came from a long line of Italian cooks on his mother's side.

"Yep. Buddy's doctor has him on a strict diet, so I've been hitting the Weight Watcher cookbook hard. Poor guy begged not to serve his favorite niece tofu spaghetti, even though the wiseass knows I never touch that stuff. But he's been so good about eating healthy, I decided we'd cheat a little. Whatever we don't eat goes home with you."

I smiled and surveyed the room. It was the same sunny yellow as when they remodeled the apartment, but the shelves covering the wall no longer held the blue and white patterned serving plates.

"Didn't Buddy say he was never selling those dishes because they reminded him of Sunday dinners at his grandma's?"

"I'm pretty sure that's why he sold them. According to your uncle's stories, his grandmother was a bitch on wheels. Plus, the buyer made *an offer we couldn't refuse.*"

I smiled at his Godfather imitation. Danny furrowed his brow in concern or confusion or some other teenage male emotion.

The irreplaceable plates had been replaced with an assortment of cut-glass vases.

"Is this the young man who's going to be our guest for a few days?"

"Pardon my manners. The smell of your sauce fogged up my brain. This is Danny Braden. Danny, this is Norm."

"Nice to meet you, sir." He stared at Norm's chest. "Your t-shirt is fierce."

I wouldn't have described Joe Walsh playing the guitar above his iconic line, "Life's been good to me so far," as fierce. But Norm beamed.

"Don't tell me you're a fan of old Joe?"

"Him and the rest of the Eagles, too. My father had about a hundred of their t-shirts, but Joe was his favorite. Dad and I spent hours with him trying to teach me to play. I was starting to get better."

"Did I hear we've got ourselves another Eagles fan in the house?" Buddy barreled through the French doors holding a squirming black and tan chihuahua. The tiny creature wriggled against Keith Richards's crinkly forehead. The last time my uncle wore the shirt, the aging guitarist's face sported fewer wrinkles due to the extra thirty or so pounds Buddy carried, mostly in his belly. Today, Keith looked like a withered apple, signaling my uncle's diet was working.

"You heard that right. A man with taste and a treasure-trove of vintage tees. Even better, the boy's got music in his blood. Lucy's brought us a winner, which is very timely. Rumor is the guitar player in Norm's band is approaching senility."

Norm tapped him on the arm with his fist before trapping him in a headlock and rubbing his knuckles across my uncle's head. The dog howled indignantly.

"Dammit, Norm! You're gonna mess up what little hair I have left. And Doris is getting seriously pissed off."

"She just wants to see her special daddy. Don't you, sweetheart?" He released Buddy and snatched the pup, who covered his face with kisses. Wild whimpers and squeals sounded from the other side of the door.

When my uncle opened it, two brown and white chihuahuas stumbled into the room. They rushed toward Danny and began dancing in between his legs, frantically pawing at his jeans.

Norm scooped them up. "This is Paco; the smaller one's Pepe. And Doris, the little hussy, is currently slobbering on my sweetheart. You can pet the boys if you want. They're real friendly."

He scratched Paco under the chin with one hand and patted Pepe's back with the other.

"You're a hit." He thrust Paco into Danny's arms. "Tell us some more about your guitar playing."

"Not much more to it. After Dad died, I packed it up with the t-shirts. I think they made my mom sad."

I suspected not only was he right about his mother, but that they saddened him as well. I searched for something to say to restore the lightness of the room and came up with nothing.

Rather than gloss over Danny's sadness, Buddy took it head on. "Your mom's lucky to have such a thoughtful kid. But I hate to see wasted talent. While you're here, you could humor a couple of old farts and try out one of Norm's guitars. He won't admit it, but he's among the best of the best pickers in Georgia. That includes the banjo and the fiddle. Course we've got plenty of time for that. Let's get you settled in the guest room before we eat."

When the others were out of earshot, I asked if he was okay with the arrangement.

"Hey, you know our philosophy: the more the merrier. As long as his mother is aware of the situation."

Within minutes, we sat down to steaming platters of spaghetti, roasted brussel sprouts, and a loaf of lightly buttered French bread.

"Don't let my diet hold you guys back." Buddy shoved the butter across the table to Danny, who helped himself to an oversized slab.

Norm grinned as his young guest dug into the heaping mound of pasta on his plate. No one spoke for a few blissful moments as we stuffed ourselves.

My uncle paused and said, "This guy here has me eating healthy. Even started walking. Tossed that damn Fitbit your mama got me for Christmas. Bossy-assed thing was just like her. Interrupting my nap by buzzing and telling me to get up and move. Good news is that I've dropped quite a few pounds. Which means this year..." He turned to Norm. "Drumroll please." An impressive rat-a-tat-tat with spoon and fork began, then died out as Buddy shouted, "Marilyn is back, baby."

"Marilyn Monroe?" Danny asked.

"Is there any other?" My uncle raised an eyebrow in mock indignation.

"I, uh, well," the boy stuttered, clearly fearful he offended Buddy.

"Don't pay him any attention. He's getting a head start on his upcoming performance." Norm patted Danny on the shoulder.

"Did Mom sign up as the buxom Miss Russell?"

"Faster than you could say diamonds are a girl's best friend."

Last year was the first in a long time when my uncle and his partner had strayed from donning his shiny-seamed iconic Marilyn dress, the one where she stands over a windy subway grate. Norm happily took backstage in the Yankee Clipper's number five jersey. Two years ago, he talked my mother into going as Jane Russell, the statuesque brunette who played Monroe's best friend in *Gentlemen Prefer Blondes*. Truthfully, that wasn't a hard sell since Mom was Juliet in high school and never let anyone forget it.

I explained to Danny who Jane Russell was, as well as the storyline of the movie. While summarizing the film, I realized how the premise of hot chicks looking for wealthy husbands must sound to a boy from his generation. To his credit, he simply smiled and nodded at the end of my synopsis.

"Any luck talking Dad into dressing as one of the rich dudes the girls are after?" My father was not into costume parties.

"I can't see him in a tuxedo. But I bet if you borrow Mateo's hat, he'd come as a misfit."

Another puzzled expression crossed Danny's face. He set his fork on his plate and stared at Buddy.

"Marilyn's last film before she died was *The Misfits* with Clark Gable, who played a cowboy. Most people remember him as Rhett Butler in—"

"*Gone with the Wind*," Danny finished for me. "My mom loves that movie. I try to tell her it isn't historically accurate, but she doesn't care."

Buddy nodded. "Lots of Southerners want to believe in all that antebellum bullshit."

Norm got up to refill Danny's plate for the third time.

When he had his back turned, my uncle scooped up a glob of butter and smeared it onto another piece of bread before Norm returned to the table.

"I can't see myself in all those hoops and petticoats, shooing suitors away with a fan."

Norm laughed and said, "Truth is most of us would have been sharecroppers coming through the back door of Tara."

"Lucy, don't forget to pick up Elsie and Hugh's invitations. And Danny, you and that little niece of hers are invited, unless the two of you already have big plans in the works." When it came to entertaining, my uncle went all out. His philosophy was the bigger, the better.

"Your party sounds way cooler than anything my friends would have. Do our costumes need to be connected to Marilyn?"

"That's what's great about being part of the aging gay population. We don't have to worry about sticking to themes to be cool. You can be anyone at all. Think you might come?" Norm asked.

"Yes, but I want to check with Cody Rae first. I think she's gonna love it."

Buddy clapped his hands. "Nothing like new blood to keep tradition alive and well."

Despite my uncle's excitement, I felt a twinge of sadness at the mention of the girl. I had no doubt she'd love anything Danny suggested if it meant being close to him. I worried that her feelings for him went much deeper than his for her. That made it easy for girls her age—hell, women my age—to forget who they were and what they wanted. I didn't believe for a second a boy as thoughtful as Danny would intentionally hurt Cody Rae. But that wouldn't make her pain any lighter.

I shook off my gloomy reaction and attributed it to me projecting my miserable experience with Lance.

Norm got up to clear the table, but Buddy stopped him.

"You sit there and talk to Danny about who's the best guitar player in the country or whatever musician stuff you discuss. Lucy and I will take care of this. Hope everybody saved room for dessert. I made Grandma Taylor's banana pudding."

I stacked up plates and followed him to the kitchen.

"Just put those in the sink. I'll do them later." He pulled out a chair and motioned for me to sit. "Norm didn't want me to say anything, but I've had the same dream vision three nights running. And, honey, it's driving me crazy. You're in it."

Most of the family either mocked my uncle to his face or behind his back when he shared his flashes of insight. Only Norm and I recognized the possibility Buddy might have a touch of what my grandmother called "the Gift." Often, his premonitions were vague enough that he took credit for their outcomes whether it made sense or not.

Like the time when I was in college, and he predicted a visit from a being in trouble who would reward anyone who helped it. That night, a fluffy cat with tiger stripes showed up in the backyard. She yowled until Norm gave her some tuna fish, which she scarfed down. When she flopped down on her side and growled, he realized she was in labor. Three hours later, they had four tiny kittens and an exhausted mother. Since my uncle was allergic to cats, Norm fixed them a spot on the porch where they spent the next eight weeks. Then he found the mama and the babies good homes.

Buddy insisted the cat gave them two months of fun with them frolicking among the fake flamingoes and elves. Whenever he told the story, Norm smiled and nodded. My mother rolled her eyes, and Dad changed the TV to the baseball channel.

I leaned toward the possibility of belief. Just because you couldn't understand or see something didn't mean it wasn't there. But was it a gift or a curse?

I thought of Cassandra, the beautiful daughter of the king and queen of Troy. She pissed off some god who gifted her with foresight, adding the stipulation nobody would believe her prophecies. She kept warning people of oncoming death and destruction, while everybody shrugged and called her crazy. It seemed odd to me no one ever put it together. But that's why it's mythology, I guess.

Today, Buddy's premonition disturbed me.

"In my dream, you and I are sitting out back looking at Venus popping up out of her clam shell. Your phone rings, and the statue starts crying. And then, dear God, her tears turn to blood."

"That is a terrible nightmare. Do you think it might have something to do with your medications?"

"If only. No, sweetheart. I don't know what it means, but have you had any strange calls lately, or maybe an unknown number?"

Strange? I thought. *Only if you count my ex-boyfriend calling from prison. What could possibly be strange about that?*

For a moment, I considered telling him about Lance. But what was the point? I answered the call. Whatever evil lurking behind those bloody tears had already been unleashed.

CHAPTER 17

Mateo didn't get home until almost ten. After he showered, he poured a glass of wine for me and a beer for himself before settling into bed.

"I don't see why you're surprised at how well Buddy and Norm got along with Danny. Those two are more like teenagers than grown-ups. I bet they keep the kid up all night with their stories. Going backstage with Dolly Parton, hunting ghosts in Oakland Cemetery, solving murders. That poor boy will never be the same."

"True, but he'll have a hell of a time. And I shouldn't worry about his mother freaking out because I explained they were a married couple, right? She doesn't seem like the type to come back later and cause trouble, but you never know."

"From what you've told me about her son, they're good people. And your uncles have stellar reputations for only being attracted to each other. Drink your wine and try to relax."

I took a sip and leaned against his chest, letting his heartbeat slow mine.

"They really are devoted to one another, at least as much as my mom and dad are, maybe more."

"Ah, my love. You wound me. What about our devotion?"

He nibbled my ear, and I spilled a drop of wine on my nightgown.

"Sorry about that. We should get you out of those wet clothes before the stain sets in." He unbuttoned the first button and was on the second when I wrapped my hand around his.

"White wine doesn't stain." I nipped at his knuckles before kissing them. "Besides, I want to hear all about your day. How was your lunch with Sofia?"

He slipped from my grasp, and I felt his body tense beside me.

"It was good. She sent her love and wanted to order a plate for you, but I was afraid of it sitting in the car too long."

"I hope everything's all right with her. She's such a sweetheart I would hate for her to be in any kind of trouble." I sat up, trying not to pummel him with questions about why the girl had asked him to stop by without including me. The request hadn't hurt my feelings. It had triggered my instinct something might be off with her.

"It's not a big deal, just a security thing with the restaurant."

His words hung heavy between us because of his obvious lie. Before we met, I insisted on total transparency in everything from my relationship with my dentist to my love life. Learning my favorite uncle, the one adult who never lied to me, had secrets he was ashamed of taught me that honesty without allowances for human frailties made for a cold, lonely existence. But I never expected to apply that knowledge to the man I loved.

Instead of being angry, I was hurt he didn't trust me enough to share Sofia's problem. Then it occurred to me he must have given his word not to tell anyone. But that didn't mean me. So, despite my urgent desire to be included in every part of Mateo's life, I stifled my follow-up interrogation. I couldn't resist a parting shot designed to evoke guilt or doubt.

"I'm glad her parents trust her with such an important decision." I kissed his cheek, then changed the subject. "I need some advice about the funeral. Like whether to act as if Buddy and are grateful insurance clients or friends of Ryan."

"Just when I was beginning to think you're only after me for my body, I discover you respect my mind. What a terrible disappointment."

I assured him I was hot for both, and he suggested we say my uncle was a long-term client who talked his niece into signing up for renter's insurance a few months ago. He warned us to stay away from the father, who might keep a close eye on new policies, but said Howard and Taylor were common enough names not to sound alarms if we did slip up.

"Should I rearrange my schedule and go with you instead of Buddy? He can be a bit of a loose cannon."

"Are you kidding? It would kill him if he didn't get to perform. He called me three times on my drive home asking which shirt went better with his gray suit and should he wear black or navy shoes."

Mateo sighed. "All right but be careful. I'm getting a bad vibe about all this mess. A sex-crazed teacher who may or may not be a murderer. Your jailbird ex and his maniac ex. Sometimes, I wish you were an accountant."

"Me, a numbers-cruncher? Isn't being good at math a requirement for that? Anyway, I've got the perfect cure for those negative feelings of yours."

Later, holding me close, he seemed to have forgotten his preference for a woman in a more sedate profession. I had almost drifted to sleep when he whispered in my ear.

"So, what kind of dog do you think we should get?"

I pretended to be asleep.

• • •

According to Norm, Buddy spent hours going through his closet in search of the perfect funeral outfit. My uncle's days in community theater and his time performing as Lady Lola onstage at Belle's Parade of Queens Cabaret developed him into somewhat of a fashion guru. He had a sixth sense about when flamboyance was appropriate and when it would frighten clueless onlookers. For him, picking out the best clothes for the occasion was as much an accomplishment as Arthur pulling the sword from the stone.

Accordingly, it had to project the dignified sorrow a slightly less than casual acquaintance might feel. Understated, yet somber. He selected a light-weight Ralph Lauren suit he bought on sale last year at Macy's and had been so excited about showing me how loose the waistband was that we ran late getting to the church.

Westview Baptist is a sprawling structure perched on top of a small hill. The main building itself looms above two annexes, one on each side. Four colossal white columns support the brick façade, giving it the appearance of a courtroom. Quite appropriate, since the minister, Reverend Lester Hightower, considered it the seat of judgment with himself serving as the major dispenser of justice.

He reigned supreme, with a cadre of five assistant ministers to take care of the mundane matters of church finance, politics, and general ministering to the flock. The man spent the majority of his time planning for televised sermons and mammoth fund-raising drives. A genius at instilling the fear of the flaming pit into those who refused to give generously, he wasn't too shabby on the pulpit either.

On the few times I visited with a college boyfriend determined to save me from sin, while he attempted to get into my pants, Hightower's "hell, fire, and brimstone" style didn't do it for me. Neither did my horny, sanctimonious companion.

I remember the congregation was a combination of old and new money. Ryan's family was old; Ashley's, new. We had to park about a mile away beside a dusty Ford pickup with an extra-large dog carrier in the back.

Buddy stepped from the car onto the pavement. "You can always tell the financial condition of a church by the physical condition of the parking lot. This one here is smoother than a baby's butt, minus the dimples. See how tall that steeple is? The taller they are, the more money the deacons have. These sons of bitches are loaded."

A few rows of cars ahead of us, a woman in an enormous saucer-shaped black hat complete with peek-a-boo veil perched at a startling angle on top of reddish orange curls stumbled on three-inch heels. A bold choice even if she'd known the lot was in pristine condition. Next to her, a sturdy man in a cowboy hat and Western-style suit reached to take her arm. She snatched it away and continued staggering on her own.

I tapped Buddy's shoulder and pointed. "That's the department head where Ashley teaches. She had a thing with Ryan about not getting back to her soon enough about insuring her husband's dog pen or something like that. I'm guessing her husband is the guy beside her."

"Dear Lord. That hat."

I nodded.

As we closed in on the entrance, a sinking spell hit me. The idea of high drama gets my adrenaline going. The reality is that tragedy isn't dramatic at all. It's small and sad. There might be a flash of fanfare, but even Juliet's mom, Lady Capulet, had to clean up the kitchen after everyone had dropped off a casserole and returned to their mansions in Verona. She and the Nurse were left sobbing by the sink.

Buddy must have sensed my reluctance to pass through the heavy white doors because he took my hand and squeezed it. "Come on, honey. We don't want to sit in the back row."

Actually, that was exactly where I wanted to be or at least far enough from the front to avoid making eye contact with the preacher or any of the choir. From my early days as a captive on the third pew at the Methodist church my mother demanded we attend, I developed the fear the man on the pulpit and his cronies could read my mind. They knew what Dennis Norton and I had been doing behind the stadium. And even though nothing underneath the blouse had taken place, their gleeful stories about sinners burning in hell seemed to be aimed directly at me.

Buddy's enthusiasm troubled me a little. He deemed himself a character actor; Norm said he was just a character. But my uncle was right. We needed a spot closer to the front, on the aisle if possible, so we could see the faces of the mourning family as they trudged to their place of honor.

As soon as we stepped into the building, an overpowering aroma of carnations sucked the air from the room. That and the crowd of heavily powdered and perfumed women with their sweaty men in dark suits brought on a wave of claustrophobia.

"Shit! I can barely breathe in here. And forget about getting a good seat." I whispered to Buddy, not as quietly as I intended if the woman who turned to stare at me in what could only be indignation indicated. I pasted a shocked expression on my face and looked over my shoulder at the eighty-something matron behind me.

"I think she might be senile," I offered with a shrug.

She sniffed and faced forward, probably looking for someone else to judge.

"Follow my lead," my uncle murmured before raising his voice. "What? You're about to faint?" Moving closer, he patted my cheeks, then announced, "Please, people. Give this little lady some air."

Everyone around us focused on me, the little lady at the center of the drama, but no one moved.

"What's that?" He put his ear close to my mouth. "Oh, Lord! She's about to upchuck." He stomped his foot, and, just like Moses parting the Red Sea, the crowd divided. While they stumbled over each other to avoid spewing vomit, we cut through the line and snagged end seats five rows behind the area marked off for the family.

"Don't stop leaning on me until the music starts," Buddy commanded, while fanning me with a program. Both thrilled and embarrassed by our performance, I happily obeyed, keeping my face covered with my hands.

As the organist hit the opening notes of "Amazing Grace," the rustling of hymnals cued us to join in with the singing.

Forced to attend a denomination that called him a sinner did nothing to dampen my uncle's fervor for belting out all the church oldies but goodies, and today's first choice was a favorite. His rich baritone caused more than a few ladies to glance his way and smile.

When we finished the stanza, the shuffle of fabric behind us as people rose from their pews signaled the show was about to begin. Hightower soared past, robes flowing. I shifted slightly in my seat, curious to see if they'd observed the tradition of having the spouse follow immediately after the officiate. They had.

Ashley wore a smaller, more tasteful version of Sue Ann's hat. Its black veil obscured over half of her face. The skin that was visible had a pale glow, which made the freckles on her nose seem as if they were painted on. Her matching long-sleeved dress and dark stockings gave her the air of a Victorian ghost.

To her left, an older lady with plump cheeks and fading blonde hair held Ashley's elbow. She was the image of what her daughter might look like in twenty or so years. A slim man with a halting gait flanked her other side.

Her movements were stiff and jerky. I wondered if it was her mother or some other well-intentioned woman who had known the right amount of Xanax to administer. Enough to dull the recipient's senses to the sharp edges of pain stabbing at her heart without transforming her into a vegetable.

There was an unexpectedly long gap between Ashley's family and the next members of the procession. Finally, well over eight rows behind, a woman I recognized from my research appeared. The local paper featured her as a sponsor of a charity event. She stood beside a sign with the name of some foundation I couldn't remember on it, holding herself ramrod straight. When I was a teenager, my mother threatened to put me in a brace if I didn't pull my shoulders back and sit up right. If Mrs. Helen Miller's mom had issued a similar command, she must have followed through.

Today, despite standing tall, she seemed diminished. Subdued highlights threaded through hair styled in a tight chignon. On another woman, it might have been referred to as a bun. On her, it was definitely a chignon. She wore a black suit tailored to fit her slender figure and matching pumps. A beige scarf tied in an intricate flowerlike knot emphasized the length of her swanlike, if somewhat crêpey, neck.

I wondered if she'd chosen the outfit or if a friend had laid out her clothes and draped the shawl across her thin shoulders. I couldn't imagine losing a child and still be able to make such a beautiful bow. She stayed focused on the stained-glass image of Jesus hanging from the cross behind the pulpit and gave no indication she was aware of the man walking with her. Only a slight tremor on her left side indicated the possibility of suppressed emotion.

Mr. Miller, taller than his wife by at least three inches, moved mechanically, carefully placing one foot in front of the other. His sharp cheekbones and hawk-like nose made him look gaunt, despite a powerful build. A tennis player probably or swimmer, or another sport that kept him toned. His pace was steady, but he turned his head from side to side, slowly searching for something or someone he never seemed to find. If not for our premium seats, I would have sworn the man was devoid of emotion. When he passed and I saw his eyes, I recognized my mistake.

While Ryan's had been pale blue, his father's were almost black, sharply contrasting with snow-white hair. Today they blazed like coals in his pallid face, dark and bottomless enough to reflect the light from the windows.

An elderly couple came next. The woman tottered on a cane; the man beside her used a walker. I guessed they were Ryan's grandparents, but age had robbed them of distinguishing family traits. What was likely to have been a nose as prominent as Miller's, had melted into his wrinkled flesh. Long ago, the wife might have been as statuesque as Mrs. Miller. Now, stooped over her walking stick, she had become another victim of time.

Buddy nudged me and pointed. "Get a load of that casket. Top of the line stainless steel. And check out the reinforced handlebars. That model is fancy as hell inside. Must have set them back three grand at least. Shame they couldn't show it off at the viewing."

"The way Ryan died, they didn't have much choice."

The puffy-haired lady in front of us glared over her shoulder. Buddy mouthed *sorry*, then stuck out his tongue when she turned back around.

I suppressed a giggle and focused on the drama playing out at the front of the church. Instead of walking into the row so Ashley would be the closest to the casket, Mrs. Miller stepped to the side and waited for her daughter-in-law to go first. The younger woman seemed unaware of the protocol, and if not for her mother's grasp, looked as if she was about to obey her mother-in-law's implicit command.

Ashley's mom pulled her aside to clear the way. For a moment, no one moved. The usher swayed from foot to foot. Mr. Miller broke the deadlock by palming his wife's elbow and guiding her forward. She swatted his hand away as if he were some insignificant but annoying insect. But she proceeded down the row. Ashley's mother filed in next, leaving a space that could have accommodated three or more people between the in-laws. Her father made sure both his wife and daughter were seated before he scooted between them.

"That group is wound tighter than a gnat's ass."

Another blistering glare from the woman in front of us. She opened her mouth to deliver what I guessed would be a warning about brimstone.

Luckily, the Reverend Hightower ascended to the pulpit, his long black robe flaring elegantly over a body that was described by his supporters as portly. His detractors referred to him with less dignified adjectives. There was no question he'd attended one too many church dinners, but he used his girth to his advantage, throwing himself with abandon into every sermon.

I imagined today would be no exception. I told myself I was no longer the frightened child, trembling at my mother's side as our minister gleefully told the congregation that we had all sinned. And if we didn't play our cards right, God would send us to the fiery pit.

I might not be that terrified little girl, but the towering figure above me still had the power to scare the hell out of me, and I hadn't killed my husband. I scanned Ashley's face in search of the terror that should be reflected on it and found only the innocence of the bland-faced doll she'd reminded me of.

CHAPTER 18

"Friends, we are gathered here today to bid a fond farewell to a golden child of God taken from us too soon. Ryan Miller radiated goodness and decency in every area of his young life. Everyone who knew him loved him."

Hightower paused for effect, unaware of the irony of his statement. If Ryan's father was right, there was at least one person who hadn't enjoyed basking in his light. The Reverend continued, a thin line of sweat forming on his upper lip.

"But the Lord truly does move in mysterious ways. It is not up to us to question His Divine Reasoning. We must be content to accept his gifts without questioning when they are no longer ours. Ryan was one of those gifts. To his family, he was a loving and dutiful son and grandson, respectful and hardworking, eager to make his folks proud."

He took a breath and raised his eyes to the heavens, more accurately to the ceiling. But the congregation got the hint and provided the requisite *Amens*.

The preacher nodded his approval and revved it up.

"His special relationship with his mother was evident to anyone who saw them together. They lit each other up and allowed those lucky enough to be near them to be part of their magic."

Buddy squirmed in his seat and whispered. "Is it me or is that whole mommy-son thing creepy?"

I elbow-jabbed him, trying to remind him we were supposed to be keeping a low profile. The longer Hightower rambled on, however, the less likely my uncle was to fly below the radar.

Unfortunately, the holy man was just getting started.

"And to Ashley, his lovely bride, he was everything: friend, partner, protector. Everyone could see that Ryan adored her. He emanated adoration, and surely God smiled on their union. Their happiness, bittersweet for its brevity, was holiness."

At the word holiness, Ryan's mother snorted, then began emitting choking sounds. Her husband offered her his handkerchief, but she waved it away impatiently and stared relentlessly at the man in the pulpit.

"It was a blessing only true children of God were worthy of. Young innocents who accept Jesus Christ as their Savior and have bathed in his Holy blood. And I'd like to ask all of you now to consider where you would be if the Lord decided to end your time on earth *right this moment.*"

The good Reverend reached a crescendo. I noticed the disapproving lady in front of me start to sway. I suspected any second she would begin speaking in tongues. My mind was stuck on the image of couples bathing in blood.

"All you must do is open your heart to God's words. Put aside worldly pride and humble yourself to the Lord's will."

A chorus of *Amens,* more enthusiastic than the previous outbursts, rippled through the congregation. I thought he was finished, but I'd forgotten those Baptist preacher false endings and, of course, the ever-popular invitational. Hightower started painting a grim picture for those of us who didn't get straight with Jesus as he set the crowd up for getting saved.

I began a list of the songs I wanted sung at my funeral: definitely "Amazing Grace" even though it was overused. Maybe someone would order a bagpipe group to sing me home. I'd always been partial to "I Come to the Garden Alone" and "When the Role is Called Up Yonder." Sort of sweet and savory.

Buddy startled me when he stood for what I prayed was the final hymn, "Nearer My God to Thee." Catchy, but the connection with the Titanic rendered it overly dramatic. I seriously doubted Ryan or Ashley had thought of preparing a playlist. I made a mental note to put mine together so I wouldn't get stuck with some morose Presbyterian send-offs.

We launched into the third stanza when a lady in a black and white flowered dress headed to the front to be rededicated. Bless her heart. I imagined it would have taken at least another three or four songs before the rededications started. A few other courageous sinners joined her while I pondered what outfit I wanted to be buried in.

At some point the preacher reached the conclusion he'd hit the limit on all the souls needing saving or refurbishing. He had not, however, concluded the service, which turned out to be a serious problem for me.

During his interminable closing prayer, I checked out the multiple floral arrangements. Too many for the pulpit area to contain, they had been artfully arranged at the ends of aisles. I took in the elaborate sprays of lilies, chrysanthemums, carnations, hyacinth, and others I didn't recognize.

A particularly large grouping did me in. Perched atop an easel was a spray made to resemble a piece of paper. Against a background of close-cropped white flowers, was what I expected to be an expression of sympathy conveyed with deep red roses. I squinted to read it both times—the first for content, the second to dispel my disbelief. Instead of a sweet sentiment about meeting again in the Great Beyond, the message was written in formal business language, like a will or property agreement or—or my dear Lord, an insurance document.

"This is to certify that the policy holder, Ryan Davis, is insured by God Almighty for all eternity. May he rest in the peace that comes from planning ahead for Salvation."

A surge of emotion rose in my chest, and suddenly, I was comedian Mary Tyler Moore in an episode I caught on late night TV. In it, well-known local entertainer Chuckles the Clown gets squashed by an elephant during a parade. Mary is not amused by her co-workers' callous jokes and asks them to show a little respect for the poor guy. At the funeral, however, she loses it, convulsing with hilarity at the clown's undignified demise.

Hysterical laughter rolled up from deep in my stomach, and only by clamping my hand firmly over my mouth was I able to suppress it. Rather than emitting peals of amusement, I spewed snorts from my nose and spit from the corners of my lips.

Buddy reacted by pulling me to his chest and stage-whispering, "There, there, honey. Everything's going to be all right."

I expected the woman who had shushed us earlier to flip out, but she was distracted by the congregation's recitation of the Lord's Prayer followed by Hightower's invitation for everyone to join the family in the reception hall for refreshments. The organist began "Here I Am, Lord" as the pallbearers took their places alongside the coffin. Thoughts of sit-coms disappeared as the finality of death washed over me.

I'd purposely kept my distance from the reality of Ryan's murder. Even though I hadn't known him, I didn't take his loss lightly. Removing myself from the immediacy of tragedy was the only way I could treat the case with any objectivity. But the men bearing the burden of their friend toward his resting place jabbed a hole in my carefully constructed cool. I pictured each of them in different scenarios with the man in the casket. Who had played tennis with him only a week ago? Did the two meet regularly to smoke cigars and play poker, or go golfing? Could one of them have been beside him in this very church when he took his wedding vows? Was there a false friend who helped him fall to his death?

I discarded that possibility, as much because it was overwhelming as it was tragic, and shifted my concentration to the scene playing out beneath the pulpit.

The new widow seemed unaware of the approaching usher and started away from him, catching her heel on the carpet. Her father caught her when she stumbled, and her mother rushed to her other side. Ashley remained motionless, then doubled over sobbing. Whatever state her marriage had been in, there was no question she was devastated by Ryan's death.

Her mom lifted the veil, kissed her daughter's forehead, and whispered something to her. This parody of a bride's first kiss seemed to soothe the younger woman, who nodded and resumed following the casket.

As Ashley passed, I decided she was either an actress worthy of an Academy Award, or her ruined face was truly an expression of agonizing grief. Her mother maintained a firm grip on her daughter's elbow. Her father stayed a step or so behind the two, possibly to provide a buffer between them and Ryan's parents.

Once again, Mrs. Miller looked to neither side. Rather than seeming totally unaware of her surroundings as she'd been on her way in, this time her gaze was alert and frightening. It was fixed on the back of Ashley's head, and I wondered how it was that her daughter-in-law, if she still retained that title after her husband's demise, didn't break into a sweat from the heat of those blazing eyes. The woman's slow and steady steps became purposeful strides that threatened to overtake the younger woman. I pictured her knocking the grieving widow to the ground and stomping her to death with her dangerously pointed heels.

I must not have been the only one sensing a deadly assault. Mr. Miller quickened his pace to catch up with his wife. He wrapped an arm around her waist, and she reacted by whirling to face him. Fury rose like heat from her body. He recoiled slightly but didn't release her.

I suppressed a shudder as I watched them walk through the columns and out the church door.

. . .

The receiving line was so long I didn't worry that someone might notice Buddy and I hadn't joined it to offer our personal condolences. Instead, we separated to eavesdrop on any possible gossip from the mourners, planning to meet outside in ten minutes.

Other than some snarky remarks about Ashley's dress being too short and her hair too blond, I didn't pick up anything useful.

I gave up on listening in to conversations that left me vaguely depressed and headed to the refreshment table. Instead of taking one of the tiny glass plates designed to hold a limited number of tinier sandwiches, I grabbed a few napkins and began wrapping up chicken salad quarters on fluffy white bread. In another napkin, I packed up brownies and cookies and stuffed them in my purse.

Turning to make a quick exit, I almost bumped into Fiona Adams. The first thing I noticed were the light blond highlights threading through her goldish-red locks. I shop at discount stores and order knock-off clothes online, but I never skimp on my hair. So, I recognized expensive work when I saw it. And Fiona's was definitely in the luxury-price line. Similar to the style in her failed engagement photo, it curled around her face and accentuated her pale blue eyes. I remembered our last visit and how empty they'd been.

But when she looked into mine today, the devastation I'd seen had been replaced with something unreadable. It didn't resemble happiness. But it was no longer the picture of grief. If forced to name it, I might have described it as peaceful with darker undercurrents, an emotional match to the variations of light and dark in her spectacular hair.

During our conversation, she hadn't struck me as overly religious. I didn't see her taking comfort in the hope she would someday reunite with her true love, while Ashley burned in Hell for leading Ryan astray. But something had softened the sharp edges I'd seen during our first meeting.

"Hello, Ms. Howard. How's that tribute article coming along? Still looking for good things to write about my ex, or should I say the dearly departed?" Her words had a harsh undertone, but her expression remained smooth and calm. I had the uncomfortable feeling she never believed there would be a newspaper story praising the guy who dumped her.

"I've just about put that piece to bed except for one last edit. I'm only here for the same reason everyone else is. To mourn the tragic loss of a young man with so much potential." Why was I channeling the Reverend with his pretentious bullshit?

Fiona's tight smile suggested she was thinking the same thing. Her next comment confused me. "Maybe you should put that article on permanent hold. You never know when a better story might come along." She excused herself before I could ask her to clarify her remark.

I spotted Buddy barreling toward me, flushed and out of breath. He took my elbow and hustled me to the car. Once inside, he cranked up the air conditioning and wiped his forehead with an over-size handkerchief.

"You go first," he commanded, while exiting the crowded lot.

"I got nada."

"Lucky you brought me, then, because Ryan's Uncle Henry turned out to be quite the talker. It probably had something to do with him being at least three sheets in the wind from sipping at the flask in his jacket. According to him, his nephew and Ashley were about as far from the ideal couple as possible. Which was exactly what everybody who was anybody expected. The family was dead set against him marrying her in the first place. Henry's sister told him they considered the poor girl NOKD. What he really said was NAKD, but I'm pretty sure he was referring to local shorthand for *not our kind dear*. He shared that he understood why Ryan hadn't been able to resist her charms but didn't see why he married her. He stopped to cup his ample bosom and make the universal sign for big boobs. I love it when dirty old straight men think I'm one of them."

He switched on the radio to a classic seventies station and sung along with "I Want to Rock and Roll All Night" before continuing. "Seems Ryan and his dad got into it at the old man's birthday party. The kid flipped out. He was so mad he and Ashley left before the cake cutting. The mom ran out after them. Henry heard her shouting something about ruining everything they'd worked for and destroying their future. My inebriated informant didn't hear how the boy planned to end the dynasty. Sorry I couldn't get more out of him."

I assured him he'd been invaluable, and I meant it. A quarrel in front of an influential audience had to embarrass the old man. Fiona had mentioned the family wanting Ryan to go into politics. I wondered if it was his dad who had his own political aspirations and if that might have had something to do with his son's death.

"Other than Henry, did you talk to anyone else?"

"Just a large-breasted woman with a bad dye job. She and two of her friends pinned me against the wall. She babbled on and on about what a beautiful voice I had and how I should join the choir. Have to hand it to the old gal; she wasn't afraid to flash a little Baptist cleavage." He chuckled. "I wonder what those lovely heifers would say if they found out one of the herd had flirted with a deviant."

Buddy insisted I come in for a drink before I headed home to Mateo. He had an arrangement of skeletons playing poker he wanted my opinion on, and led me to the table with its creepy assortment of card players seated around it.

"Is the mustache too much?"

"No, but the saloon girl's hair might be a little too orange."

He frowned, but before he could respond, guitar music sounded from the apartment in the back. It was a rendition of Credence Clearwater Revival's song "Bad Moon on the Rise."

All smiles now, he said, "Norm's been working on that tune for months, but it never came out right. Guess all he needed was harmony."

It was easy to tell the difference between the older man's husky blues voice and Danny's straight-forward vocals. They were good together.

But unless I could help prove the kid had nothing to do with Ryan's murder, their harmonizing days wouldn't last long.

CHAPTER 19

I dragged myself inside to the den where Mateo yelled at a bad call against the Braves. He muted the announcer and patted the sofa beside him.

"You look beat. Sit. I'll make you a Cosmo."

Fifteen minutes later, I was moaning in ecstasy as he hit the sweet spot between my arch and heel, a place often ignored by your run-of-the-mill foot masseuse. I sipped on the pale pink drink and marveled at his ability to read me, to respond to my needs, sometimes when I had no idea what they were.

Whereas I would have bombarded him with questions about the investigation, he gave me time to decompress. When I thought of his lunch with Sofia, a flash of déjà vu came over me. For a moment, it was as if my ex and I were together with me doubting him.

Mateo is not Lance, I reminded myself, annoyed I'd slipped back into the old Lucy. The one who refused to accept anything other than total transparency. Hadn't I learned how much more important it was to love without reservation? But self-destructive habits die hard.

Determined not to return to them, I didn't mention his cousin. When my glass was half empty, I started to share the details of Ryan's farewell ceremony.

"Hold on a second while I grab my notebook."

After his years in law enforcement, he never left home without a spiral pad. I pointed out the memo feature, both text and recording options, on his phone, but he said he loved the feeling of control that came with carefully writing information on the blue-lined pages—even if it was only a grocery list or the title of a novel he wanted to read. I accused him of documenting the details of our sex life, such as what worked and what needed improving. He smiled and scribbled something down.

Today, he returned with a brand-new paper tablet and signaled for me to begin.

I described the main mourners, emphasizing how genuinely devastated Ashley appeared. He held up his pen to stop me.

"Didn't you say she seemed manipulative during your visit to her home?"

"Yes, but this was different. Everything about her looked miserable."

"Maybe she's miserable because she's guilty."

I admitted he had a point, then lightened the mood with the part of my story where I lost control during the Lord's Prayer.

"Buddy did even better than I expected. He made friends with Ryan's drunken uncle, dished some dirt about a big fight at a party with some political hotshots in attendance. And some choir ladies tried to pick him up."

Mateo burst out laughing, sending his beer down the wrong way. I patted him on the back until he stopped coughing.

"So, what's your next step?"

"Good question. I hate to admit it, but we're no closer to proving Ashley's innocence or guilt. I'm pretty sure identifying the writing on the matchbook and the napkin would help us find out what was going on in Ryan's secret life. But that's harder than it sounds."

"Speaking of secrets, have you given any thought about the one hidden in your house?"

"Honestly, I don't even know if it's true. But why would Lance would conjure up a story like that?"

"From what I've heard about the guy, he doesn't need a reason to lie, just someone to listen to it."

"I suppose. But lying to his attorney is plain stupid, and he's not that dumb."

"He lost you, didn't he? That's the dumbest thing I've heard of."

"Excellent point. How about I make nachos, and we watch the game together?"

His grin confirmed what I already knew. Joining him on the sofa to cheer on his favorite team was as much an aphrodisiac for him as the foot massage was for me. I doubted we'd see more than another inning or two, regardless of how close the score was.

. . .

Raindrops pelted the bathroom window as I stepped out of the shower. I towel-dried my hair and pulled it into a ponytail before slipping on lightweight black pants and a loose-fitting white shirt.

The buttery combination of cinnamon and sugar filled the kitchen.

"Oh, my God. Is that French toast?"

"Not just any French toast. It's my vanilla cream recipe." He scooped two thick slabs onto my plate before serving himself.

After polishing off a third piece and reluctantly refusing a fourth, I pushed away from the table. "What did I do to deserve that?" I wiggled my eyebrows. "Never mind. I remember."

He laughed, and we finished our coffee together.

"If I had my way, we'd go back to bed and stay there, but I should check in at the office. What's your schedule like?"

Before he answered, my cell phone rang.

"Please, Lucy. Don't hang up." It was Lance, and this time, the call came through with no prison system switchboard involved.

I mouthed his name to Mateo and hit speaker.

"You have sixty seconds, starting now."

"I didn't want to leave town without telling you how sorry I am for the way I treated you. I had a good woman and—"

"Wait a second. Did you say *leave town*?"

"Yes, but that's not why I called. If I hadn't cheated on you, none of this would have happened."

"Well, you did cheat, and I'm glad. Otherwise, I might have wasted more time on you. But let's return to that part about you leaving." I thought of Janelle's escape. "You didn't break out, did you?"

"Of course not. I gave the Feds information on Janelle to help them find out who she was working for."

"So, you're not worried about the key to the safe deposit box getting into the wrong hands?"

"What key? I put the original in the safe my dad gave me. Remember that monstrosity? He kept his gun collection in it until Mom made him sell everything off after she found him in front of the full-length mirror practicing his quick draw. I stuck a few confidential files in it, then asked my cousin if I could store it in his basement. Not first cousin, possibly second once removed? Hell, I have no idea how we're related. I gave him some bullshit story about keeping important family documents in there and paid him a few bucks a month. I thought he might question me when I got arrested, but no. He's not the brightest tool in the shed."

"Sharpest. It's sharpest tool."

Mateo closed his eyes and shook his head.

"No, babe. I'm pretty sure it's brightest. Anyway, I gave my attorney the combination to the safe to set up my deal."

"Hold on. Your lawyer said the only hard copies were in a safe deposit box. That's why he called to ask me to look for the key."

"Sorry, Lucy. I don't know what you're talking about. And Myra Gordon is a she, not a he."

"Who the hell is Myra Gordon?"

"*She's* my attorney."

CHAPTER 20

One of the many things I admired about Mateo from the start was his laser-like ability to stay focused. Whether he was delving into details about Uncle Buddy's colorful past or taking aim at bad guys, he never lost sight of the mission.

Lance's revelation that his attorney was a woman stunned me and disturbed my concentration. Mateo took up where I couldn't. He asked the big question: if Simon Elliott didn't represent him, who the hell was he and what was he really hoping to find in my apartment? Half an hour after Lance hung up, I still needed clarification on the facts.

"Why call me? Obviously, he wasn't aware there was somebody out here impersonating his lawyer. Did he just want to gloat about getting out of jail?"

"He said he wanted to apologize for the way he treated you."

"What a load of crap. Please, don't tell me you bought it."

"Do I believe he's sorry he hurt you? Not so much. More like he hates losing. But that part about him hating that he put you in danger? I can see that."

"Well, it doesn't matter now. Since there's no mysterious key, we can stop worrying about it."

The look on his face made me doubt my safety.

"You're probably right, but I'll feel better once Janelle's back in custody."

"Didn't he say the information in his files would help them catch her?"

"Not exactly. But it should make it easier to get to the people who set up the organ trading scheme. His real attorney has to be really good, and what Crawford has to trade must be valuable. Otherwise, there's no way she would've been able to finagle him into WITSEC."

"It figures that jerk would end up getting off scot free. The doctor and Roberta are dead, Janelle's on the run, and Lance is going to be living it up as a ski instructor in Colorado."

"When did he take up skiing?"

"He hasn't, but I can see him on the slopes picking up lonely women."

"That's not the way witness protection works. The Feds won't go out of their way to get them a cushy job or location. Lance will never be a lawyer again or do anything remotely connected to the legal field. Unless he has some other marketable skills, he'll have a hard time finding a job that would keep him in the style he's used to. I see him being miserable."

"I hope you're right."

On my drive to work, I caught myself humming a nameless tune and smiling. My mood was a direct result of the mental image of running into my former boyfriend slinging burgers at a fast-food joint or behind the wheel of a Roto-Rooter truck.

My smile faded as I pulled in between Hugh's and Elsie's vehicles. My boss would share my anger over Lance's luck. The inability to get to the man who had gotten off so easy would put him in a foul mood, one that would have a negative effect on the entire office. Plus, I'd been so sidetracked by the news, I forgot about the Miller case. Luckily, I had Mateo's notes recapping the funeral.

The last thing I expected to hear was the sound of booming laughter, followed by girlish giggling.

Seated at the reception desk, twirling a lock of long, dark hair and smiling, was Codie Rae. Elsie stood beside her, staring with her mouth open in the direction of our boss, who was grinning at the girl.

"Lucy," he called. "We've finally got somebody here who appreciates my jokes."

It was my turn to stare with open mouth. Not at him, but at Cody Rae. Somehow, the witchy little creature had charmed the man immune to charm. I glanced at Elsie, who only shrugged.

Afraid of breaking the spell, I faked a smile of my own. "Wow. We are lucky."

"Yeah. I was just telling the girls how surprised I was at the Miller wake. Boy, those Baptists throw one hell of a going-away party. Fruit punch and soft drinks. Thank God for closed caskets and open flasks."

The girl giggled again, and I vowed to put her in for a bonus.

But even the power of adolescent approval waned as Hugh returned to himself.

"What's new on the Miller case?" He turned and lumbered toward his office before I had a chance to respond. "Well," he said over his shoulder. "Are you waiting for a formal invitation?"

I sighed and followed.

Once seated, I asked, "How do you want it? Most recent to back in time or chronological, starting with Bethany and me at Ashley's?"

"Hell, I don't know. You pick."

"Well, the first approach offers a different perspective. But the second is easier to follow because—"

"For the love of all that's holy, get on with it."

"Chronological it is, then."

I began with our trip to Ashley's house, then scrambled in my purse. "Look. This is the matchbook the intern dug out, and this is the napkin Ashley found. Check out the handwriting."

He studied them and grunted. "This suggests Miller was playing around with at least one satisfied woman other than his wife, who suspected the affair. Possibly a motive, but if she was banging her students, would she begrudge the husband a little fun on the side?"

"Unless it was more than that." I told him about Fiona and suggested she might be back in the picture. "But I didn't get that feeling when we talked. More like she was still pissed at being dumped for someone she considered beneath her."

"Why is it rich, good-looking people never seem content?"

This insight surprised me coming from a man with no romantic entanglements in his life. None I was aware of, at least.

I picked up my narrative with Bethany and me at the Broadview Motel. "The manager was an ass, but we got him to admit Ryan had been a regular until a few months ago. We had to squeeze him pretty hard to get him to show us the name he signed in under."

"Poor guy. Getting squeezed by you and your hot friend."

I ignored the remark, took out my phone, and scrolled to the pictures of the signatures. "Listen to this. Lord and Lady Chatterly." Expecting the same look as Bethany had given me, I began to summarize the novel.

"Yeah, yeah. The rich broad falls for the sexy gardener."

I must have been the one with the blank expression.

"What? You don't think I ever read a book? All that talk about female parts got me going, especially after *Robinson Crusoe* and the rest of that Victorian literature shit."

"You took Victorian Lit?"

"My college course schedule isn't relevant to the case, so can you please get on with it?"

"Right. I have a hard time imagining Ryan Miller reading D. H. Lawrence and thought it meant his lover was more highbrow." I didn't add that Hugh's revelation about his educational background made me question that conclusion.

"We got any high-class women who match that theory?"

"I suppose Fiona does. And pushing someone out a window is more impulse than premeditation. But he had to outweigh her by fifty pounds. I guess she could have gotten a running start. No, wait. Wouldn't that make it premeditated?"

"Maybe, but that's not the biggest problem. Whether it was planned out or spur of the moment, our guy could have said the wrong thing at the wrong time to anybody."

I remembered how angry Sue Ann had been about Ryan's lack of interest in writing a policy for her dog pen and told Hugh about the conversation.

"She made it sound as if her husband took his hunting dogs seriously but surely not enough to kill over them."

"What if there was more to the Porter woman's anger than some crappy kennel falling apart? Plus, there's the possibility somebody else he did business with might have knocked him off."

"Did you get anything from the viewing other than a buzz from your flask?"

"Are you kidding? Those church ladies were sniffing all over me. I swear they all had booze detectors."

"I'd say it was more like they had single-men detectors. Don't let it go to your head, though. Uncle Buddy got mobbed, too. And he came away with some juicy information."

I told him about the drunken relative and the fight at the party with all the bigwigs.

"Interesting, but how would it lead to Ryan's death?" He rolled back and propped his feet on the desk. "Thanks to you, Nancy Drew, we're up to our asses in suspects. And I'm running out of ideas on how to narrow the field, what's less prove the wife did it. Elsie's been fielding calls from Grover since early yesterday. I dread telling him we haven't found anything solid to implicate his daughter-in-law."

"Speaking of new suspects. Simon Elliott isn't Lance's attorney."

I mentioned the phone call from my ex and included Lance's denial of there being a safe deposit box. Then I waited for the explosion. What came in its place frightened me more than any raging outburst.

Hugh's normally ruddy complexion turned a grayish pale. In a voice barely over a whisper, he said, "Just because Crawford denies it doesn't mean something isn't there. But Elliott's the one who worries me. Until we find out who the hell he is, you're going to need a full-time bodyguard."

"Aren't you overreacting a little? Besides, I have Mateo."

"He's good, but more is better. And so is a professional who isn't crazy about you."

. . .

My head was spinning with possible murderers or impulse killers or whoever the hell had helped poor Ryan out of the upstairs window. On the way to my office, I thought of my favorite method of sorting out a parade of random thoughts swirling in my brain. The spreadsheet.

I scrolled through the entries in "Suspects in the Miller Case," stopping with the last one, Cody Rae. The more I was around her, the less sure I was she belonged on the list. It seemed obvious she was interested in Danny as more than a friend, but from my observations, they hadn't taken their relationship to the next level. Killing Ashley's husband made no sense at all. She would have whacked her rival instead. Unless she came to the office expecting to find his wife, and Ryan caught her. But why did she think Ashley was going to be there? I filled in the "Motive" column with wrong place/wrong time and a question mark.

I puzzled over Sue Ann's name before deciding to add Big Ron to the list. As her husband, he had an obligation to support her in the insurance debacle. If she had been furious with Ryan over something more personal, jealousy could be his reason for murder.

Hugh's suggestion some dissatisfied client had taken action against his agent annoyed me with the vagueness of this possibility.

This was an area for someone with access to his records, so I left it off and hit save.

A light tap on my open door saved me from continuing to pound my head against the invisible brick wall this case had become. It was Cody Rae.

"Did I catch you at a bad time?" She shifted from one foot to the other.

"Not at all. You just may have preserved what little sanity I have left."

She drew her brows together and kept her distance.

"What I meant to say is please come in."

She entered and shut the door behind her. She perched on the edge of her chair, like a baby bird debating whether to take flight. I closed the spreadsheet. "What can I do for you?"

"It's more me helping you."

"Is it about Mrs. Miller and her tutoring style?"

"That and a whole lot more."

Her offer excited my curiosity. I resisted the urge to hurry her and spoke as calmly as possible, fearful I might startle her into soaring away. "Can you be more specific?"

"That school is filled with secrets, and Mrs. Miller isn't the only teacher who'd do just about anything to keep them from coming out."

She explained the person I needed to speak with was a friend of hers and Danny's who had been afraid to talk until she realized how serious the situation had become. Cody Rae set up a meeting but was worried if we waited too long, the fear would outweigh her concern.

"So, should we go right after work?" I asked.

"We need to go now."

CHAPTER 21

When Cody Rae suggested the meeting, I assumed we'd walk to the coffee shop on the corner. Instead, we drove twenty minutes across town to a smoothie joint that sat next to a thrift store in a half-deserted strip mall.

A boy in a hot pink shirt with the words Suzee's Smoothzees emblazoned in bright purple stood at the counter.

Without looking up, he said, "Welcome to Suzee's."

"Hey, Lionel," Cody Rae responded.

At the sound of her voice, he turned and grinned before tipping over the stack of plastic cups to his right. He scrambled to pick them up as he mumbled, "She's over there."

His directions were unnecessary since she was the only one in the place, but I suspected both the information and the clumsiness had something to do with my companion. She rewarded him with a "thank you" and her half smile, and he ran into the specials sign hanging on the wall.

We walked toward my braided guide, who sat with a frothy yellow drink. She wore the same shirt as the boy who greeted us. Her face was buried behind the paperback she held.

"You know Kanisha?" I asked.

She ignored my question and made her way through the maze of empty tables. The girl remained engrossed in her book until her we stood in front of her.

"You guys have met, right?" Cody Rae pulled up a chair and sat in it.

I followed suite, unsure if the girl with the golden threads in her hair would remember me or if I fell into the category of easily forgotten and boring adults, I responded first. "We did. If not for Kanisha, I doubt I would have made it through the halls."

"You can call me Nisha, and I think you would have been fine without me."

There was an undertone in her voice, but I couldn't tell if it was complimentary or if she'd known from the start I had an ulterior motive to my inquiries.

Cody Rae flipped the book over, *The Bluest Eye* by Toni Morrison. "Haven't you read this at least a hundred times?"

"And I would read it a thousand more if I could change the ending."

I closed my eyes and thought of my junior year in college when I studied the same novel. It took a moment to recall the conclusion, which was filled with madness and death. Then I shared her desire to provide a happy ending for the tortured characters. Now I realized rewriting a book that shed light on a dark part of the nation's past would be the same as editing history.

"Nisha's the biggest nerd I know." She tapped her friend on the shoulder with her fist. "And the smartest."

Our server arrived with two berry-colored smoothies. "On the house." He kept his eyes glued on Cody Rae.

"That's really sweet," she said.

Nisha snorted, and he scurried away.

"That boy is all about you, girl. I've told him you're taken, but he can't seem to get it."

"What are you talking about? You know Danny and I are just friends."

"Uh huh. Keep telling yourself that."

I interrupted. "Thanks for meeting us here. I hear you have some information that might be helpful in figuring out what happened to Mrs. Miller's husband."

"That worst thing was marrying that woman in the first place," Cody Rae said. "Well, the second worst, I suppose."

I stopped myself from pointing out that technically it was impossible to have a second worst and addressed Nisha. "About that information?"

She picked up a backpack from the floor and removed a folder with *Confidential* written in red marker on the front. "This is from the file cabinet in Mr. Parnell's office. There were a bunch of others like it, but I was afraid he'd notice if I took too many."

"Parnell's our principal. He's a real dick head," Cody Rae explained.

I reached out, then pulled my hands away as if I'd touched hot lava. "This is scary stuff, girls. You could get in a lot of trouble for taking school property. It might be better if you put it back."

"No. You take it, but don't open it here. When you see what's inside, you'll understand why it's not me who should be worrying about getting in trouble."

. . .

When we returned to Farewell and Associates, I hustled Cody Rae into my office. Inhaling a deep breath, I peeked into the folder and stared at the contents.

"Holy shit! Sorry about that, but my God!"

"That's exactly what I said when Nisha showed them to me."

The photos were in black and white with bad lighting and blurred faces, but their purpose was crystal clear. We were looking at what had to be the prelude to an orgy or at least some kind of sex thing. And it wasn't pretty.

Around five or six topless women wearing masks appeared to be strutting in front of similarly masked men in their boxers or briefs. Except for a few well-muscled guys, most of them should have kept their shirts on. Their female counter parts sported an assortment of breast types, from modest A-cups to bosoms large enough to smother any unsuspecting person who passed too close.

"The one with the super skinny legs and the gigantic potbelly is Mr. Parnell. You can tell by his gross comb-over."

"My, God. What kind of school do you go to?"

"The usual, I guess. The woman with her hair pulled into a bun could be the drama teacher. Her boobs are about the right size. And the dude behind her looks like Mr. Miller."

"How in the world did Nisha find these?"

"She sneaks into Parnell's office because he leaves it unlocked half the time, as if he doesn't consider her a threat or forgets she's there. She says it's because of her being black. I said it's because she's a girl. Guess we're both right. She goes through his desk and cabinets whenever she gets bored. His secretary's, too. Mostly, she only finds to-do lists or receipts. Stuff like that. But she overheard him talking on the phone about what a wild time he had at some party he went to. He mentioned something about the costumes or lack of them being a big hit and how much he appreciated the special packet. She peeked around the corner and noticed him stick a folder in here."

She pointed to the top right drawer. "It's supposed to lock automatically when you close it. Only it doesn't because Nisha stuck silly putty in the hole her second day as his student assistant."

I had to admit the girl was resourceful. Possibly a future addition to Farewell and Associates.

The photos were gross but interesting. I wished we were able to identify more of the partygoers. I pressed Cody Rae.

"I think that's the media specialist. And this might be the football coach."

I picked up the last one in the stack and zeroed in on a tall woman with an impressive chest. She'd wrapped a scarf around her hair, but she looked familiar. Even in black and white, her dark, thin lips stood out.

Using the magnifier Hugh bought me for examining signatures, I zoomed in on her face and there, almost lost between her breasts, dangled a gold locket, the same one worn by Sue Ann Porter.

I dropped both magnifying glass and photo onto the desktop.

"What? What did you see?" She reached for the picture, but I shoved it back with the others.

"Nothing important, just disgusting. But I'll hold on to this for now."

She gave me a narrow-eyed gaze but didn't protest. "Whatever. I better get out front or Mr. Farewell might fall out of love with me."

When she was out of earshot, I dialed Elsie's extension.

"Are you up for paying someone a visit? We'll be back in time for you to pick up Cody Rae."

She jumped at the chance, and within ten minutes we were on the road.

. . .

"So, where are we going and who should I pretend to be?" Elsie turned the visor down to run a brush through her shiny silver bob and to apply a shade of light coral lipstick.

At a stop sign, I risked a glance in the rearview mirror and decided not to bother trying to tame my thick curls. I would go as myself—a harried investigator with no time to work on her appearance.

I told Elsie about the folder with the naughty photos and pointed to my bag in the back seat. "Take a look inside."

She thumbed through the contents. Except for an occasional grunt of disgust, she examined the pictures in silence.

"Dear God. What a bunch of perverts. Imagine seeing her teachers running around as if they were sex-crazed nudists. She may never get that image out of her head."

"That makes two of us." I told her about recognizing Sue Ann's necklace. "After I saw the locket, it was obvious it was her."

"Do you think she murdered that poor man?"

"Poor man? He was a player and a pervert. She's as likely to have killed him as anyone on my list, maybe more so. At first, the only definite connection she had with Ryan was her husband's fancy kennel. And exorbitant premiums are hardly a motive for murder. Now that I've seen her cavorting around naked in front of her insurance salesman, I'm betting there's more to her story."

"True, but didn't you say there were five or six women there?"

"Yes, and any of them could have had good reason to want him dead. Trouble is I have no idea who they are. Neither did the girls."

"What about identifying marks?"

I wrinkled my nose at the prospect of inspecting naked bodies looking for tattoos or scars with two teenage females but admitted to myself it might come to that.

"I don't know about you, dear, but seeing your spouse parading around like that is a good motivation for murder. Especially if he or she were there without me."

"The question is which spouse."

CHAPTER 22

My GPS announced we were nearing our destination. I had no real plan of attack, so I decided to wing it.

"We'll say you're my partner. You came to record a backup of the conversation. If she balks at being recorded, you take notes. Ideally, we can do both. That way, you'll be able to write down her physical and facial reactions."

"Pretty soon we're going to have enough material for a Netflix docuseries. Don't know about you, but I'm going to play myself."

"Hell yes, you will." I laughed at the idea of a heavily made-up Elsie handcuffing a suspect.

The Porter's subdivision was a settled-in neighborhood with lots of sprawling old oak trees. Not far ahead, a husky man in a Braves cap leaned against the trunk of one of them. Its thick roots rippled underneath his generous behind. I recognized him from the picture on Sue Ann's desk.

I eased into the driveway. "There's Big Ron. That's what his wife calls him, for obvious reasons. He doesn't remind me of anyone in the nudie pics. How about you?"

She shook her head as we watched him struggle to stand up. He continued his attempts while we headed up the walkway, welcomed by the sound of barking dogs.

"It's okay, Mr. Porter. Please, don't get up. We're here to talk to Sue Ann."

When the wind blew in our direction, it brought with it a familiar foul odor. The closer we got to Big Ron, the stronger the smell became.

"I apologize for my sorry state, ladies. It just hasn't been my day. I'm sure we've never met because I wouldn't have forgotten two beautiful gals like you." He bellowed a command for the dogs to get quiet, and the howls faded away.

Despite his miserable condition, he poured on the charm. Unfortunately, it competed with the smell of poop. The poop won out. We stopped at the edge of the lawn.

I explained we wanted to interview his wife on the follow-up story of the one memorializing Ryan Miller, confident Big Ron had no interest in feature articles, even if they subscribed to the local paper.

"'Fraid you missed her. She probably wouldn't have been too much help anyway. That woman was madder than a wet hen when she left." He closed his eyes and shook his head.

"That's a shame. Do you have any idea when she might be back?"

Elsie spoke up. "I bet that depends on how angry she was. Am I right, Mr. Porter?"

"You sure are, little lady. Call me Ron."

"Okay, Ron," she smiled, "what did you do to make your wife unhappy?"

He sniffed and swiped his hand across his beet-red nose. "Nothing. At least, not on purpose. You see, I was supposed to be waiting for the man to bring wood for the new pen. Then she wanted me to get cleaned up to meet her sister and her blockhead husband for dinner. I may have had more to drink than I should have. Anyway, I was helping the delivery guy unload, and I slipped in some dog shit. Dammit, I did it again." He tilted the can to his lips, then tossed it aside and stared into the horizon.

"Swearing doesn't bother us, Ron. Please, go on," Elsie coaxed in a soft, honeyed voice.

"Sue Ann got ticked off and locked me out of the house. I told her I wouldn't be able to get inside to clean up without a key. She said I should hose off like the hounds. Then she jumped in her car and took off. I tried, but the grass was too slippery, and damned if I didn't fall down. I can't say I'm sorry about missing dinner with my high-faluting in-laws, but I hate getting Sue Ann riled up. That woman is the sweetest little thing in the world 'til you piss her off. Then, it's Katie bar the door."

He paused, scratched his head, and repeated, "Katie bar the door. Wonder who the hell Katie is and what door she's barring?" After a few seconds, he gave up on the mystery and asked, "You don't happen to be carrying a cold one, do you?"

"Sorry, but we left in a hurry and forgot to bring the cooler."

By now, the air was rank, and all I wanted to do was leave as quickly as possible. But finding the drunken husband of a suspect, who might be in that category himself, offered an opportunity we couldn't ignore.

"Maybe you can answer a few questions for us, so we don't have to go back to our editor with nothing." I tried to sound pitiful.

For the first time since our arrival, a slice of clarity appeared on Ron's face. His previously unfocused stare sharpened as his blurry eyes met mine. "Sue Ann said I'm not supposed to talk about that teacher and what happened to her husband."

Elsie stepped in. "Well, we wouldn't want you to disobey the missus. Especially with you already in such an awful situation. It's a shame she got so angry, though. Anybody with half a brain can see it was an accident, and you're the victim. Come on, Ms. Howard. We certainly understand about being afraid of the boss."

"Goddammit! Sue Ann is not the boss of me," he growled and pushed his back against the tree. Using it as leverage, he struggled to his feet.

When Elsie reached for his arm to help him maintain his balance, I expected him to shake her off. But he accepted the assistance and thanked her. My little con woman dazzled him with another smile and shook her head.

"Of course, you're not. I bet a man like you isn't afraid of anything." Rather than sounding flirtatious, Elsie's words came across as soft and melodic as a lullaby a mother might sing while putting her reluctant baby to bed.

"Damn right I'm not. You ladies take a seat on the porch while I try the hose again." He stumbled onto the walkway and disappeared around the back of the house. The dogs greeted him with squeals of joy.

"What a mess." I brushed leaves off the top step and sat.

"No shit." Elsie grinned and eased down beside me.

"You've been spending too much time with Hugh. But that was a good one."

"It was more wishful thinking than a joke."

A snort of laughter escaped from my lips. Within seconds, a giggling spell overtook us. When it passed, I wiped my eyes. "Detective work is not as glamorous as they said it would be."

"At least it's not boring. The worst thing about getting older is the tedium of daily life. Before I started working with the agency, making it through the days by myself was a challenge."

"You seemed to find plenty of ways to entertain yourself." I remembered the pictures on the white board I'd used to prove she was defrauding insurance companies. Photos of her bowling, line dancing, riding a mower with a beer in one hand.

"I'm not saying I didn't have any fun. But it was an effort. The only time I felt really alive was when I turned to a life of crime."

The wistful expression on her face worried me a little. "Speaking of crime, do you think Big Ron had something to do with Miller's death?"

"If he found out about those orgies, it makes sense he might confront Ryan and lose control. But he strikes me as the passive type. More whiny than explosive."

Renewed barking signaled Ron's approach. Still unsteady, he'd shed his shoes and exchanged his smelly clothes for a pair of dirty coveralls. Despite the wiry tufts of salt and pepper chest hair sticking out the top and sides of his outfit, the look was an improvement.

"I found these draped over the fence out back. I forgot I took 'em off after mowing the lawn yesterday."

The image of Ron traipsing around clad in his boxers and nothing else flashed through my brain. I shook it away, stood and offered my hand to Elsie, who was already halfway to her feet.

"I believe you ladies had some questions you wanted to ask. Before we get down to it, I need to feed the dogs and check on the new pups."

"Puppies," she gushed. "Would it be okay if we came with you? I absolutely adore puppies."

I tried to picture her bipolar cat, Dr. Jekyll, next to a squirming pup and conjured up Mr. Hyde, teeth bared and claws out. Then I realized she'd done it again, established another connection with Big Ron. Pretty soon he'd be spilling his guts, happily unaware she'd played him.

He grinned his approval. "Nothing like a litter of puppies to brighten your day."

As we walked to the back, he began discussing which dog breed was the best overall for hunting.

"I've raised beagles and Brittanys and Goldens. Great dogs. But about ten years ago, a friend of mine brought this little pup over. You could carry her in one hand, but she was the feistiest thing I'd ever seen. Bit my thumb and when I set her down, she grabbed hold of my pants leg and wouldn't let go. I fell in love and never looked back. Sheba, the sweetest, craziest Jack Russell terrier. But man, that dog could hunt."

He launched into a tribute to the creature who captured his heart and made him swear off any other breed. When he got to the part where Sheba died from an inoperable tumor, his voice broke. I had to turn away to stop from crying. But Elsie let her tears fall freely. If she was faking, she deserved an Oscar.

"Watch where you step. I clean the kennel three times a day and still can't keep up with the little boogers."

Instead of the chain link enclosure I expected to see, Ron led us to an elaborate structure constructed of wrought-iron posts enclosing an area with wooden planks raised several inches above ground. At the far end of the pen, sat a playhouse tall enough to accommodate most adults. It was divided duplex-style.

A fluffy tan and white dog ran to the fence, growling between yips and howls.

"That's the proud dad, Bruiser." Ron took a key from his back pocket, unlocked the gate, eased the dog away from the entrance, and motioned us to join him. "Don't worry. His bark is worse than his bite—most of the time."

Elsie entered first, cooing softly to the diminutive guard dog. "You're just taking care of your children and their mommy, aren't you, sweet boy?" The baby-daddy eyed her for a few seconds before scampering over to sniff her extended hand. She kneeled and scratched his ear, sending him into a wriggling frenzy of delight.

Ron whistled, and a smaller dog with the same coloring but a rougher coat stuck out her head, then bounded toward her master. Three fat, white puppies with brown spots trailed her, tripping over one another as they stumbled out of their house.

"Don't be shy, guys." He squatted and tapped the wooden flooring. Two more pups with identical patterns emerged. Ron reached inside and snapped his fingers, coaxing the smallest of the litter out. Wobbling behind the group, this little female only vaguely resembled her siblings. Her black coat was smooth except for tufts of wiry white fur sticking up randomly.

He picked her up and held her to his chest. "This here's the runt and the spoiler." His lips turned down as he nuzzled the dog.

"She's adorable."

"Want to hold her."

He handed Elsie the puppy, who sniffed her silver hair and licked her face. She laughed and lapsed into baby talk.

"Definitely a cutie." I ran my finger across the creature's fat belly. "But what do you mean by spoiler?"

"Bruiser there was supposed to sire the litter, and he did his part. Didn't you, boy?" The dog responded by standing on his hind legs, pawing at Ron's pants. "But Sue Ann insisted on boarding a bunch of poodles the owners planned to breed. One of the horny bastards must have snuck in when we weren't looking."

"I've never heard of two daddies in the same batch. And a poodle with a Jack Russell? I bet they're precious. Who will she look like, the mother or the dad?"

"Hard to say. If I had, I'd guess she's going to take after the momma, except for the color."

"I don't understand why you couldn't offer a deal on the purebred pups."

"It's against the AKC regulations. Sue Ann said we could just not tell them, but if anybody found out, our reputation would be shot."

Worrying about the doggie equivalent of a Jerry Springer paternity reveal seemed ridiculous to me.

"Personally, I think this one is the cutest of them all. Don't you?" Elsie thrust the squirming creature into my arms. The puppy nuzzled against my chest and stared at me with slightly unfocused eyes. I ran my fingers over her tiny muzzle, then handed her to her owner.

"What's going to happen to her and the rest of the litter?"

Big Ron assured us they would work something out and suggested we step out of the pen while he filled dog bowls. Since the babies were too young for solid food, he scooped them up and eased them back inside their little home, allowing the parents to eat in peace.

Once they were finished and the mama was reunited with her brood, he locked up, and we went to the front of the house.

"Can't see as how I'll be of help since I barely knew the guy. Met him at a faculty picnic, the kind where no drinking's allowed, not even beer. Sue Ann was pissed at me the whole time because I snuck in a flask and ended up sharing it with the librarian. She's the one who introduced me to the Millers. That Ashley's as cute as a bug. I never understood why my wife hates her so much."

"Was that when you went to Ryan about getting a policy on the kennel run after you made improvements?"

He scratched his head. "I suppose I might have mentioned the plan for sprucing things up out there."

Elsie looked up from her notepad and tucked the pen behind her ear.

"I could have sworn Sue Ann said she asked Ryan about increasing the value of your policy."

He emitted a sound between a grunt and a laugh. "The only interest that woman has in my babies is trying to find ways to cut corners. She didn't give a rat's ass about their living conditions. No, if she was talking to him, it sure as hell wasn't about insurance."

"I guess I misheard your wife. Thanks for clearing that up for me." I took out a business card and handed it to him. "Would you ask Sue Ann to call us when she gets home?"

Once we were on the road, Elsie asked if I thought she would get in touch.

"That woman's hard to predict. I imagine she won't like Ron's exposing her lie about the dog pen. My question is why she lied in the first place. And if she did, what really made her so angry with Ryan? Because she wasn't faking it."

"Maybe he's too drunk to remember." She flipped through her notebook.

"It's possible, but drunk or sober, I don't seem him forgetting details about his dogs, especially if his little old lady is as tight-fisted as he says when it comes to taking care of them."

"True." Elsie stuck the pad in her purse. "Then I suppose the more important question isn't what got her so angry. It's whether it made her mad enough to kill."

CHAPTER 23

We made it back to the office a few minutes before closing time.

"That took longer than I expected. And we're no closer to narrowing down the suspect list."

Elsie patted my arm. "Maybe not so far away. Big Ron is too crazy about those dogs to risk going to jail and leaving them in Cruella Deville's clutches." She unbuckled her seat belt. "I'm getting Cody Rae and heading out before Hugh notices we're gone. I suggest you go home to that hot fella of yours and forget about murder and pornographic pictures."

We knew each other well enough to be aware that forgetting Ryan Miller's death and the educator orgies would be impossible.

"Not a bad idea. I planned on running some errands, but it's nothing that can't wait until tomorrow. Mateo and I have been working some long hours, and I'm sure he doesn't expect me home until late. I'll surprise him. Tell Cody Rae I said hi."

I pushed back the thoughts of our victim diving to the earth without a net and faculty nasty bits and fixated on the dynamics between and among the lovers in the unfolding drama that had fallen into my lap. More importantly, I zeroed in on how happy couples devolved into miserable ones.

The light dancing in Fiona's eyes in her engagement picture and the easy smile on Ryan's face portrayed the essence of a couple destined for eternal married bliss. And they hadn't even made it to the altar. Picturing Sue Ann as a blushing bride next to a beaming

Ron was challenging, but there must have been a time when they gazed at each other with longing.

The dewy-eyed photo of Ashley from the wedding on display at her home didn't give off the same happily ever after vibe as her predecessor's had. But her distant stare might have reflected her dreamy approach to the marriage, while Fiona's showed an understanding of what it would really mean to be Mrs. Miller. Neither realized the promise of their separate viewpoints.

Far from the glamor shots of Ryan and his ladies, my parents' wedding pictures were traditional bordering on cliched. The gleam in the groom's eyes when the bride walked down the aisle. The first dance and cutting the cake. Typical moments on what was supposed to be the happiest day of their lives. And they were happy, so maybe cliches aren't so bad after all.

Watching the daily affirmations of their love—Dad tucking a strand of Mom's hair behind her ear, Mom slipping Dad's glasses off his face when he fell asleep reading, a thousand tiny touches and smiles—gave me hope for the possibility of a long-lasting relationship. The kind I wanted to have with Mateo.

But thoughts of the short-lived happiness of the couples surrounding this case fogged my brain with pessimism. Up until a few days ago, I would have attributed my melancholy to the natural glass-half-empty philosophy that came from picking and prodding until I discovered the rotten core of each and every situation.

Despite my negative approach, I hadn't really expected to discover rot in my relationship with Mateo. But when he told me his meeting with his cousin had been to discuss restaurant security, the same annoying alarm that turned my love life into a never-ending state of doubt sounded. I wondered if I should be relieved or disgusted that he was terrible at deception. Not only was he unable to look me in the eye while delivering his falsehood, but the lie itself was lame.

The likelihood of Sofia dealing with tightening security in the family-owned business was slim to none. Her father, or even her mother, would have been the logical choice.

Instead of suspecting Mateo of anything more than protecting his cousin's privacy, I'd only been hurt that she didn't trust me enough to share her problem. The deceit and pain from my current case caused doubts to bombard my brain. By believing my interpretation of the situation, was I falling back into the same pattern as when I accepted Lance's lies as truth? Was the man I loved seeing another woman? Was he using Sofia's name as code for some hussy?

"No." I spoke so loudly I startled myself. "Mateo is nothing like my ex. He would never cheat on me, and I totally suck as a girlfriend for suspecting him."

In my eagerness to make it up to him, I bolted from the car and raced into the house, where I closed the door as softly as possible. My plan was to find him and cover him with kisses before dragging him into the bedroom.

The TV sounded from the den and I tiptoed toward it. Halfway there, I realized the voices I heard weren't from the television. A man and woman spoke too low for me to make out their words. I eased into the room and discovered a couple locked in a passionate embrace. The female was barely visible, but her slender hands confirmed her gender. His identity was perfectly clear.

I took two involuntary steps back and most likely would have continued with my exit as if I were the one caught in a compromising position. Although less humiliating than walking in on Lance with a big-bosomed floozy on his lap, this was far more painful, and I had no desire to look today's lovers in the face.

I was in the process of making a clean get-away when my phone buzzed from inside my purse. Mateo turned around. His body still blocked my view of the other woman.

"You're home early." His seemingly delighted grin shocked me until his partner in crime stepped from behind him. It was Sofia.

Her tear-streaked face further proved their embrace had nothing to do with passion. He had only been comforting her. She swiped at her eyes and attempted a smile. I ran to them, drew them into a group hug, and held on as tightly as possible.

"Easy, there, girl. You must be working out." He unwrapped me, laughed, then kissed me on the forehead. "Your timing is perfect. We have some things to tell you. Right, cuz?"

She nodded, and I suggested we go to the kitchen to talk. On the way, I struggled to slow my breathing. Seeing his cousin released a flood of adrenaline into my already over-stimulated system. To suspect your boyfriend of cheating one minute and realizing he was being the kind, loving man I loved the next did a number on me.

Although happy to be wrong, the suspicion itself left a bitter taste in the back of my throat. What sort of person is so easily convinced her lover is capable of such callous cruelty? Especially when it's obvious how incredibly sweet and gentle he was. The answer was tragic but simple. It was someone incapable of being in a successful relationship.

I busied myself making coffee and avoided eye contact with them. My hands shook so badly, I sloshed hot liquid onto the table when I placed the cup in front of Mateo.

"Are you okay?" He tapped my hand with his index finger.

"Yes, everything's fine. I'm just concerned about what's been bothering Sofia."

He raised his eyebrows. If he doubted me, he let it go and turned to his cousin.

"I can tell her if you want me to," he offered.

"No. This is all on me."

With most of her makeup washed away, she looked much younger than her twenty years.

"I got involved with an older man. He came into the restaurant for lunch at least two or three times a week. He said I was too smart and pretty to be a waitress. When I explained about my family needing my help, he apologized and complimented me for being loyal. He left outrageous tips that I should have refused. The first time he asked me if I would have dinner with him, I made up an excuse. But he didn't give up. Instead, he began bringing gifts. Nothing terribly expensive. If I mentioned liking an author, he brought me her latest novel. I told him about wanting to go to see the turtles on the Galapagos Islands, and he gave me a bronze replica of Lonesome George, the poor old guy who was the last of his species."

"I remember reading about him. A hundred and one when he died, wasn't he?"

She smiled at me and nodded. "It sounds silly, but when I talked about anything I was interested in, he really listened to me. So, when he asked me to go to an art exhibit with him, I said yes. I am such an idiot."

"You're not stupid, querida. He's a pendejo."

"Mateo's right. Women like you should never let some jerk make them feel bad about being trusting."

My stomach lurched when I remembered my recent lack of trust. But this wasn't about me. It was about the broken-hearted girl sitting across the table.

"We dated for about three months. He told me he loved me, and I believed him. I'm not sure why, but I could never say it back, even though I think I did love him." She separated several locks of her silky black hair and twisted them into a tight braid, then untwisted them and sighed.

"We started meeting at his condo in midtown, one of those tall buildings with an incredible view of the city. The place was amazing but kind of cold. Nothing personal like pictures or refrigerator magnets. He said it was because he traveled so much. I stole his spare key and made myself a copy, then bought him a plant and promised to water it when he was out of town. I'm sure the poor thing's dead and gone."

The mention of her gift brought more tears, and this time she surrendered, laying her head on her arms and hiding under the curtain of cascading hair.

Mateo picked up the story although I'd already guessed the ending. Not only did she catch her aging Casanova with another woman one night when she came over to water the plant, but she also discovered he had a wife and three teenage children in the suburbs. She confronted him, but he laughed and said if there was any breaking up to do, he would do it. That's when things turned ugly. She tried to leave, and he slapped her and threw her on the bed.

"I'll tell this part." She sat up and smiled. "I didn't realize how much he had to drink, which was a good thing for me. When he stumbled on top of me, I grabbed the lamp on the table and slammed it against his head and got the hell out of there. For a while, I looked over my shoulder for the police. But I realized he'd never do anything to alert his wife about his affairs. I thought that would be the last of it. But he called day and night, sometimes begging me to see him, other times to shout obscenities and threaten to kidnap me. He started showing up wherever I was. The mall, the grocery store, at school. That's when I turned to Mateo. I shouldn't have asked him to keep it a secret. I was just so ashamed."

"You have no reason to feel that way, especially not with someone as messed up as I've been."

"Thank you for saying that, but you're the most put-together person I know."

I laughed and promised to tell her sometime how un-put-together I really was. "So, exactly how did Mateo take care of the situation?"

He shrugged. "That's another reason we didn't want to involve you. It seemed better to keep the details of my questionable methods from you."

"You're right about that. Only it's not the methods I don't approve of. I'm all about them. Please tell me about every single body blow and face punch because what pisses me off is not getting to kick him in the crotch."

"Oh, my God." He rocketed from his chair and pulled me from mine. "Do you know how turned on I am right now?"

"Sorry, guys, but there's not much worse than seeing your elderly cousin get all sexed up. I'm out of here."

I hugged her, and Mateo walked her to the door. While they said their goodbyes, I considered the realization that the Old Lucy Howard, the girl who couldn't leave well enough alone, had not been banished. She still insisted on poking and prodding at every good thing that happened to her. New Lucy hadn't driven her out with the understanding that total transparency was both impossible and unnecessary when love was involved.

The worst part of the equation was that I did love Mateo and believed with all my heart he loved me back. So why had it been so easy for me to suspect him of being with another woman? Until I uncovered the answer, it wasn't fair for me to be with him. He deserved better than a girlfriend so insecure she evaluated situations based on past experiences and flew into a tailspin of doubt and distrust.

If I explained all this when he returned to the kitchen, things might have turned out differently. But the words clotted in my throat, and all I managed to eek out was my declaration that we needed to spend some time apart.

I'm not sure what I wanted or expected Mateo to do or say or what reaction I wanted from him. When he learned a favorite aunt had died, he'd gone quiet. I sat beside him, leaning into him, and waited out the silence. The afternoon I told him Lance had gotten rough with me, he pounded the steering wheel, then clenched his fingers around it so tightly his knuckles turned white. Occasionally, a client problem made him swear. But he kept his emotions on a tight leash.

His reaction surprised me.

"I've been expecting this moment ever since we started talking about moving in together. I'd almost talked myself into believing things were going so well with us it wasn't coming. But that's what's scares you, isn't it? You're always looking for the catch, some dark secret or lie behind whatever positive thing comes your way. Because we're good together. Only you don't trust yourself to be happy, do you? Or do you not believe you deserve happiness?

As confused and miserable as I felt, I recognized his question was rhetorical and traced the butterfly on the cheerful placemat in front of me without responding.

"If it's okay with you, I'll come back tomorrow to pick up my things." He stood and gently tilted my chin toward him. "I have no idea how to help you work out whatever's going on inside that beautiful head. Apparently, loving you isn't enough. And I love you, Lucy Howard and always will."

I whispered, "I love you, too." But he was already out the door.

CHAPTER 24

Instead of pulling a tissue from the box on the counter, I wiped my tears away intentionally with a rough paper towel that scratched my skin because I deserved to suffer. Mateo hit a nerve when he said I feared happiness. But he was wrong about me ferreting out non-existent deceptions because I expected to find them. My erratic behavior was how I dealt with the knowledge I would never be worthy of a man like him.

I imagined this explained how I ended up with Lance. I considered him so far out of my league that, despite the dismissive way he treated me, I might very well have stayed with him, thinking I'd never do any better, trapped in a marriage filled with lies, while trying to be someone I wasn't.

"What the hell have you done?" I slapped the table in disgust and shoved back my chair, unable to stand another second alone. I automatically thought of Bethany, but halfway to my car, I remembered it was after ten on a Friday night. Even if she were home, she would say the same thing she always did when I was drowning in self-doubt. She'd give me a stern pep talk about what a great catch Mateo was and how perfect he was for me, followed by a reminder that he was also incredibly lucky to have me.

Usually, her encouragement lifted me from whatever dark place I might be in. Tonight, I'd fallen too deep into the pity pit.

My mother was a possibility but crossing that line would unleash more trouble than Pandora's box. She would regale me with stories of acquaintances who'd thrown away opportunities for love and lived to regret it. And she would worry, then share the info with Dad, who would also worry. Then she would pull out another card with the name of a doctor who specialized in harvesting women's eggs.

The best choice was the person who wouldn't give advice or pass judgment, but she was already embroiled in problems of her own. Selfishly, I didn't care. I decided to at least be considerate enough to wait until morning to visit my wisest friend.

As expected, I tossed and turned until past two, falling into a restless sleep filled with snippets of vague dreams that resonated like nightmares. I woke a little after six and checked the clock every fifteen minutes or so until eight when I showered and dressed. Elsie rose early. So, instead of calling, I took my chances I'd catch her before she headed out to run errands.

The black BMW sedan parked in her driveway wasn't familiar. I did, however, recognize the voice booming from within as I stood on the front porch ringing the doorbell. Cody Rae opened the door and stepped outside.

"It's that creepy douche bag from the office," she whispered. "Groover or Grover or something. He was waiting on the steps. Started talking to me in the way adults do to make you feel stupid, saying he and Elsie had a meeting scheduled and that she said it was okay if he waited inside. Obviously, that was a lie, but he was blocking the door, so I stalled by digging around in my backpack, acting like I couldn't find my keys."

Cody Rae's hand shook as she tucked a loose strand of hair behind her ear.

"He kept getting closer until he almost backed me off the porch. He reached for my bag. I yanked it back, and all my stuff fell out. He yelled at me to get out of the way, bent over, and went through my things. His face got redder and redder when he couldn't find my keys. No surprise since they were in my pocket, but I admit he scared me. That was when Elsie pulled up."

She took a deep breath. "My aunt was frickin' amazing. Asked him who the hell he thought he was showing up uninvited, dumping out a teenage girl's bag all over the place. She said she was going to call the police if he didn't leave. He apologized fast and begged her to hear him out. She agreed to give him five minutes, let him inside, and told me to wait in the hallway."

A reverberating "Goddammit" sounded from within. Cody Rae shoved the door open, and I stumbled in behind her. We dashed to the kitchen where Elsie stood, hands on hips, looking up at the angry man who dwarfed her. Red-faced, he waved his fist in her face. She didn't give an inch.

I pushed past the girl. "Mr. Grover, I'm certain you're aware that showing up at an investigator's home is against policy. It's an infraction that constitutes nullification of the contract between our firm and yours."

Lance always hated the calm tone I used when facing down a bully. At the time, his distaste for my rational approach confused me. Now, I realized he was a bully himself and feared I would eventually focus my passive, logical attention on him.

Grover's mouth hung open, as if he were a fat bass gasping on the hook. Sweat beads gathered on his forehead as he laser-beamed fury in my directions. At the office, his bland face with its pleasant features struck me as pleasing. Now, the wide-set eyes were narrowed in a fierce squint, and the full lips tightened into a thin, harsh line.

He seemed not to recognize me. After a few seconds, he shook his head as if to clear it, moved away from Elsie, and unclenched his fists. He relaxed his jaw and flashed a simian grin.

"Miss Howard, no one told me you'd be joining us. As for nullifying contracts, that wouldn't benefit anybody. Ms. Erickson and I were discussing where I might find the Braden boy. Why don't we all take it down a notch, sit down, and talk about how we can help each other get to the bottom of what happened to Ryan

Miller?" The purplish-red hue on his face faded to a less stroke-indicating crimson.

"First, that's what you hired Farewell and Associates to do—discover who's responsible for his death. My understanding is you don't want to be directly involved with the evidence gathering. Second, the only one in the room who needs to calm down is you. Third, we're not ready to share the whereabouts of any potential witnesses or suspects or information about the case. That includes Danny Braden. Now, you need to gather your things and leave immediately."

Elsie handed him a leather briefcase, took his arm, and led him into the hallway, where Cody Rae was standing.

"I would say it's been a pleasure, but a lady tries to keep her lies to a minimum." The older woman gave him a push and slammed the door before he had the chance to respond.

"When I grow up, I want to be exactly like you two." She hugged me, then her great-aunt.

The compliment turned me into one of the cool girls—something I rarely experienced in school or beyond. Elsie smiled and suggested we have lemonade and cookies while she and her niece shared what Grover said before I arrived.

Cody Rae insisted on serving us. I doubted my elevated stature would last long but intended to enjoy it before it evaporated, and I returned to dorky adult status.

I took a sip, then asked if he offered an explanation for his visit.

Elsie picked up a cookie from the napkin in front of her but put it back before taking a bite. "That's the weird part. He said he wanted to talk to Danny."

Cody Rae sloshed her drink on the tablecloth. "I don't get it. They've never even met." Her response hit an off note with me.

The likely answer was that our obnoxious client had grown impatient with Farewell and Associates and had decided to do some snooping of his own. The only possible reason for him to be interested in Danny would be the boy's connection to Ashley. He had been obvious in his need to please her father-in-law and might plan to use their affair to encourage the police to see it as a motive for murder.

I hated to bring it up but needed to hear why he suspected she could direct him to Danny.

Elsie explained. "Apparently, everybody's into everybody else's business at school. Grover spoke to the football coach. That fellow gave him an earful concerning rumors about Danny and Mrs. Miller. The busybody also said he'd seen him with Cody Rae."

"How did he figure out she was staying with you?"

She shook her head.

"It had to be the same perve who told him Danny and I were good friends. Coach." There was a tremble to the girl's voice, but she powered through. "He's always coming up to the girls asking cringy questions. He asked me if my boyfriend was treating me right. Only the way he sounded made me want to take a shower. He kept pushing, teasing me about who I was dating. When I told him nobody special, he grinned and agreed that the Braden kid was nobody special. He got real close and whispered in me ear that I should try a real man who could make me feel special. Barf. I should have smacked him, but I just wanted to get out of there as fast as I could."

"We should report that son-of-a-bitch," Elsie growled.

I almost suggested having Mateo pay him a visit, then remembered I pushed him out of my life the same way the killer had shoved Ryan out the window. "Does the Coach have access to your address?"

"You mean did he find out Aunt Elsie's the only person who would take me in?"

"Honey, that's not true." She took a few minutes to extoll her niece's many virtues and insisted anyone who didn't want her had to be crazy.

When she placed her creased hand over the girl's smooth one, Cody Rae sniffled, and I turned away from them. I waited for the intensity of the moment to pass and said what everyone had probably been thinking.

"Chuck Grover won't stop until he finds Danny. So, let's give him what he wants, or let him think he is. I'll call Uncle Buddy to clue him in on the situation in case we run into problems. All that clutter at the shop makes it the perfect place to hide."

"What's your plan?" Cody Rae fixed a lighter version of her death stare on me. I suspected anything that didn't include her seeing Danny wouldn't be acceptable.

"Grover looks and acts like a moron, but he isn't stupid when it comes to tracking people down. My suspicion is he's parked around the corner, waiting for you to lead him to Danny."

She shifted her gaze to the right, then down, adding to my belief that running to her friend was exactly what she had in mind.

"When you leave, odds are, he'll be behind you. Instead of the antique shop, you'll take him on a wild goose chase. Drive to the school, park in the lot, and call Kanisha. Stop at the mall. Check out a few stores." I reached into my wallet and pulled out two twenties. "Buy something before you head to her house. Text me if he's still tailing you. If it's okay with her mom, spend the night at your friend's. If not, call when you're on the way. And this is really important. Don't go off script. If Grover thinks we're playing with him, there's no telling what he might do."

She promised to follow my exact instructions.

"Elsie, I want you to use my car to drive to the office. I left a baseball cap in the front seat. Wear it. If Grover doesn't take the bait with Cody Rae, he should be interested in where I'm—you're—going."

"Got it. But please don't tell me your part involves something dangerous."

"Not at all. I'll take your car to the MARTA station and ride to the stop a few blocks from Uncle Buddy's place. I'll walk the rest of the way because it'll be easier to spot him if he tries to follow me."

"Why can't you call to let Danny in on what's happening?"

"I'm going to do that, too. But I need to revisit a conversation we had earlier. He'll be more likely to answer if it's only the two of us."

I expected Cody Rae to ask what I wanted to discuss with him, but she only nodded and gathered up her keys and purse.

Elsie closed the door behind her niece and leaned against it. "Can she handle all this?"

"Are you kidding me? That kid is tough, which is no surprise. Look who she comes from."

She smiled. "I realized we never asked what made you stop by when you did?"

"Instinct," I lied. Or maybe it wasn't a total lie. I had instinctively turned to my friend for emotional support. Possibly, it was only a coincidence she needed me at the same time for the physical kind. Or even better, it was possible a little of Buddy's ESP had rubbed off on me.

CHAPTER 25

When I called my uncle to update him on the situation, he reacted with his usual enthusiasm for drama.

"Lucybird, don't you worry about a thing." Then he stuck me on hold while he shouted for Norm to grab his shotgun and head to the kitchen.

"Shotgun?" I repeated.

In the background, Norm yelled, "What the hell's gotten into you?" Then, from closer to the phone, "Slow down and put Lucy on speaker."

"Hey, Norm. Please tell Buddy there's no need for weapons." I lowered my voice. "Is Danny there?"

"He's playing some bloody-ass game on the internet. Doubt if he'd notice anything less than the house blowing up underneath him."

"Good. It's better not to mention I'm coming." My real reason was to ambush the boy with sensitive questions regarding the nature of his relationship with Ashley. But admitting that made me sound like a terrible person. Unlike my uncle, Norm rarely pressed an issue. If he wondered why I wanted to keep my visit a secret, he didn't ask.

I summarized our encounter with Grover, emphasizing his determination to talk to Danny. Next, I explained the plan, including the part where I'd be arriving on foot after taking the train.

"This is some serious spy-level shit, girl. I have to say, I'm impressed." Unlike my uncle, he was easily impressed.

"I can't imagine Grover will be tailing me. But I'll keep my eyes open and call you if we need to change plans."

The ride on MARTA gave me time to replay what I learned about Ryan Miller's death. Without my spreadsheet to fall back on, however, I was at a disadvantage. One of my psychology professors recommended a trick to help with memory. Instead of relying completely on right-brained strategies like my beloved Excel, he suggested we access our creative side. The idea was to expand understanding by approaching the topic from another viewpoint.

I figured I had nothing to lose, so I removed my trusty spiral notebook from my purse, drew a thick-trunked tree, and added stick figures of a bride and groom at the top. I labeled them Ryan and Ashley. Rather than adding offspring on my perverted ancestry tree, I stuck suspects on the branches.

To save time and space, I paired some of Ryan's potential killers. While it seemed unlikely they would work together after we dropped the bomb about his wife's lies concerning her dealings with Ryan, I sketched a bosomy woman and a large-bellied man and put them—Sue Ann and Big Ron—on the same sagging limb.

The image of the poor guy covered in dog poop, exiled by his not-so-loving wife, made me wonder if their union had ever been a happy one. If so, had they been sucked into the vortex of misery their marriage seemed to have become without realizing what they'd lost? Did that mean they stayed together out of habit or convenience? More important to my investigation was Sue Ann's connection to the dead man. She hadn't discussed kennel insurance with him, but I remained clueless about the true nature of their relationship. No matter how hard I tried, I couldn't imagine them as lovers, but stranger stuff had happened.

Thoughts of strange things led me to Chuck Grover. His recent interest in Danny indicated a different level of involvement in his quest to prove Ashley was a murderer. He might suspect the two of them had conspired to kill her husband, but I didn't buy it. The boy was far too sweet to wittingly set up a murder. And even if she were an incredible actress, her performance as a painfully naïve ingenue disguised as a murderous femme fatale was brilliant.

I sketched a broad-shouldered stick man with evil-slanted eyebrows for Grover and made him sit alone on his branch.

Although it seemed disloyal, I had to include Cody Rae with her silky hair half-covering her face alongside a guitar-playing Danny. I didn't believe she had been part of a plot, but I had the undeniable impression she would do anything to protect him.

The picture of the lovely, jilted woman sadly sorting supplies in the church basement came to mind. That image contrasted drastically with her eerily peaceful expression at the funeral. I remembered the information Elsie got from the cranky lady about Fiona having a secret lover. If that were true, would it make her more or less likely to be involved with her ex's death? Whether she still carried a grudge or a torch, a boyfriend would be a helpful accomplice. The idea of this frail society girl committing a murder by her own sweet self no longer seemed too far-fetched. I added her avatar with a faceless companion I named "Mr. Plus One."

As we reached my stop, I closed my eyes and visualized my spreadsheet. All the featured extras in the columns faded away. I had all but rejected the theory some random over-sexed teenage boy pushed his rival out the window. That was more a Lifetime movie. Nor did I think Ashley had the stamina to carry on with multiple underage lovers or the inclination to have a fling with an adult staff member.

Ryan was a different story. He dropped his high school sweetheart for a far less suitable woman. Would it be beneath him to reconnect with his jilted lover or some other impressionable female?

It could have been my need for order and control, but I believed the killer or killers were in front of me. Instead of reassuring me, it sent a shiver up my spine. It emphasized the impossibility of overriding the chaos that resulted whenever anyone became willing to take the life of another person.

My brief experience with people in that category had been with unpleasant antiques fanatics—as in those involved in the murder of my uncle's nemesis—and cheerful psychopaths—like Janelle and her lover. The first group acted primarily from greed. Their motivations were troubling but logical in a debased fashion. While the second set shared a love of money, their sense of entitlement played a bigger role in their depravity. They saw what they wanted and took it, reveling in the hurt it might cause others.

The men who would kill to possess old stuff with limited value had been too ridiculous to scare me. As for the deadly duo, events moved so quickly I operated primarily on adrenaline, dealing with fear after the fact, which was chilling but removed.

My drawing of potential murderers reminded me of artwork from one of those horror movies where a kid is possessed by a demon. Like a train wreck—poor choice of simile—I couldn't stop staring at my bizarre little masterpiece. It helped me acknowledge the possibility Ryan's murder had been part of a cold-blooded scheme to get rid of him but didn't make it any easier to wrap my head around the idea. The act of shoving someone and watching them plummet to a nasty death screamed rage.

That level of fury came from a dark, fiery place that Cody Rae and Danny were too young to have visited. Then I remembered the shoe outline on her sweatshirt and the abuse she'd suffered at the hands of the adults in her life. If her mother's latest live-in boyfriend had been the one lying broken on the ground, I'd be more flexible in my opinion of the girl. But there was no reason for her to want Ryan dead.

As for Danny, he appeared to be more sad and confused about Ashley than angry and dangerous. The first time I questioned him, his answers rang true, but something was missing.

The more I tried to impose logic and order on the investigation, the less sense it made. Worse, it signaled a return to my behavior before I met Mateo. My emotional picking and prodding helped me maintain distance, even from the people who cared the most about me. Of course, looking into a possible murder required attention to detail, but getting lost in those details could be debilitating. I needed to step back and look at the big picture, both with this case and my relationship with the man I loved.

. . .

I entered through the front of the shop, where Buddy stood next to a woman with the tightest, whitest perm I'd ever seen. He opened and shut the drawers of a black, six-foot china cabinet, smiling with every move.

"It's amazing how well made this old girl is, especially for the price." When he saw me, he patted his potential client on the shoulder. "You know I'm not one of those pushy salespeople, so I'll let you check it out for yourself."

She gave him a side-eyed gaze as if suspicious of the motives behind his departure and began a closer inspection. From my brief foray into the world of conniving antique dealers, I learned they were a cagey group and wondered if this woman suspected my uncle might be trying to put something over on her.

Buddy abbreviated his usual enthusiastic hug and led me to the door of their oversized apartment adjoining the shop.

"You scoot on in, honey. I'll get rid of the old biddy."

"I don't want you to miss a sale."

"Are you kidding? Lady Lookey-loo shows up every week and never buys a thing."

He half-shoved me inside, where Norm waited.

"Good timing. The kid gave up on his game of mass destruction. He's in the kitchen cleaning out last night's leftovers. Help yourself to a cold drink." He kissed the top of my head and joined his partner in the shop.

Although talking to Danny with no one else around was the way to go, I didn't relish asking a teenage boy about his sex life. More like the sexual abuse he'd suffered but youth and inexperience and puppy love blinded him to the truth.

With Chuck Grover on his trail, I had no choice. I had to find out as much as possible about his relationship with Ashley Miller. The idea of there being anything physical between them triggered my gag reflex.

"Stop acting like a big baby," I whispered to myself and strode to the kitchen with a fake swagger I doubted Danny would buy.

His immediate smile when I stepped into the room made me feel worse.

"Hey, Miss Howard. I mean Lucy." He put down the spoon with a glob of banana pudding on it and impressed me by standing up. Until Mateo, none of the men I dated observed the dying tradition of rising when a lady enters. Often when challenged on the issue, they cited not wanting to appear sexist. I attributed it to general laziness. Had this been one of the sweet mannerisms that attracted Ashley to Danny? Or had his youthful enthusiasm called up memories of better days?

"Can I get you something? I ate most of the pudding, but there's still some of Norm's oatmeal cookies left."

"I'm good. Sit back down and finish. I came over to make sure you're okay." The lie coated my tongue.

"The guys are great, and the food's unbelievable. It's just, well, not home." He scraped the sides of the bowl with his empty spoon.

I wanted to tell him I understood. That things would return to normal soon. But I didn't have the stomach for more lying.

"I can see you have a lot on your mind, but we still need to discuss the nature of your relationship with Mrs. Miller."

His blank look reminded me that despite the adult situation he was in, Danny Braden was only a kid.

"What I'm trying to ask is exactly how close the two of you became."

"Close?"

I sighed. "Why don't we come back to that later?" I planned to hit him with the tough questions about sex at him first, then drop Grover like a dirty bomb. Obviously, I needed to alter that plan, so I reversed it.

"Have you ever met Chuck Grover?"

He seemed genuinely confused. "There's a Mr. Rover who teaches geography, but I wasn't in his class."

"Chuck Grover isn't a teacher. He's involved in the Miller investigation and is looking for you."

"Me? What for?"

"I hoped you could tell me."

"I swear I never heard of anybody with that name. Could he be a friend of Mrs. Miller? I bet he's searching for clues because he knows she's innocent."

The expression on Grover's face when he hired me to prove Ashley murdered his boss's son came to mind. "No, that's definitely not the reason. Don't worry. He doesn't know where you are, and for at least the next few days, we're going to keep it that way."

He assured me he was cool hanging with Buddy and Norm. Then he leaned back in his chair. Catching him off-guard was working, so why did I feel like a conniving bitch? Easy answer. Because I was one. But I had to discover how Ashley picked Danny as her underaged lover.

"Why don't we start with how you and Mrs. Miller got acquainted better than, um, say, you and your math teacher?"

He laughed. "We call her Madame Obtuse, after the angle, and because she's totally clueless about anything but geometry."

I related to the obtuse portion of that equation. "But your English teacher's different. She's more in touch with her students, isn't she?"

"Yeah, I guess."

So much for what I considered one of my smoothest moves, easing into the hard part. I decided to be direct. "How about you? Is she in tune with you?"

I didn't wait for an answer. "Did she approach you first?"

"Approach?"

Unless he'd been taking acting classes from Uncle Buddy, he appeared to be genuinely clueless. It was time to rip the band aid off.

"You said nothing special went on between the two of you, but are you being completely honest with me? It has to be embarrassing discussing your sex life with someone like me. But if anything intimate occurred, it wasn't your fault. It's important for me to understand how it all began."

Danny's face paled, and I worried he might pass out. He shook his head slowly. "You mean doing it?"

I sighed. "Yes, doing it. Did she come out and ask you to do it, or was she more subtle? Brushing up against you, touching your thigh, that kind of stuff."

"You've got it all wrong." He shut his eyes and whispered, "It was all about my poetry."

Too stunned to respond, my fingers itched to take out my spiral notebook to review what I recorded of the last conversation the boy and I had. But any interruption might put him off, so I pushed for clarification.

"So, all you guys did was discuss your poetry?"

When he blushed, I assumed I caught him in a lie. I soon realized it was because I'd exposed him as a poet.

"It's not cool for a boy like me to write poetry, but I can't help it. After Dad died, it just started coming out of me. The more I wrote, the more I had to say. Every time I finished a poem, the pain got duller. More an ache than a stab. I never showed them to anybody, not even Mom. And I wouldn't have shown them to Mrs. Miller if she hadn't assigned us the poetry notebook project."

When he gave the name of the assignment, his tone reminded me of a judge pronouncing the death sentence in a murder trial. In a way, I supposed exposing his secret was the same as killing off a part of himself. Hopefully, someday he'd understand it was more of an acknowledgment of the birth of something wonderful.

"What did your teacher think about your work?"

Another blush. "She liked it a lot, even more than some of the stuff in our textbook. She wanted to see more." He turned away, but not before a smile broke through.

Had that been the reason for his initial attraction to Ashley? For him, she'd been more than the object of adolescent lust. She filled Danny's need for affirmation by praising a talent he hadn't recognized or understood.

But had she been sincere or simply skillful in the art of seduction? Because I still had trouble processing the concept their only passion involved writing.

"When the two of you got together, all you did was discuss your poetry?" I didn't try to disguise my skepticism.

"Well, not all. Sometimes we ordered pizza." He studied his fingers, and I pounced at his hesitancy.

"What else, Danny?"

"A few times, she talked about being sad."

"What made her feel that way?" Finally, he looked directly at me.

"Private stuff."

"I hate to say it, but once the police find out you were meeting after school, nothing will be private. If you tell me now, I might be able to help."

"Okay, but it sounds bad. She thought he had a girlfriend and didn't love her anymore. She mentioned some parties he begged her to go to, but she wouldn't. Then she started crying."

His vague comment indicated ignorance on his part. The image of the two of them on the sofa, Danny's poems tossed to the floor while she sobbed on his shoulder, had replaced my memory of the shocking photos from the educators' orgy. Despite his denials, I refused to accept a boy his age could resist a damsel in distress.

"It's perfectly understandable you'd want to comfort her, but she shouldn't have taken advantage of the situation."

"She didn't. Especially not after she found out the truth about me."

Was the boy about to tell me he was gay? Because if he was, I needed to take my gaydar in for a tune up.

"What truth?"

"I haven't told anyone but Cody Rae, Mrs. Miller, and now, you. She and I never had sex. I've never done it with anyone. Guess you could say I'm the last living sixteen-year-old male virgin in the state of Georgia, maybe the Southeastern conference."

My mouth dropped open, not so much as a reaction to his revelation. And certainly not because I accepted his self-proclaimed status about there not being other boys like him. Because if what he said was true—and I didn't for one second think a boy his age would have made such a confession if it weren't—it destroyed my theory of the case.

I searched unsuccessfully for words to lessen his embarrassment and ease the growing tension in the room. My phone rescued me with a message notification. I excused myself to step from the kitchen to listen, leaving what I saw as a very relieved young man alone at the table.

Most unknown callers didn't leave messages. This one had.

"It's Chuck Grover here, inviting you to stop whatever the hell you're doing and get your ass over to Cody Rae's little friend's house. What's your name again, sweetheart?" A muffled voice sounded in the background, too soft for me to make out her words.

"Kanisha," Grover repeated. "You know her, right? Smart-mouth bitch, reminds me of you. Anyway, she and Cody Rae and me have been partying, but it's not much fun without you and that snot-nosed Braden kid. I'm texting the address now. If you don't want things to turn ugly, the two of you will get over here before I decide to take the party to the bedroom." The sound of his laughter filled me with horror.

CHAPTER 26

After lying to Danny about my boss wanting to see me immediately, my first impulse was to call Mateo. But how could I ask him to put himself in danger after shutting him out of my life? Instead, I dialed Hugh. For once, he picked up.

"Thank God! I don't have time to explain, but I need to meet you at the address I'm sending. I'll forward a voicemail that will fill in the details."

To his credit, the only question he asked was if Mateo would be with me.

"No, just me. So, hurry."

I gave the guys the same excuse about an emergency at the office and promised to check in later, hoping I wasn't being unrealistically optimistic.

My GPS indicated Kanisha's house was forty-one minutes away. The perky Australian guide on my phone hadn't taken my desperation into account as I held myself to no more than fifteen miles over the speed limit. Even with a series of annoying traffic signs, I made it in a little under thirty-eight.

Flashing lights a few blocks ahead filled me with fear my timing wasn't good enough. When I reached Kanisha's address, the ambulance and police vehicle parked in her narrow driveway sickened me. I launched myself from my car onto the street and hurtled toward the house. An officer stopped me at the porch steps.

"Please, I have to see the girls." I feinted right, then pivoted left and up the stairs, yelling for Cody Rae as I raced inside.

Two paramedics blocked my view of the person lying on the floor. From behind, someone put a hand on my shoulder. I broke free and skirted the group in front of me.

The tip of a blood-soaked bandage was wrapped around the upper third of the victim's head. I couldn't tell who it was, but at least it hadn't been covered with a sheet. I released the breath I didn't realize I'd been holding.

Ignoring the shouting, I dashed past the EMTs. A ragged sob of relief escaped my lips. The battered body belonged to Chuck Grover.

Cody Rae appeared from nowhere and threw her arms around me. The same cop who greeted me at the door ordered us to follow her to the kitchen, where Kanisha sat, wrapped in a blanket.

"Oh, my, God. Are you okay?" I ran to her and noticed a smear of blood on her cheek. "Is she all right?" I repeated to the policeman seated beside the shivering girl.

"She's a hell of a lot better than the guy getting loaded onto the stretcher." He jerked his thumb toward the room where the paramedics were carrying Grover out.

"What in the name of Jesus, Mary, and Joseph is going on?"

At the sound of Hugh's deep growl, more tears flowed. No surprise that the cop knew my boss. He took him aside, and they began talking.

Cody Rae squatted by her friend and murmured that everything would be okay now that I was there. Her confidence shamed me into swiping my eyes and trying to assume the role of adult in charge.

"How about I make some hot tea? Elsie always says it's the best thing to stop a case of the shivers. Cody Rae, can you explain what went on here while I boil some water?"

Apparently, I hadn't given Grover enough credit. He must have figured out we were taking him on a wild goose chase and stayed with Cody Rae at the mall. He followed her to Kanisha's, where he barged through the back door before they locked it.

She paused to add several heaping teaspoons of sugar to the steaming cup I set on her placemat. Kanisha took a sip of hers and wrinkled her nose. Wordlessly, her friend passed the bowl to her, then continued the story at the point where Grover arrived.

"Dude started yelling right away asking where Danny was and threatening all the things he was going to do if we didn't tell him. What an asshole."

No longer shivering, Kanisha snorted. "You should have seen her. Cool as she could be, she says Grover's mistaken. She and Danny barely know each other. The douchebag called her a liar and got in her face. Then our girl turned on him as if she stepped out of a horror movie. The typical story, where the sweet little heroine gets possessed by pure evil. I'd say it was straight up gangster but nobody talks like that anymore."

She glanced at me, and I wondered if her reference to outdated slang was directed at the clueless white woman in the room.

"Seriously, CR. Where'd you learn to stare down?"

"Picked it up in the rough hallways of high school. Remember when those snotty cheerleaders laughed at your t-shirt? It had *I'm talking* written on it."

"It was *Excuse me, I'm speaking* with Kamala's picture on it."

"That's it. Anyway, I told them to fu...uh, to get lost. They puffed like angry pigeons. And they left. We cracked up. Later, she said I needed to work on my attitude because I wasn't scary enough. That my resting bitch face was weak. So, I practiced in the mirror until it was solid. I'll never be Nisha, but I'm getting there."

I suspected years of dealing with her mother and the sketchy losers coming and going from her home made it easy to develop an expression with the power to terrify grown men. "Got it, but I doubt you were able to lay Grover out with a death stare."

"That was all Nisha. While that creep was threatening me, she came up behind him with a baseball bat and whacked him on the back of the head. He dropped to the floor and stayed there. At first, we thought he might be dead."

"A baseball bat?"

"Momma says it's a single woman's security system. We've got them all over the house."

Kanisha's mom would probably laugh at my single-bat set up, the one Dad gave me when I moved out. Even after Mateo began staying over, I kept it under my bed. But it wouldn't do much good if an assailant trapped me downstairs. I made a note to stop by the local sporting goods store as soon as possible.

A woman's angry voice demanded an account of what was going on in her house. Before I heard an answer, she cried out, "Oh God! Where's my baby girl?"

The quick switch from fury to anguish first startled me. After a few seconds, I got it. How many mothers like her associated police presence with children who were wounded or worse?

The tall broad-shouldered woman shared the same high cheek bones and regal bearing as her daughter. She rushed to Kanisha and tilted the girl's face to hers.

"Is that blood?" She took a napkin from its holder, spit on it, and rubbed the tissue over the bloodstain. "Did somebody hurt you?"

"It's okay, Mama. I'm fine. I used the kitchen bat on the guy they're loading in the ambulance."

"Good girl. Is he dead?" She stood with her arms crossed over her chest.

"No, ma'am." Hugh answered from behind me.

He had ended his conversation with his police friend, and I wondered how much of the girls' account he'd heard.

"At this point, the medics are saying it's most likely a concussion. They expect him to regain consciousness in the next few hours."

I doubted the EMTs would make that kind of prediction but was proud of my boss for his reassuring lie.

"The cops want you and your mom to come to the station tomorrow morning. Probably wouldn't hurt to bring a lawyer with you."

The idea Kanisha needed an attorney troubled me. If Danny and his mom couldn't afford one, would the same be true for her?

Her mother quickly eased my mind. "My brother's a public defender."

"Good. Until then, don't say anything to anybody else."

"If you're okay, baby, I'm going to get in touch with your uncle."

"Smart woman. You girls gotta be like her. That means you talk to nobody about this." He turned to Cody Rae, who looked away a little too fast.

"Especially not Danny." I added, with what I hoped was a stern expression, then, in a softer tone, "It's as much for his protection as for yours."

She nodded, but I had trouble accepting her acquiescence. In a way, it was like asking me to keep something important from Mateo. Or once upon a time, it had been like that.

. . .

Cody Rae decided to go home to Elsie. She said it was because her great-aunt would be pissed if somebody didn't update her on the investigation. I imagined she needed the comfort of being with someone who returned her unconditional love.

Hugh stopped me at my car and asked me to meet him at the office to figure out what Grover had been up to and the reason for his desperation to find Danny.

On the drive, I considered what might be so important that a grown man would threaten teenager girls over. Had the boy seen or possessed something that would implicate the dirtbag or one of his colleagues? The idea of good old Chuck playing well with others took me out of the moment. No, he wouldn't give a damn about protecting anyone but himself. But that wasn't completely accurate. As part of his own best interest, he would care about keeping his employer out of trouble.

It came to me so suddenly I almost ran through a stop sign. Because Grover hired us on the behest of Ryan's father, I never considered the possibility the senior Miller might not be the only one good old Chuck reported to.

I stepped on the accelerator hard. My tires squealed in protest as I scolded myself for not thinking of it sooner.

Then I excused my omission because if I was right, the answer to the question of who killed the younger Miller was too dreadful to imagine.

CHAPTER 27

Seated in Hugh's office, my story sounded more like a Greek tragedy than a murder mystery. When I finished, neither of us spoke for a long time. He didn't even reach for his bottle of bourbon.

Finally, he broke the silence. "It would seem we've stepped in a steaming pile of horseshit. And the only way to wash off the stink is to make sure you're on the right track before we mention anything to the police."

I was disappointed at his reaction. I wanted him to point out all the reasons I was wrong because the alternative was unthinkable. But once I said the words and he validated the possibility they were true, I couldn't take them back.

Hugh continued, saying we needed hard evidence to advance my theory. He agreed when I said finding out Grover's reason for coming after Danny would be a step in that direction.

"The problem with that is the kid insists he never heard of Chuck Grover, and I believe him."

"Then we've got to find out what he assumes the boy has against him, which means we have to get into the hospital to talk to him. I checked on his condition, and he's still unconscious. They're running tests and waiting. I guess that's what we'll have to do, too. Wait. Go home and rest."

"Sounds like an excellent idea." But how could I when so much depended on finding answers?

Since I hadn't gotten any better at either of Hugh's options, I decided to do what I was best at: research. I would delve into Chuck Grover's background to find a clue to explain his actions and motivations by exposing his weaknesses.

Elsie's car in the driveway put my plan on hold.

"My favorite ladies!" I greeted them as they stepped out. I had to fake my enthusiasm. Not that I wasn't happy to see them. But I had the strong impression this was no social call.

"I hope we're not keep you from anything terribly important, but we have something to show you."

"Nothing that I can't do later."

Elsie put her arm around her niece and they followed me into the house.

"Let's go to the den. Can I get you guys a drink? I don't have any homemade cookies, but I've got some chocolate-covered store-bought ones."

They both declined, which worried me even more.

Once we settled in, Elsie said, "Cody Rae has it. It's okay, honey. Tell her where you found it."

The girl reached into her jacket pocket and took out a flash drive. I immediately thought of Janelle. I'd become so involved with the Miller case I forgot about her and her hoax about hiding something in my place. A woman with her keen survival skills was most likely long gone by now.

"This is probably what he wants." She handed it to me. "He must have guessed Danny's the one who picked it up when he left Mrs. Miller's house. But he's wrong. I know because I was following him. I'm not proud of it. I just had to find out if there was something funny going on with him and her. Turns out, he stopped at the mailbox and stuck a notebook in it. A door slammed, and I turned around in time to see Grover get out of a black car. I pulled my cap down and slumped in my seat."

She propped her elbows on the table and dropped her head into her hands, once again only half visible behind a curtain of dark hair.

Elsie patted her shoulder. "Since she was at the wheel wearing Danny's hat, he mistook her for the boy."

I turned to her. "How did you get the drive?"

"The alarm went off, and he came running out of the house." She grinned. "Dumbass tripped over that creepy little statue of the dude with the pointed head and fell to his knees. A folder tore open and all these papers flew out. He stuffed everything back in and got the hell out of there. I noticed the drive when it fell and ran up to get it. Then I took off, too."

I stifled remarks about the risks of being in the front yard of a house with the alarm blaring. Elsie's expression suggested she might be doing the same thing. If so, she, too, kept it to herself.

"So, should we look at it or call Hugh first?"

They correctly assumed my question was rhetorical, and we raced each other to my office in the sunroom.

While we waited for my laptop to boot up, I asked Cody Rae if she could remember anything Grover might have said other than his threats to Danny.

"He mentioned something about them being in terrible trouble if they wouldn't cooperate. Nisha laughed at him, and he screamed at her to shut up. He shouldn't have done that. She doesn't like it when people scream at her."

My computer blinked to life, and I inserted the drive. File folders named household budget, renovation projections, repairs, and entertainment costs lined up.

"I can't believe this could be something worth kidnapping teenage girls for," Elsie said.

I clicked on the budget folder and stared at the screen as five files appeared. I chose *groceries*, and a series of spreadsheets popped up. I had no idea what I was looking at, but it sure as hell wasn't a list of items needed to make lasagna.

"Woah," she exclaimed. "Let me see it."

Her hands flew across the keyboard as she opened one, scrolled through it, then repeated the process until she examined each file. Finally, she pushed away from the table and slid her glasses onto the top of her head.

"It looks like some kind of business plan. If so, we could be looking at a pretty strong motive for murder. Now might be a good time to involve Hugh."

"Probably so, but I wish we had more to go on." My cell buzzed, and I showed Elsie the screen with our boss's face.

"I was just going to—"

"Forget the chit chat. Grover's conscious. We need to get to him before he talks to the cops. Meet me at the hospital."

. . .

Hugh instructed me to go to the emergency room entrance because the chaotic atmosphere made it easy to slip by unnoticed. He was right.

"My nurse friend sent me a text telling me our guy's awake. That means we have about an hour or so before they determine he's stable enough to talk to the police."

On the long winding walk to the elevators, I told him about the drive and our suspicion Ryan Miller was siphoning off cash to start his own business. He grunted his acknowledgement of the possibility but seemed too preoccupied to explore the idea.

We reached our destination and watched the light flash as the elevator descended. Once inside, he jabbed the fourth-floor button repeatedly. "Jesus, this is like sailing through molasses."

"Won't we have trouble getting past the officer posted outside his room?"

"You watch too much television. The police department is operating on a shoestring budget with a shortage of money and cops. Hospital security checks in a few times an hour, and Chucky boy is handcuffed to the bed rail. If anyone questions us, we're his cousins."

I wasn't keen on pretending to be related to the Grover clan, but the doors opened and he strode through them before I could protest. He stopped at the nurses' station. The woman behind the desk glanced up with a tight-lipped expression that softened when she saw my boss. He leaned in and spoke too softly for me to hear. But at one point she threw her head back and laughed. He touched her hand before returning to me.

"Another member of the Hugh Farewell fan club?"

"Just an old friend. Grover's in room 423."

This *old friend* business made me curious, but I'd have to bring it up later.

For a stocky guy, he moved fast, and I broke into a half run to keep up. As predicted, no one was outside his door. Without announcing his appearance, Hugh burst in and threw back the privacy curtain. I sent up a little prayer requesting that Chuck Grover wouldn't be sitting on the bedpan.

The man in the bed looked more like the loser in a bar fight than a sleazy thug who bullied teenage girls. His head was bandaged, and his right eye was haloed in shades of purple and black. Kanisha's whack wasn't the only blow he suffered. I struggled with being alarmed at the possibility Cody Rae had gotten into the action or become indifferent to the girl's use of excessive force. Did excessive force even exist when it pertained to such a man?

"Nice shiner, Chuck." Hugh read my mind. "Which one of the teeny boppers gave it to you?"

"How did you get in? I'm not supposed to talk to anyone but my lawyer. I will say those two little bitches are demons. They attacked me! My attorney's filing charges now." He raised an arm to shake his fist, taking his IV tube with him. He winced and dropped an f-bomb.

When he finished his tirade, I said, "Don't kid yourself. It's obviously a case of self-defense. And it was only a little crack on the head. The judge will take one look at you beside those girls and laugh in your face."

"Is that what they told you? A crack on the head? That crazy white girl went ballistic on me. Kicked me when I was down. I may have a broken rib. Thank God I blacked out."

I made a note to address Cody Rae's anger issues.

"Take it easy." He sidled up to the bed. "That's not a very comfortable position. Why don't we adjust this for you?" He reached for the controls and began pressing buttons.

Grover howled as my boss kept going until the patient's upper body was almost touching his thighs.

"I've got a concussion," he whined and his cuffed hand clinked against the bedrail.

Hugh bumped into the bed, hard. "Oh no. All your pillows fell to the floor. Lucy, would you mind picking those up and fluffing them?"

I smiled, nodded, and retrieved the errant pillows. "Before we get you situated, we have some questions for you."

"My head is killing me, and I can't reach the goddamn button for the nurse. Can you please lean me back?"

"Answers first." I shoved a pillow underneath his shoulder.

He shifted his position and groaned. "All right, already. That kid swiped something that belonged to my client. I wasn't really going to hurt those little hell cats."

"Waving a gun at minors is a funny way of showing how harmless you are." Hugh adjusted the bed again, positioning it flat, with the patient staring at the ceiling.

Grover shrieked as he lurched upright.

"You son-of-a-bitch! I could get a brain bleed."

"He's right. We don't want him to stroke out. Ease him back a little and I'll fix these pillows." I turned away to hide my grin. The good cop, bad cop routine always made me smile.

My boss snorted but maneuvered him into a more humane position.

"There now. Isn't that better?" I tapped the hand attached to the tubes and he yelped. "Oops. Sorry about that. The sooner we start, the faster you get your pain meds."

I sat on the edge of the bed, enjoying it as he scooted away from me. With Hugh on the other side, he couldn't scoot far.

"What was so important that you risked going to jail for?"

"It's confidential."

"Okay, I'll rephrase my question. What mattered so much about a set of business plans and possible evidence of a little double billing to siphon money from Ryan's daddy?"

"I knew it," he shouted, then closed his eyes and fell back. After a few moans he continued. "What did he do? Sell it to you or did you have those she-devils work him over for it?"

I remembered my conversation with Hugh when we first took the case. I hadn't understood why Grover came to us instead of handling it himself, but I felt as if I were getting closer to the reason.

"How come you didn't say anything about Ryan's involvement in embezzling his dad from the start of this mess?"

"Because the old man is clueless, and his wife wants to keep it that way. She's the one who fired him up over the daughter-in-law."

"Wait," Hugh held up his hand. "Are you telling me our part of the investigation's been nothing more than a distraction to save the father's feelings because that's really going to piss me off?"

Grover shook his head. "You got it all wrong. Mrs. Miller is certifiable when it comes to her daughter-in-law. I don't know if she believes the girl killed the kid or not, but she sure as shit hates her. As for making the old dude feel better? Except for running hot at the mention of her son's wife, I doubt she cares about much of anything. But who knows? Maybe that's the way rich people are supposed to act, as if they're above it all."

I had so many questions. First, if it wasn't to protect her husband from his son's treachery, why did she care about keeping the documents secret? And how long had she known about them? Most important, how far was she willing to go to get them?

"Are you saying she hired you to steal the information?"

"Smart girl. And it's not stealing if it belongs to you in the first place. But it wasn't just the drive. She gave me a list of everything she wanted, including a bunch of folders with hard copies and a couple of flash drives. I didn't notice one was missing until later. I retraced my steps, but it was gone. That's when I figured out that boy must have stayed behind and snatched it. If I ever get my hands on that little bastard—"

"Forget about him. Tell me more about how the wife convinced a sharp old man like Edward Miller that a hundred-and-ten-pound woman pushed a guy with more than fifty pounds on her out the window?" Hugh dragged a chair closer to the bed and sat.

"People believe what they want to. I'd say he just didn't give a damn anymore. I've known him for over twenty years, and all he ever talked about was his *empire*, how he was king and someday it would belong to his sons and grandchildren. After Ryan got killed, all he did was sit in his office staring at pictures of him and the kid. The walls are filled with them. Golfing together, shaking hands with the mayor, sailing on his boat. He had the shrine ready before the son was dead."

Hugh looked at the window, and I stared at the screen with the patient's vitals. Grover picked at the crumbs on his sheet. Even he seemed affected by his bleak portrayal of a lifetime dream destroyed by an unexplained act of violence. The heavy silence gave me a chance to process Mrs. Miller's fury and her husband's despair. Something about the story bothered me, but I couldn't quite pin it down.

My boss cleared his throat. "This is fascinating information. But it's not getting us any closer to whether Ryan Miller was pushed or jumped out of the window. And it doesn't answer the question of why his mom is hell bent on proving Ashley killed him or why a drive belonging to a dead man is so important."

"That's it." Both men started and turned my way. "You said you can't steal something that belongs to you. Don't you see? It didn't belong to Ryan. It belongs to his mother."

CHAPTER 28

The arrival of Hugh's nurse friend, followed by two men in suits, signaled the end of our visit with cousin Chuck.

Hugh pushed the button with less urgency than before and said, "That was some shit."

The elevator arrived, and the crowded space prevented me from adding to his assessment of our conversation with Grover.

Our lumbering journey to the first floor gave me time to consider what little I knew of the relationship between Ryan's parents. I recalled Mrs. Miller's furious expression as she watched Ashley on their solemn walk out of the church sanctuary. I expected her to leap on her unsuspecting daughter-in-law and, at the very least, snatch her bald. When her husband put his hand on her shoulder as if to hold her back, she froze for a moment. Then she turned to face him—eyes narrowed, lips drawn, gums exposed. He released her and acted as if nothing out of the ordinary had happened. And if she hated him as much as I thought, her reaction wasn't unusual.

As they passed, a Robert Frost poem crossed my mind. The poet wonders if the world will end by fire or ice. Ryan's father had more than a casual relationship with both, and I was curious about his preference. Go up in fiery flames or slowly growing numb in a deep freeze. My guess was his wife had stuck him in the freezer before he had the chance to contemplate his options.

"Let's grab coffee and sort out this mess."

"Don't remember how you take it, so I picked up everything." He spread an array of packets onto the table before maneuvering into the tight space between table and chair.

I stirred sweetener and cream into the coffee I didn't really want, while postponing a conversation I couldn't imagine having. An afternoon chat about fratricide—no, that's when a brother kills his sibling. Patri and matri weren't right, and infanticide had an age limit. I dug deep into my ninth-grade Latin and found it—filicide, the act of killing of one's child. Naming it made it no less incomprehensible.

While I blew on the steaming liquid, the surrounding tables began to empty, but the room was still too crowded to speak freely about my terrible suspicions. I was clueless as to how to begin, and Hugh's unusual reticence offered no help. When he spoke, it took me a moment to comprehend him because his voice was too low. I leaned closer and asked him to repeat his comment. When he did, I realized he was whispering, a decibel level I'd never heard from him before.

"This isn't a good place to talk." He shoved himself back from the table and stood. "Come on. I'll walk you out."

Whispers and chivalry, too. If not for the abrupt departure and lumbering gait, I would have sworn someone swapped my boss for a more enlightened model.

We reached my car, and he said, "What exactly did you mean about not being able to steal something that belongs to you?"

"Chuck said it about Mrs. Miller sending him to get the drive—that it wasn't stealing if already belonged to you. I think she was the one with the second set of books. What do we know about her? Her husband comes from old money, but does she? Wouldn't he make her sign a pre-nup, something to appease his parents for marrying below his station? It's possible she wanted out of the marriage but didn't want to give up her standard of living."

"You think Momma had plans to start her own company and take her husband's clients with him?"

"It sounds crazy when you say it out loud."

"Not really. But it is hard to stomach. The idea a wife could hate her husband enough to use his son against him."

His acceptance of my case theory made me a little light-headed, so I proceeded with caution. "What if Ryan didn't know about her plans or decided he couldn't go through with them? I bet his mom would have flipped out."

"The question is did she get mad enough to kill."

I slid behind the steering wheel without shutting the door. There were no words to express the extent of a fury like that. My boss stared at a spot beyond the horizon.

Inaction threatened to unhinge me. Finally, I asked, "Shouldn't we do something? Call the police or Mr. Miller?"

"And tell them what? We have reason to believe the well-respected wife of a prominent businessman pushed her own son out of a window because she wasn't satisfied with being rich. She had to take it all."

My expression must have been as forlorn as my emotional state because he took pity on me.

"I wouldn't be concerned. In situations like this, people have a tendency to get what's coming to them. As of now, nobody knows Grover's in police custody. Dear old mom is waiting for him to contact her and turn over the drive. He'll keep her on the hook until he figures out how to use her as a bargaining chip. You and I will have front row seats at the cage fight of the century."

He shut my door and turned, then stopped to signal me to open my window. I lowered it, expecting another comment about the case.

"It's none of my business, and I don't need details, but if Mateo hurt you in any way at all, say the word and he's toast. If not, for God's sake, talk to the guy."

• • •

On the way home, I stuck in an old Patsy Cline CD and hummed along to "Walking after Midnight." The mournful ballad reminded me of Hugh's plea for me about Mateo. But what would I say? Nothing had changed since I went off the rails when I saw him embracing another woman. It made no difference that he was only comforting his niece because it was about my lack of trust, not his lack of trustworthiness. How was I supposed to welcome someone as kind and good and sexy as hell into a life riddled with self-doubt and baseless suspicion?

My stomach growled over the music, reminding me I hadn't eaten since breakfast. Sometimes the only cure for heartache is a burger combo. I placed my order at the drive-through line, adding a chocolate milkshake in case the carbs and sodium didn't do the trick. Too hungry to wait, I devoured the fries and half the shake before turning into my driveway.

Disappointment stabbed me in the gut at the spot where Mateo's car should have been. Or maybe it was the onion causing my discomfort. Either way, despair followed me into my dark, empty home.

Inside, I began flipping switches, blaming Mateo for forgetting to leave the hall light on. Then I remembered he didn't live there anymore, and I stomped into the kitchen for a beer. Drinking alone after midnight made my misery worse, and I poured most of the bottle down the sink before heading for bed.

My earlier rush of adrenaline from discovering Mrs. Miller might be behind the events leading to her son's death had dissolved into an exhaustion so complete I had trouble brushing my teeth. I dragged a washcloth across my face, ran a brush through my hair, and put on a worn pair of pajamas. But as soon as my head fell onto my pillow, I realized this bone-crushing tiredness wasn't the good kind that would catapult me into a black, dreamless slumber. No, this was a curse that would lull me into a false sense of safety, promising sleep that hovered on the edges of my consciousness. It would awaken pinpricks of nerves set to jerk me upright at the exact moment my frenzied thoughts began to ease.

Rather than endure hours of torture, I reached for the laptop on my bedside table and turned to the comfort of my spreadsheets. Normally, scrolling through clearly defined data covered me with a warm glow. Each column served as a guidepost to logical conclusions and solutions. Tonight, the screen mocked me for assuming human failings and emotions could be wrangled into a cold computer program.

In a fit of rebellion, I closed the cover without properly shutting down, shoved the laptop underneath my bed, and rolled onto Mateo's side. I wrapped my arms around his pillow, breathing in the faint musky aroma of his aftershave. Then, I fell asleep.

• • •

A little after seven, I awoke to the rhythm of rain pelting against my window. For a few lovely seconds, I lay there listening for soft intakes of breath. But like the taste of raw onion, last night's melancholy returned. Before I gave into heavy-duty wallowing, the insistent beeping of my dying phone sounded.

Shit. Hugh said he would call first thing in the morning. For him, that was six or six-thirty at the latest. Sure enough, when I plugged it in, my voicemail notification pinged with a message from my boss.

Mercifully, he informed me my presence wasn't required for a meeting he arranged with one of his friends on the force. He suggested I dig into Mrs. Miller's background.

After a shower and my second cup of coffee, I decided to follow his instruction about checking into the older woman's past. But my restlessness made it impossible for me to consider spending the morning behind a desk, googling her. The best approach to uncovering dirty secrets would be to talk to someone in the family.

An interview with Ryan's father was out of the question. Even if he was nowhere near as out of it as Grover indicated, after losing his son and possibly his business, the poor guy didn't deserve to be picked at by me. Besides, with his high society view of the world, I doubted he would dish the dirt on his wife, regardless of the state of their marriage. No, I wanted someone who disliked her. But not just anyone. Someone denied entry into the inner circle because Mrs. Miller refused to welcome her into the family. An abused daughter-in-law would be more than happy to spill the tea. Hell, she might drop the hammer on her dead husband's hateful mother.

The polite thing to do would be to call her first. But good manners and good investigations had little in common. My surprise attack on Danny worked well, so I approached Ashley the same way.

When Bethany and I spoke to her, she wore almost no makeup and did nothing to conceal the dark shadows under her eyes. Yet her natural prettiness had been evident, and she had dressed in fashionably torn jeans and an off-the-shoulder top. After staring into my far less fashionable array of clothing and sensible shoes, I selected an oversized burnt-orange sweater and navy leggings with leopard print trainers in case I had to make a quick get-away.

After rummaging in the pantry, I settled on an uncooked toaster pastry. Fallen leaves once again covered my windshield. But I was in too big of a hurry to care about streaks or smudges and scooped them up with my hands before starting the car. My stomach flipped-flopped as I headed for the person I hoped would provide the key to what motivated a woman to turn against her husband and possibly her own son.

On the way, I realized my previous cover story was out. So, I worked on another one about the paper wanting to know more about the women in Ryan's life as an auxiliary piece to my original tall tale. If she didn't buy it, I could go completely wild and tell her the truth or some version of it since I wouldn't include the awkward part where her father-in-law wanted to prove she was a murderer.

I reached her neighborhood a few minutes past ten. The only cars on the block were mine and another parked on the curb across the street. Rather than turn into the driveway, I stopped two houses away, planning to stroll by to see if her car was in the garage. If so, I would pretend to be a spur-of-the moment visitor.

Apparently, I wasn't the only one surprising Ashley. At the top of the three narrow steps leading into the house, stood a woman with her back to me. Dark blonde hair threaded with silver highlights hung loose against her neck in a style popular to a thousand or more women over the age of sixty in my zip code. It was the ramrod straight line of her spine that gave her away. Helen Miller had come calling on her son's widow, and I doubted it was to comfort her during her time of grief. When she reached into her Gucci handbag and took out a small pistol, all doubt as to her intentions disappeared.

CHAPTER 29

If not for the shriek of alarm followed by frantic poodle barking, I might have remained glued to my spot, a hypnotized bystander at a traffic accident. Only this was no accident. And Ashley's scream reminded me I was no bystander.

I considered calling 911 or Hugh, but my growing sense of urgency overrode my natural caution and any advice my boss had ever given me. A quick surveillance of the interior of the garage revealed the side door was ajar. Ashley's mother-in-law must have walked around the house and come through this second entry point. The cheerful serenity of the subdivision made it easy to understand why residents didn't worry much about home security.

After checking for passersby, I ran to the same spot the intruder had and slipped inside. The barking ceased, hopefully as the result of her owner cradling Taffy in her arms and not because of something less benign. Helen hadn't closed the door to the mudroom.

"Sit down, dear." The icy quality of those three words voice transformed what should have been a pleasant request into a sinister command. She continued in a slow, steady fashion as if she had all the time in the world. "We have a lot to talk about, don't we, especially now that you and that oversized rat are all alone?"

As if she sensed the insult, Taffy emitted a low-throated growl. Ashley immediately began soothing her. "It's all right. Nobody's here to hurt you."

The shaky delivery made me doubt the confidence behind her attempt to reassure the dog. Taffy's continued growling indicated she didn't buy it either. The following high-pitched snort of laughter from her owner's mother-in-law underscored the volatility of the situation.

"Of course, no one wants to hurt you. What a shame you weren't as kind to my son."

"I don't understand, Helen. You have to know how much I loved him."

Good job, Ashley. I thought. *Calling your captor by her first name is an excellent hostage negotiating technique.*

"I'm sure you did. It's just you had a strange way of showing it. Screwing around with those young studs you tutored while trying to turn my son against me."

"I never cheated on Ryan." She spoke defiantly and with a conviction that sounded genuine.

It didn't go over as well with Helen. "You lying, little slut!"

Taffy let out a howl, eerily close in pitch to Ashley's mother-in-law's.

"Don't you dare call me that!" Her defiance morphed into anger almost as unnerving as the older woman's. I worried things were escalating too quickly but had no idea how to stop them.

The resounding crack of hand on flesh jolted me out of my observation mode into the pre-action phase. Still unsure of how I might disarm an enraged mother hell-bent on revenge, I took a few cautious steps in the direction of the kitchen and peeked around the corner.

Ashley sat in a floral cushioned chair, clutching her shivering dog with one hand, trying to cover a red hot spot on her face. Helen Miller stood several feet in front of her daughter-in-law. She was too far away for me to rush and tackle her, which was probably for the best as I only played flag football and would toss the rag toward anyone coming at me, then run to the sidelines.

Ducking back into the mud room, I dropped to my knees and crawled around in search of a weapon or something to use as a distraction. Ryan must not have been much of a handy man as there were no tools on the bench, only a pink gym bag and a pair of tennis shoes small enough for a fifth grader. Underneath the seat, there was a dusty copy of *Glamour Magazine* and a candy wrapper. I eased down and leaned against the wall, brushing up against the straw end of a broom.

How the hell had I missed it? I removed it from the hook, debating whether I should reveal myself to Ashley or surprise them both. I settled on a compromise tactic.

I squat-walked to the entrance, dragging the broom behind. It made a soft swishing like troops marching in ballet shoes. I tiptoed inside, holding my finger to my lips, hoping Ashley's wide eyes and raised brows wouldn't alert Helen to my approach. I'm not Catholic, but it seemed as good a time as any to send a prayer up to Saint Francis, patron of animals, asking him to keep Taffy from giving me away. He must have been listening because other than wagging her tail, the poodle remained quiet.

When I was within a broom's length of Helen, I poked her in the back with the handle, praying she wouldn't know the difference between a household cleaning tool and a dangerous weapon.

"Hold it right there, Mrs. Miller. I've never shot anyone, and I don't want to start now."

For several long seconds, she said nothing. Then she laughed, more of a most unsettling cackle. But I kept the broom steady and played it tough.

"What's so funny about having a gun held against your spinal cord?"

"You're absolutely correct. That wouldn't be the least bit humorous. But expecting someone who grew up with firearms to mistake a broom for a pistol is hilarious." She whirled and pointed her gun at me.

Without thinking, I whacked the wooden handle as hard as I could against her wrist, sending the weapon flying. She yelped, but the pain didn't slow her down.

The pistol bounced off the pale blue cabinet above the sink and landed in front of the dish washer. We both dove for it. She reached for it a second before I did but must have been distracted by Ashley's scream. I took the opportunity to grab it by the barrel, not the best position to be in, especially since my opponent held it by the grip. Lucky for me, I had smacked her dominant hand. She managed to take it from me but couldn't maintain her hold. It came loose and slid halfway underneath the refrigerator.

She reared onto her knees and catapulted forward, pinning me face first on the cool tile. From there, she snatched a handful of my hair and smashed my head against the linoleum. When she prepared to do it again, I used her momentum to slam into her forehead.

"You little bitch," she growled, releasing me just long enough that I could slip out from under her and sit on her chest.

Normally, when given a choice between fight or flight, my amygdala signals for me to run faster than the wind. But this woman had taken my free will. Under a less stressful situation, I might still have decided to hop off Helen and yell for Ashley to follow me to safety. But I didn't want to. I wanted to slam my fist into my attacker's face until blood spurted onto her perfectly ironed blouse. My urge to kill or maim faded when I discovered that even when I punched her the way my self-defense instructor suggested, two blows and my hand hurt like hell.

While I paused to shake away the pain, she tried to wriggle from my grasp. It was my turn to do some hair-snatching and head bashing. I drove my fingers into her scalp, surprised at how hard it was to separate the lacquered locks. As I struggled to get a better grip, she screeched impressive obscenities, arched her back, and used her legs to gain leverage.

My God. The woman was a freaking beast. I got in one solid whack before she started to scream.

Ashley must have released her hold on the pup because the feisty little creature locked onto Helen's calf and, despite being flung about as her victim swung her leg, refused to let go. I slid down her body, stopping to put all my weight on her lower abdomen. She twisted her torso, demanding we call off the brute, and eventually I heard Ashley issue a command to "Drop it," as if Helen were something nasty Taffy dragged into the house.

More Marvel heroine than grieving widow, she stood over us, holding Helen's gun and a pair of what appeared to be police handcuffs.

"Roll her over and cuff her," she said, cradling her bloody-muzzled pup as if she held an infant. "And don't try anything funny, Mrs. Miller, because right now, I'd kinda like to shoot you."

Once we had our prisoner cuffed and shoved against the cabinet, I relaxed a bit.

"Ashely, it would be a good idea to—"

"I already called 911. The operator was super nice, but her advice was useless. She said we should get out of the house and run to a neighbor's. I fibbed and told her we would. Then I got the handcuffs from my bedside table, and here we are."

"Yes, here we are." I resisted the urge to ask why she kept restraints by her bed. Instead, I stared at the trussed up, broken woman on the floor and wondered how she could have been so menacing. It occurred to me she might be faking, and I spoke in the iciest voice I could muster. "Before the police get here, I want to know what happened between you and Ryan and your husband."

"And why should I tell you anything?" She spit blood at me.

"Well, confession is supposed to be good for the soul. Since you seem to be missing that particular human component, how about bragging is good for your evil ego? Wouldn't it be wonderful to share with someone how you almost pulled off the perfect crime? Neither of us are law enforcement, so nothing you say can be used against you in court. Secondly, if you don't talk, she'll sic Taffy on you again. Right, Ashley?"

She nodded and kneeled, still holding the dog. "If I let her go, I'm going to give her the eat-your-face command."

I had trouble picturing her unleashing the apricot hell hound on her mother-in-law. Helen was more imaginative.

"Okay, okay." She drew her legs into her body. "It actually is a quite excellent plan if I say so myself. You see, I've hated my husband far longer than I ever loved him. People mistake him for a kind man and brilliant businessman. What a joke. He was always cruel to me and Ryan as well."

She paused to ask for water and I held a cup to her lips. Then she continued with a story of what she suffered at the hands of Edward Miller. She characterized it as emotional abuse, but it sounded to me as if she had gradually come to recognize exactly who she'd chosen to spend the rest of her life with, and it was slowly eating her from the inside out.

"Every morning I woke up dreading the moment the lump beside me would roll over and yawn his hideous breath in my direction. When I requested he move to the guest room, he laughed in my face. I was his wife and, by God, we would continue the charade our marriage had become, both in public and private because servants gossip."

I asked why she didn't file for divorce and get out from under his control.

"Believe it or not, at the beginning, I loved Edward. I was young and very foolish. When he gave me the pre-nuptial agreement to sign, he called it a mere technicality required by his family's corporation. I agreed without a second thought."

Years later, when she was ready to leave him, her attorney told her the bad news. She would receive forty percent of the sale price of their house and a small monthly allowance until she remarried, unless, of course, she had been unfaithful. In that case, she got nothing except her expensive wardrobe.

"This information freed me to hate the man openly with every fiber of my being. Ryan was twelve and already showing signs of taking after his father. I prayed it wasn't too late for him. I suppose timing is everything, isn't it? Anyway. As I said, guns have always been a part of my past. Daddy insisted my sister and I learn to shoot as soon as we were tall enough to hold a shotgun. Sissy hated the noise and the smell, but it was different for me. The sequence of events—aiming, squeezing the trigger, waiting for the explosion, and the burst of heat and hot metallic smoke—brought me an overwhelming sense of power."

She closed her eyes and smiled, as if remembering a lover's tender touch.

After realizing ending her marriage would be significantly downsizing her style of living, she chose another direction.

"It had been a while since I'd been to the practice range, but I went the day after I discovered Edward's deception. After hitting bullseye several times, I returned home, made Ryan a sandwich and sent him to a friend's house to work on a school project. When his father arrived, I followed him to his office and told him we needed to talk."

She infuriated him by taking the power seat behind his desk. When he protested, she removed the gun from her purse and placed it in front of her. He stayed on his feet, glowering down until she picked it up and pointed it at him.

"It was one of the few times I had his undivided attention." Before continuing her account of a cold and miserable existence, she leaned her head against the cabinet, once again seeming to relive a favorite memory.

Then she explained that moment changed the trajectory of their relationship. She outlined their rules of engagement, or non-engagement. First, he would immediately vacate their bedroom. Second, he would never refer to her in public or private as the "little wifey." And most importantly, he would stop taking Ryan to the office with him. In general, she asserted he would limit his involvement to dinner conversations and any other situations where he couldn't reasonably avoid talking to his son. He was to show affection but keep his opinions on everything from politics to choice of attire to himself. To ensure there would be limited contact, she planned to enroll the boy in a fancy residential school.

When Edward protested the expense, she waved the pistol in his face and reminded him they weren't having a negotiation. At that point, his anger got the better of his judgment and he attempted to call her bluff.

"He said I would never shoot him and risk prison. That's when I shot him in the foot. I knew the exact spot that would cause pain but no serious damage."

She stopped the bleeding and drove him to the emergency room. On the drive, she dictated the explanation he was to give. Carelessly cleaning his gun without properly examining it.

"Poor Edward. The idea of a scandal terrified him more than the possibility I might shoot him again. On the way to the hospital, I talked about accounts of random break-ins in our area and how easy it would be to make his death appear as the result of a robbery gone horribly wrong. You should have seen his face."

Her girlish giggle sent a chill up my spine, as did the speed with which her mirth changed to rage. "I should have known he would get at me somehow. Ryan continued to emulate his father and eventually joined the firm. The bastard charmed my son away from me, then paid him just enough to make sure he got hooked on a lifestyle he wouldn't have been able to sustain without his daddy's money."

It was about that time Ashley entered his life. Even in her precarious situation, Helen couldn't keep the sneer off her face when she added her daughter-in-law to the story.

"It's no secret I opposed the marriage, but he was besotted with his sweet little schoolteacher. It wasn't so much that she was of a completely different social class although I had hoped for someone closer to our status. It was more that she had nothing to bring to the union and in her profession, she would never make the kind of money needed to help Ryan escape his father's clutches."

I wondered what line Helen Miller had been willing to cross to win back her son. Whatever it was, it hadn't worked.

"You hateful, selfish woman." Ashley startled me with the fury in her voice. "We had a plan to get out from under you both."

"Are you talking about his brilliant idea to start his own firm, taking his clients with him?"

Ashley's flushed face faded eggshell pale.

"Silly girl. Did you really think Ryan was capable of coming up with something like that on his own? I proposed that he and I become partners. You see, his father hadn't been totally forthright with the IRS for years. But I needed evidence to prove it. And he had to have cash to start his own firm. He gave me the necessary passwords."

She looked at the pear-shaped enamel clock on the wall as if hypnotized by the slowly moving pendulum. If given the opportunity to turn back time, would she accept it, or simply try to come up with a better way to get what she wanted.

Just as I was about to ask her what happened to spoil her plans, she fixed her eyes on Ashley and arched like an angry cat.

"This is all your fault, you stupid, stupid girl. We were so close, but you couldn't stand that I had more influence on Ryan than you ever would. Imagine my surprise when out of nowhere he starts saying he doesn't want to blackmail or steal from his father. He insisted we return the money and come clean to Edward. He sounded like a middle-class schoolteacher himself, talking about ethics and doing the right thing. You put those ridiculous thoughts in his head. Ideas that would destroy everything I ... we, worked so hard for. Of course, that was never going to happen."

My heartbeat pulsed in my ears, and Ashley sank into her chair. I didn't have the breath to ask the obvious next question, but knew if I didn't speak up, we might never learn the truth about that terrible day.

Helen seemed to have grown smaller as she stared at the bronze chandelier above the kitchen table. I almost felt sorry for her. Almost.

"Mrs. Miller, how did you keep your son from ruining your plan?"

She stayed focused on the light fixture. I cleared my throat in preparation for repeating the question, but she continued on her own.

"I sent that inept oaf Grover to reclaim the files, but he completely botched it. He brought one of the drives but somehow left the backup behind. When I came into the office, Ryan was standing at the window doing the breathing exercises he picked up in *couples yoga*."

She made the fitness class sound like a devil-worshiping cult.

"He turned when he heard me come in. In one hand, he held the folder containing the records I'd taken from his father's. When I asked for them, he gave me the most dreadful look, as if I were responsible for the bleak lifestyle we endured at the hands of his father. My son had the nerve to say he was going to give Edward the files and tell him everything. You understand I had to stop him, don't you?"

She tilted her head from me to Ashley. "Of course not. You're not bright enough to comprehend the complexity of my situation. And neither of you is old enough to realize what it's like to lose the only thing that raises you above the others. You have your whole lives ahead of you. All I've ever had is my standard of living."

Ashley gasped. "Your standard of living? That's what mattered the most to you. You vicious witch."

I feared the girl would attack her mother-in-law, but she staggered back to the table and sank into her seat as if the outburst had sapped all her energy.

Fearful the interruption might stop Helen's story before we got to its horrific climax, I stepped closer to the woman on the floor and reached out to tap her on the shoulder. There was no reason to worry. Her words came out in a flood like bleeding from an open wound.

"I never meant to hurt my son. I only wanted him to give me the folder. He sat on the windowsill trying to convince me what we were doing was wrong. I reminded him of all the years I spent cowering underneath that cold, cold man. But he kept yammering about how once we did it, we could never go back. As if I would ever do that."

She took several deep breaths before shaking her head and sighing.

"Everything happened so fast, but when I think about it now, it's as if it was in slow motion. I grabbed his arm and tried to pull him inside. But he was too heavy. All I managed to save was the folder."

CHAPTER 30

After her admission that she had been responsible for her son catapulting out of the window, Helen ran out of material.

I texted Hugh and sat with Ashley waiting for the police. My boss must have been nearby because he barged through the garage entrance before the cops arrived. When he saw Mrs. Miller splayed out, handcuffed and bloody, he stopped and stood with his mouth open.

"What the hell, Lucy?" He pointed at the gun next to Ashley's pumpkin centerpiece.

I recounted how we disarmed Ryan's mother and held her prisoner while she spilled her guts. Even my hardened boss seemed shocked at the story's tragic conclusion.

Two officers came through the unlocked front door. They hauled Helen to her feet. "Could somebody get these cuffs off, so we can put ours on?"

Ashley moved toward her mother-in-law, key in hand, but the older women hissed and stepped away, dragging one of the cops with her. He tightened his grip, then handled the handcuff replacement.

The other officer got our contact information and said someone would be in touch about taking formal statements.

Hugh gave me a brief lecture about calling for backup but agreed, in this instance, I hadn't had time to do anything but move forward.

Once the kitchen was cleared of loud male voices of authority and the shrill, frightening cries of a woman gone mad, Ashley offered me coffee.

"I really should be going." The room might have grown quiet, but echoes of Helen Miller's terrible revelations ruffled the frilly curtains, and what looked like a greasy outline of a gun appeared on the surface of the table. Even Taffy, with her frothy pink muzzle, seemed more a dangerous alien species than man's or woman's best friend.

"Please, stay."

Her usually sleek blonde hair hung in tangled clumps, and her baby-doll eyes were red rimmed. Streaks of mascara ran down her cheeks. Despite her disheveled state, she projected a childlike innocence. If what Danny said was true, she was innocent of having sexual contact with him. But she had led him on in ways he couldn't comprehend. Ashley, however, did. She purposely sought out the adoration of the boy, and I wanted to know why.

"Sure, but no coffee this late. Do you have wine?"

She rushed to the refrigerator, as if afraid I'd change my mind, and removed two bottles.

"Sweet or dry?"

I chose sweet. Taffy whined at the door, and Ashley stepped out with her to the small patio area off the kitchen.

While waiting, I replayed portions of Helen's story. The part where she accused her daughter-in-law of being behind Ryan's attack of conscience interested me almost as much as her involvement with Danny.

When she returned, I suggested we toast the little dog for her bravery.

She hoisted the squirming creature and answered for her. "She says she would like that."

I raised my glass. "To Taffy, the most extraordinarily courageous poodle I've ever met."

We clinked glasses, and went to the den. I welcomed the chance to escape the faint scent of sulfur Helen Miller left in her wake.

Once we settled onto the oversized navy-blue leather sofa, I decided to be direct. "There are a few things I don't understand. Would you mind if I asked you some questions?"

Instead of her usual tendency for compliance, I sensed some resistance in her hesitancy and tight-lipped expression. Rather than push her, I let the silence work for me. After a few seconds, she nodded.

"You already know more about my life than anyone, including my mother. But go ahead, ask."

"If this is too painful, you don't have to answer, but is there anything to all that stuff Helen said about you influencing Ryan to tell his father what was going on?"

She snorted and smoothed her hair back. "Honestly, I was shocked when he told me about wanting to start his own firm. He never talked to me about business. Whenever I asked, he repeated something I heard his dad say: reasonable boundaries make a marriage stronger. Maybe if he had opened up about what his mother wanted him to do, things would have turned out differently."

A line from the famous poem about building a wall came to mind. How good fences made for good neighbors. Only the narrator didn't agree with that premise. I remembered how Mateo and I shared pretty much everything about our days. Except for my nagging doubts about my ability to sustain a relationship. That, I kept fenced up.

"I'm sure he wanted to keep you out of his parent's problems."

She pulled a tissue from her pocket and swiped at her eyes. "That's a nice thing to believe, isn't it?"

She startled me with what I perceived as a sharp insight into the way people comfort themselves with hollow words.

She asked if I wanted more wine, and I agreed to half a glass. She filled both of ours to the top.

"Do you have more questions? I assume none of them are for your article memorializing my husband."

I felt a rush of heat traveling from my chest up to my neck and wondered how long it had taken her to figure out Bethany and I lied to her.

"It was wrong to mislead you like that. I hope you'll forgive me."

"We all do things we regret. Some are worse than others."

Was Danny Braden one of hers? If so, where did he fall on the scale? I took a healthy swallow of alcohol and jumped in.

"It's about Danny."

It was her turn to blush. "What about Danny?"

When she said his name, it was in a church whisper.

"What sort of relationship did the two of you have?"

"Not the kind you mean."

"I don't know what to think, Ashley, other than he was your student, and you were alone with him outside of class."

"I'm sure you realize he's special. I may have only been teaching for a few years, but I recognized his potential immediately."

Bethany would have nudged me with an elbow to my ribs and wriggled her eyebrows at the naughty possibilities behind the mention of the boy's potential. But I no longer accepted the theory of Ashley as criminally seductive. I believed the boy. Still, I needed her to verify it.

"Weren't you worried about how it might look spending so much time together? What if someone saw him leaving your house at night? Did you consider what that could do to your reputation?"

"I guess I didn't really think about it. I tutored lots of kids after school, mostly football players the coach sent to me. Most of them were almost illiterate, but I worked hard to help them get their grades up, not the way some of the teachers did. They—"

She covered her mouth with her hand, as if she were a child holding back a secret.

"What was it they did?"

"Nothing important."

I suspected it was but not to me. So, when she spoke again, I put those questions aside.

"No one could write like Danny. Essays, news stories, and poetry. He did it all."

She sighed and stayed quiet for so long I was afraid she'd reached the end. She hadn't.

"But it was his poetry that made me forget everything—what people thought, the age difference between us. I even forgot about Ryan."

I did my best to maintain a neutral expression while I waited for her to remember her previous declaration concerning their non-relationship.

"Forgetting about your husband is serious. Did that mean there was more between you and Danny than an appreciation of writing?"

Her cheeks pinkened again, and her eyes glistened with unshed tears.

"Not really. I just had this silly dream that someday he would dedicate a novel or Pulitzer or whatever great thing he accomplished to me. Pathetic, isn't it? But my whole life all I ever wanted was to be somebody's muse."

CHAPTER 31

Shortly after midnight, I burrowed under the quilt Elsie gave me. The sunshine yellows, soft blues, and creams comforted me on normal nights. Nothing about this night or day had been normal. I wasn't supposed to be lying here alone. I never signed on for dealing with a mother who passively watched as her son fell to his death. Or worse, encouraged him to topple out the window because of her greed and a desire for revenge.

The self-defense course Hugh sent me to hadn't prepared me for disarming an assailant determined to shoot me. When the evil nurse and her partner Janelle attempted to kill me, Elsie did the disarming. She had been fearless. Me? Not so much.

I relied on the men in my life to do the heavy lifting. Today, I crossed a line in what most people would call a positive way. So why no sense of triumph? Yes, I pulled off being a genuine badass. If I were being totally honest, tackling Helen Miller and smacking her around tapped into a savagery that excited me. Worse, I liked it. But it did nothing to fill the empty spot beside me.

I rolled onto Mateo's side, trying to recover the warm feeling of his body, only to find it cold. Instead of the scent of cologne on his pillow, I breathed in the smell of generic fabric softener. The thoroughness of my washing him away hit hard, and I reached for my phone on the bedside table.

But what would I say if he answered? Something like, "Mateo, I'm just as messed up and emotionally unreliable, but I hate being alone."

I was in love limbo, unable to conquer my self-doubts, yet fearful if I couldn't resolve them soon, he wouldn't be waiting for me.

It wasn't fair to call him. I loved him too much to yoyo him in and out of my life. I tried to push aside thoughts of how fantastic he was. My mind drifted to Elsie's incredible rescue of me and Lance in his office. That brought me to Janelle's spot on Memory Lane. Hugh promised to pass on any updates as to her whereabouts, and I trusted him to keep his word. which meant no news. It seemed as if she vanished in a puff of smoke.

But I knew with a strange certainty she hadn't. A bond developed between us when she insinuated herself into my life. I never expected to be her friend, but I understood her, at least to some extent. Not her seduction of my boyfriend, nor the countless—okay, three for sure—old guys she wrangled into her bed before murdering them. And not her involvement in distributing stolen organs.

I related to the unheard part of her. Like most beautiful women and a good proportion of the rest, men desired her, but they weren't interested in her ambitions or values. If any of her victims had delved into her mind, they might have been saved. As for other females, the majority viewed her as a cheap threat to their personal relationships. But they didn't recognize what made her truly dangerous. They discounted her intelligence, her devious brilliance. And they overlooked or ignored her determination to get what she wanted, no matter who got hurt.

Despite the false nature of her visit when she came to warn me about Lance, I believed that woman was the real Janelle. Treacherous, yes. But also insightful, competent, and vulnerable. Unless she had suckered me into falling for another fake front.

Regardless of the basis for our brief relationship, its intensity inexplicitly connected us. If she had fled the vicinity, I would still catch the scent of brimstone left in her wake. No. Janelle hadn't gone far because we weren't finished with each other.

. . .

Elsie greeted me. Her usually calm demeanor had been replaced with an electric energy that was almost palpable.

"Hugh called to say he's ten minutes out. Fill me in on what the newspaper didn't cover before he gets her."

She thrust the local section of the paper across her desk. While the rest of the world got information from online sources, our boss liked the old-fashioned, print copy-in-hand approach. I understood his point. The sensation of touching a story in which I played an important role thrilled me in a way an electronic device couldn't match.

I skimmed the account, relieved not to be mentioned by name. The last time I was heralded as the heroine who helped bring a killer to justice, my parents flipped out. Nothing in this article should alarm them. My mother, however, possessed a little of what Buddy called the family gift, so I made a mental note to call her in case her extra sensory notification pinged.

Elsie tapped a pen on the desk and cleared her throat. I sat beside her and related the awful events of the previous evening.

"Dear God. I can't imagine living with the guilt of being responsible for your only child's death."

I bit my lip, trying to recall the expression on Helen Miller's face when she explained how her son had ended up on the pavement. There had definitely been anger but guilt?

"I didn't detect any remorse. More irritation that if Ryan had gone along with her plan, he'd still be alive."

Hugh interrupted our mutual confusion over the woman's failed attempt at being a mother. He grunted and motioned for me to follow him.

"Looks like the sexy teacher is off the hook." He leaned back in his chair and put his feet on the desk.

"I never really considered her as being capable of murder. But I was wrong about one thing. She's no seductress luring young boys to her bed. She only wanted to inspire creativity, to be someone's muse."

"I'm guessing being her husband's inspiration to sell insurance wasn't enough." He shook his head. "Whatever. We found the killer for poor old Edward Miller. Grover will probably try to stiff us for the bill, what with you helping to stick him behind bars. I invoiced them myself before they file for bankruptcy. Either way, we should get something out of that crook."

"I'm sorry. Did I miss the part where you said, 'Great job, Lucy'?"

He grinned. "You did all right. I've already sent Cody Rae an email about getting it out on all the social stuff about how we solved the case. Oughta bring in clients." His face returned to its normal state of gloom. "Turns out we helped uncover more than Ryan Miller's killer."

"What else did *we* find out?"

"Do you know anything about some disappearing photos?"

"Photographs?"

"Right. I got a call at home from the Georgia Professional Standards Commission. Never heard of them before, but they investigate ethics issues in the public school system. They've been looking into what the lady on the phone called an epidemic of grade changing violations. Know anything about that?"

Happily, my negative answer was one hundred percent honest. But I wondered if this was what Ashley stopped herself from revealing about other members of the faculty. I congratulated myself on not wasting time with that line of questioning and with getting Hugh off the subject with my innocent reaction to the missing pictures. My congrats were short lived.

"The lady from the standards department told me they were still looking into the record altering. But were concentrating on a juicier scandal. Seems like somebody stole some naughty photos from the principal's office."

I resisted the urge to come clean about the folder Kanisha had stolen. They had nothing to do with our case and everything to do with keeping her friend out of trouble.

When I didn't volunteer information, Hugh shrugged. "I told her we had no interest in internal affairs at the school. We don't, do we?" He narrowed his eyes and stared into mine.

"Absolutely no interest at all." That much was true.

"Good. I got the impression there was going to be a big turnover at Brookdale High, and we want no part of it."

I wondered if Ashley would be part of the change in faculty and couldn't decide if that would be a good or bad thing.

CHAPTER 32

Other than a phone call from Bethany announcing my sex toy party was scheduled for Saturday from four to six, the beginning of the week was ordinary. I filed paperwork about Helen Miller's role in Ryan's death and a police interview about what happened at Ashley's house. The officer who questioned me remained unimpressed with what I considered a tale worthy of a made-for-TV movie. I should have been pleased at a return to normalcy, even if it included an embarrassing, upcoming foray into helping women reach fulfillment. Instead, a vague sense of gloom crept over me.

By Wednesday, I began scouring the newspaper for stories requiring investigative assistance. Other than a dog snatching ring in a ritzy area of Atlanta and an exotic dancer who stabbed a customer, the articles were the usual car jackings, random shootings, and a few robberies. I tore out the canine kidnapping story since most rich people insured their fancy purebreds. Although it was unlikely the stripper episode had anything to do with insurance of any kind, unless the victim died, I saved it, too. Mostly because I liked the idea of an objectified woman literally sticking it to the man.

Cody Rae's school break ended, but she charmed Hugh into sponsoring her for an internship credit, which meant she would be in the office half-days on Monday, Wednesday, and Friday, starting next week. Elsie shared some of her niece's relationship status but not enough to satisfy my curiosity.

The girl never accepted Danny had been involved in a student-teacher affair. She did, however, suspect he harbored serious feelings for the older woman. This, coupled with his seeming lack of romantic interest in her, led to a state of mild despair. I guessed Elsie knew more but was keeping quiet out of loyalty. I respected her position but couldn't wait to get Cody Rae alone and subtly grill her. Hardly admirable, but I needed the practice and really did care about her. Plus, I was incredibly bored.

On Thursday, I began to question my decision about the job with the Atlanta Historical Society. Elsie must have sensed my restlessness and insisted I leave early.

"See what's up with those missing mutts. Or better yet, pay a visit to the titty bar and check out what an angry stripper looks like."

I giggled at the colorful slang, so unlike my sophisticated accomplice and left the office in a slightly lighter mood. It lasted until I was halfway home when Bethany's lovely face flashed on caller ID. Rather than refuse the call, I answered, planning to use the fact I was driving to dispense with her quickly.

She didn't give me the chance. "I'm emailing you a list of stuff to buy for the party. The trick to being successful in the pleasure industry is to tailor everything toward sales. In the snack department, that means no hardline phallic foods. Get it? Hardline? So, no pigs in a blanket."

I rolled my eyes. A few years back, I brought those delicious little pastry-wrapped wieners to one of her Christmas parties and never heard the end of it.

While I'd been reliving my past party-food failures, Bethany had continued outlining what not to serve.

"Wait. Aren't you bringing everything?"

"All but the refreshments. With the discount I offer on products, you'll make more than enough to cover it."

After a few more minutes of instructions she would send later in an email, she turned the conversation to the Miller case, or escapade, as she called it.

"I saw the story in the paper and recognized the players. It sounds like the senior Mrs. Miller's a real bitch."

Bethany's ability to cut to the chase always amazed me. Today, it made me smile. I promised to give her all the details when she came over to help with set-up for the party.

Then I stopped for a giant chicken sandwich from Zaxby's and ate it at my home while researching strippers gone rogue.

After piddling away over an hour in a deep rabbit hole of dancing ladies and their efforts to unionize and a seemingly never-ending list of websites featuring exotic performers of both sexes for hire, I dragged out my dusty yoga mat. In the middle of a very shaky downward dog, the doorbell rang.

Even when viewed from the distorted view of the peephole, he made me go weak in the knees. I shook my hair from its ponytail and reached around back to check for unsightly wedgies. When I opened the door, I leaned against the frame, assuming a cool and casual pose. The tremor in my voice when I greeted him gave me away.

"I should have called but couldn't risk you saying no. If you want me to leave, I will. But I really need to talk to you."

I motioned him inside and tried to catch my breath.

"I'm glad you came by." To temper this admission, I sat in the recliner, a safe distance from his place on the sofa.

"I know I promised to give you space." He leaned his head back, exposing his unshaven throat.

How many times had I kissed the spot less than an inch below his jaw?

A growl escaped his lips as he bolted upright. Something feral ignited inside me, making it impossible not to touch him. Within seconds, I straddled him and bit his lip before covering his mouth with mine.

He grasped my breast. Desperate for his hands on my flesh, I pulled my sweater over my head, then unclasped my bra. He slid the straps down my shoulders and cupped both breasts, teasing them with his tongue.

"Goddammit, Lucy." His breath was hot against my skin.

"Don't talk. Don't even think," I commanded.

It turned out not thinking wasn't as easy as expected. Although I spent most of the next hour or so operating on sensory memory, my frontal lobe—where logical thought resides—refused to stay silent. Questions about where Mateo and I would go from here interrupted sensations from the hypothalamus and various other regions of the brain that trigger and maintain arousal.

Somewhere in the process, however, desire beat the hell out of the frontal lobe, and I lost myself in wave after wave of pleasure.

What began on the sofa ended in my bed with Mateo curled around me, our breathing slowly returning to normal. I bought myself time by pretending to sleep, suspecting he might be doing the same thing until he spoke.

"This wasn't what I had in mind when I came over."

I wanted to shush him—to tell him I didn't care why he stopped by. All that mattered was he was here now.

"It wasn't what I had in mind when I let you in, but I'm glad it happened. Aren't you?" Obviously, this was a trick question. What man can honestly say he's sorry he had mind-blowing sex?

"Of course. But I've been doing a lot of thinking, alone late at night. I almost decided that I would settle for a more casual relationship if it was the only way for this to work."

I turned toward him and wrapped my leg around his. Another sneaky move. "That's not what I want."

"Good because I said almost." He unwrapped himself and stuck a pillow between us. "I came over to tell you I'm a patient man. If you say you need more time, I'll wait. But not forever. These past few weeks have been like living in a nightmare that only being with you can end. At some point, not being sure about where we're going means we'll never be together. The longer I put off that reality, the harder it will be to move on."

He leaned over to kiss my cheek before rolling away. I reached for him, but he was too quick. I wanted to tell him to stay, that I was done with doubting whether I had the ability to accept his love. When I saw him embracing another woman, I jumped to the conclusion I had lost him to someone prettier, smarter, better. It confirmed my belief that I wasn't enough.

Discovering he was simply comforting his cousin proved to me I was unworthy of a man like Mateo. Would an afternoon of being the object of his desire quell my self-doubt? If not, how many would it take? Until I answered that question, how could I promise him the stability he needed?

So, I watched him gather his clothes and listened as he closed the door on his way out.

CHAPTER 33

I woke around five thirty and gave up trying to fall back to sleep a few minutes after six. The woman who stared at me from the bathroom mirror startled me with her mascara-streaked face and puffy eyes. I traced her swollen lips with my index finger, sending flickers of heat throughout my body as I remembered the urgency that hurled me into Mateo's arms. I stood under the hot shower while waves of sudsy water cascaded over me. Only when the spray cooled, did I stagger to the bedroom and fling my towel-draped self onto the bed.

Would this sense of loss, this hollow spot in my heart, greet me every morning spent without Mateo?

And who was to blame if it did? My brutally honest alter ego pointed her finger at me. I wanted to ask where the hell she'd been when I let him desert me. Too emotionally fragile to argue with myself, I surrendered.

What I needed was an investigation. Hugh would reject looking into the exotic dancer story unless the victim filed a claim against the bar owners. Since I was on the side of the stripper, that approach had no appeal to me.

That left the kidnapped canines. Rescuing animals had a noble ring to it. Unfortunately, my boss would most likely laugh me out of his office if I mentioned it to him.

I was so desperate I considered asking for more coursework in collecting evidence but couldn't imagine sitting in a stuffy classroom with Sherlock Holmes wanna-bes. So, I prowled through files at work.

The runway lights in the hallway added to the gloom of the empty office, but I welcomed the shadowy pall. It matched my mood far better than a sunlit corridor would. My colleagues weren't due in for at least another hour. If I worked in semi-darkness and stayed quiet, no one would realize I was there.

While scrolling through my emails, I noticed Bethany's message. The subject line read *Guest List, Preparation Instructions, Snack Requirements.* My original intent had been to ignore all such directives and follow my own. I would run the vacuum and dust, buy a jumbo package of pigs in a blanket, and call it a day. It was a testament to the extent of my restless depression that I opened the email with more than a little excitement.

I skimmed through it and decided to pick up a veggie platter in addition to the teeny wienies. The prep work session began with a directive about the best places to put the fresh flower arrangement, so I skipped ahead to the guest list.

The first ten women must have been Bethany's friends, as I didn't recognize any of them. The next five included names from my previous place of employment. I still talked to the receptionist on a semi-regular basis. If she'd been telling the truth in the breakroom, she had a remarkably adventurous sex life. She might show up to make sure there wasn't anything she was missing. The others were probably talking among themselves about the depths of depravity into which I'd fallen.

I breathed a sigh of relief when neither Elsie nor my mother made the cut. But the last two names threw me into a panic. I forgot all about my plan to keep quiet. I called Bethany and shouted at her when she answered.

"What were you thinking, inviting Ashley and Fiona?"

"Is it my fault that you don't have enough friends for a decent sex toy party? Seriously, girl, you need to expand your circles. Or in your case, find a circle."

"Oh, no. You're not turning this around on me like you always do. This is going to be a disaster, having Ryan's ex-fiancé and his widow in the same room. It wouldn't surprise if a cat fight broke out."

"Would that be so bad? But I bet neither one shows up. And if they do, they'll just sling backhanded compliments at each other until one or both develop eating disorders. But there's no reason for you to be so selfish."

"Selfish? What the hell are you talking about?"

"Since you're more or less a single woman yourself, I'm shocked at your lack of empathy for your sex-starved sisters. Why deny them the path to self-fulfillment?"

I groaned.

"And you should give me credit for not inviting that dreadful Porter person. It's not too late for me to send a last-minute email."

"I'd rather watch Ashley and Friona duke it out."

In case she wasn't bluffing about Sue Ann, I added, "I do appreciate you putting this together. Nobody does it better than you."

The rest of the week alternated between frustration and regret, which I discovered were basically two sides of the same trick coin. By the time Saturday morning arrived, I no longer dreaded the party. I didn't look forward to passing around warm-up glow from one sweaty-palmed woman to another, but at least it would be a distraction. And with no interesting cases and exhausting myself trying, unsuccessfully, to avoid crying over Mateo, I welcomed it.

The ladies weren't arriving until two, but Bethany came at noon to help. I hid the pigs-in-a-blanket under a frozen bag of Brussel sprouts, planning to stick them into the oven when my friend wasn't looking.

"I brought brie and honey, shrimp and veggie skewers, and baby bundt cakes, so don't bother trying to sneak out those miniature wieners. On second thought, cook those suckers. They might remind some of our guests that their husbands lean more toward tiny hotdogs than my newest, boldest product: the Stallion.”

She reached into her Vera Bradley duffel bag and removed a dildo of such exaggerated proportions I began to fear personal injury lawsuits from her new clients or alienation of affection filings.

“Keep that away from the food.”

“No worries. It’s fresh from the package. Speaking of packages, have you heard from that Latin stud?”

“He came by last night to discuss our relationship.” I could feel a flush traveling from my chest upward and tried to hide it by pulling my sweater higher. I wasn’t fast enough.

“I bet you did more than that, you naughty girl. I demand details.”

“After the party, please.”

She raised an eyebrow but agreed that after the festivities would be a better time to dissect my break-up or getting-back-together sex.

“And don’t let me forget to check out your previous purchase. I’m really surprised you’re having trouble with it. It’s a best seller.”

I’d almost forgotten about my glow-in-the dark dud but knew it was useless to tell her it didn’t matter to me whether it worked or not.

At one forty-five on the dot, the dining room table I inherited from Grandma Taylor held enough finger foods to feed a horde of pot-fueled teens. Elegant bottle chillers contained rose and white wine. A burgundy Merlot filled an oversized decanter.

Bethany set up her display in the den. Sixteen featured products sat on top of a folding table covered with a pink cloth. Her presentation included a brief description of what the devices promised to deliver. Once her guests were on the edge of their seats—or looking for a corner to crawl into in my case—she would expose each with a flourish. Then she would instruct me to assist in passing the product among them to increase levels of curiosity or terror.

I removed a bottle of backup white from the refrigerator and opened it.

"What are you doing?" Bethany's normally sultry voice rose to an unpleasantly shrill note. "Pour from the wine on the table and use the glass with your name stenciled on it."

"I don't need a glass." To demonstrate my point, I took a deep swig directly from the bottle. The doorbell saved me from another shriek of disapproval.

For the next ten minutes, clusters of two or three guests arrived. I gauged their level of discomfort based on the excitement they projected. A few of the hands I shook trembled with what I would call nerves; Bethany took it as a sign of sweet anticipation. Several wore stiff smiles and clung to their purses as if they wanted to be prepared to make a quick escape at the first hint the morality police were coming. I affected an air of calm, which came more easily than expected since I recently discovered a close connection between being in a state of relaxation and one of being in shock. There was also the wine.

At two ten, I breathed a sigh of relief. Both of my unwanted invitees struck me as punctual types. A teacher lives and dies by the bell. And Fiona seemed too well bred to arrive late. When the doorbell rang at twenty-five minutes past lift off, I fought back the panic that came from realizing my theories on my guests and their need for promptness was baseless. If I was wrong about something so simple, how many other misconceptions had I been operating under? And what might be the consequences?

CHAPTER 34

Ashley stood with her finger on the doorbell. Fiona lingered on the middle porch step, her lips drawn in an expression that might have been a smile or a grimace.

"Lucy, would you get that? We're all warmed up and ready to go."

Giggles followed her double entendre. I gritted my teeth and swung open the door.

"Ashley, Fiona. So good to see you both. Please, come in."

"I brought wine," Ashley said as I led her inside. I wanted to use the fancy living room no one ever sat in, but Bethany insisted the less formal setting of the den would put people more at ease. She believed relaxed customers tended to spend more, especially when her devices offered to relax them even more.

Fiona held out a sparkly bag. "In case someone's in the mood to celebrate."

I took it and removed a bottle of champagne, the expensive kind.

I guided the duo to the table and suggested they have something to eat and drink. Fiona headed straight for the wine, then sat next to a woman Bethany and I had gone to high school with. I couldn't remember her name and avoided introducing them by hanging with Ashley. For such a little person, the girl had an enormous sweet tooth.

She finished loading her plate with mini muffins, cinnamon rolls, and one pig in a blanket and scurried back to her seat to hear Bethany's spiel.

Her introduction brought with it a sense of déjà vu for the time Janelle accompanied me to a Sensual Secrets party. After she came to warn me Lance was dangerous, we formed a tenuous and temporary bond based on contempt for our ex-boyfriend. I invited her to be my guest. That night, I hid in the bedroom to escape the sales pitch. Today, as the hostess, I forced myself to participate in the fun.

Bethany started with her usual party trick. She passed around a warming gel and instructed everyone to squirt a small amount into our palms and wait for the heat. I wondered if the goo might help with my lower back pain.

Once we were properly fired up, she introduced an assortment of toys. Our leader began with a harmless-looking cylindrical toy smaller than a cell phone. Bethany promised no scams. She progressed to the Friends with Benefits model and culminated with the product of the year, the formidable Stallion. Audible gasps greeted our equestrian friend.

Phase three included a private consultation with the purveyor of pleasure. She had prepped my bedroom by laying out her merchandise on the bed. After a brief review of the products, including creams and gels, she sat beside her unsuspecting victims and sweet-talked them into revealing personal details geared to increase sales.

I was assigned the task of plying the rest of the group with alcohol, making them easier marks. They were doing a pretty good job themselves, freeing me to guzzle from my hidden bottle.

Voices from within the kitchen stopped me from entering. Reluctant to interrupt what could have been a private discussion about product selection, I peeked around the corner. Instead of discovering a saucy exchange over what to buy, I discovered Fiona and Ashley, one on each side of the granite island. They spoke in a conversational tone that would probably pass as harmless to the casual observer.

There was, however, nothing casual about the two women who had shared the same man, alone in a room filled with sharp objects. The safer option would be for me to join them, hoping my presence would ward off open hostilities. A few months ago, I would have intervened. Now? Not so much. So, rather than make a cheerful entrance, I remained out of sight to eavesdrop.

"At first, I hated you for stealing him from me. We were so perfect together. Of course, even in high school, he was a serial cheater. Back then, I assumed he'd change once we married. Later, I surprised myself with how little his indiscretions bothered me. My father played around, and my mother ignored it. Rather than taking vows of holy matrimony, they made a bargain. She maintained her social position and wealth. He did whatever or whoever he wanted. I accepted we'd have the same agreement. Then you came along."

She refilled her glass from a bottle of Jack Daniels Hugh gave me for Christmas. *Dammit!* Miss Fancy Pants had raided my liquor cabinet.

While Fiona slugged down my booze, Ashley spoke.

"I didn't know about his engagement when we met. I like to think it would have made a difference, but he was so charming. Then I got pregnant."

Fiona snorted bourbon out of her nose and erupted into a coughing spasm. Ashley waited for it to pass before continuing.

"Mrs. Miller called me a liar, but I was telling the truth. We lost the baby a month after the wedding." She turned away from Fiona to stare out the window. "Everybody said I tricked him into getting married, but we both wanted that child. Things might have been different if she hadn't died."

The finality of her words startled me. Like most people, I placed a miscarriage in its own category. It was more of a nonevent than a death. The tears welling in Ashley's eyes told me I'd been mistaken.

Fiona set down her drink, and I held my breath, hoping she would spare the other woman more harsh words. And, in a way, I suppose she did.

"I have troubling imagining Ryan as a father. Not that it's all his fault he was such a self-centered prick. His parents were the worst at being role models. And unlike you, I certainly would have made a terrible mother. Back to my original point. I stopped hating you about six months into your marriage. That's when he called me. Poor fool assumed my letting him into my bed meant I still loved him when the truth was I wanted to destroy him. My plan included exposing him for the lying bastard he was. Then a funny thing happened. Instead of being angry with either of you. I realized I couldn't care less, so I ended the affair."

Ashley swiped at her eyes and drained her glass of bourbon. "I knew he was cheating but didn't suspect it was with you. I found motel matches in his jacket pocket. At first, I thought he was smoking again and was worried he might get cancer. But his clothes and car weren't stinky. So, I went to that horrible place. The man behind the desk was disgusting, but I showed him Ryan's picture. He admitted he recognized him. Then I got him to describe the woman he'd been bringing there."

Bethany was going to flip out when I told her Ashley had gotten through to good old Earl when we hadn't.

"He said she looked like a country music singer with curly red hair and big boobs."

I jumped when, in unison, both women shouted, "Sue Ann Porter" and burst out laughing.

Fiona explained the teacher played a part in her breakup with Ryan. "I followed him to that same sleazy motel and waited until his tacky floozy joined him. Just for fun, I confronted him about her, and he swore they'd only had sex three or four times. Said he was finished with her and that stupid book she kept reading to him. The one with the horny owner of the manor and her nasty gardener."

Once again, the ladies spoke in unison, "*Lady Chatterley's Lover*" and broke into another round of giggling.

"He told me the same thing, and I was such a fool." Ashley wrinkled her nose. "After that, though, I had a hard time, uh, well, uh…"

"Reaching fulfillment?" Fiona offered, and both collapsed into gulping belly laughs.

I gave up on retrieving my bottle of wine and tiptoed back to the festivities.

. . .

"Your receptionist friend is a sexual dynamo. She cleaned me out of gel and ordered the Stallion and the Rocket. And she volunteered to host a party."

"You're welcome." I helped her refold the product table and take it to her mom's SUV.

We cleared the kitchen and shared sips of wine from my newly recovered bottle. I relayed the conversation between Ashley and Fiona as we worked.

"All's well that ends well, I suppose."

"Not so much for the Miller family," I reminded her.

"True, but don't you think their budding friendship is a testament to women everywhere?" Bethany ran a hand over her perfectly smooth hair.

"Not sure what you mean. Let's sit while you explain." I grabbed a bag of chips from the pantry and motioned for her to follow me into the den.

"It's simple." She propped her feet on the coffee table. "Imagine Ashley and Fiona were men fighting over the same woman. Can you see them drinking and laughing together about what fools they were? It'd never happen. You know why?" She crunched a chip. "Testosterone, that's why."

We spent the next few minutes discussing how the female psyche is superior to its male counterpart and how much better the world would be if we returned to a matriarchal society.

It was our turn to chime in at the same time with the disclaimer, "Not that we don't love men" and to enjoy our own moment of hilarity.

Then she suggested I bring out my inoperable toy, so she could check it out before bestowing me with my hostess gift. I sighed in resignation, then got the box from my bedside table. I carried it with both hands, much like the way one might an offering to an angry goddess.

She was struggling to take it apart when the doorbell rang.

"Probably somebody coming back to order more," I said.

But when I opened the door, no soon-to-be satisfied customer awaited me. It was Janelle Ragsdale, a pistol at the end of her right arm.

CHAPTER 35

Prison had not been kind to her. The creamy-skinned redhead who seduced my boyfriend was no longer either. Dark blotches across her cheeks and nose aged her by at least ten years. Someone, possibly a fellow inmate, had hacked off her long locks, and the perfect highlights were imperfect strands of dingy gray. If not for her flashing eyes and haughty demeanor, I wouldn't have recognized her.

"My invitation must have gotten lost in the mail, but I'm here now." Jolene waved the gun at me, and I stepped back. She motioned me inside.

When we reached the den, she smiled at Bethany and asked, "How's the dildo business?"

I braced myself for her usual response to what she referred to as a "crude misunderstanding of what amounted to a type of public service." She clinched her fists then released them. She might be passionate about the integrity of her calling, but she was more passionate about not getting shot.

She couldn't, however, resist a quick jab. "Not bad. How's the killing old men for money gig going?"

Janelle laughed and used her free hand to smooth back a greasy strand of hair from her face.

I took a beat to enjoy the image of our captor in the shower with industrial soap and saggy-breasted women. Small comfort but better than none.

"Things have been slow for me. But I didn't come here to talk business."

My moment of gloating over the shitty life she'd been living empowered me enough to ask, "Why are you here?"

"Have a seat and I promise to tell you everything although you may wish I hadn't."

We settled close to each other on the sofa. Janelle took a few backward steps in the direction of the recliner without glancing away from us.

"Instead of story time where I do all the talking, let's have a little Q and A. You toss me a question, and I'll decide whether to answer or not."

The obvious question was what she'd hidden in my place. But that would be what she expected. I wanted to take her by surprise, to change whatever plan she had for us. So, I went with what I saw as her biggest vulnerability—Roberta.

"I've been wondering how you arranged Roberta's *suicide*."

"Why, Lucy Howard, I didn't realize you had such a nasty little mind. I like it, so I won't pretend not to know what you're talking about. Believe it or not, I got no joy from the woman's death. Unfortunately, she was decidedly unreliable. And confinement brought out the worst in her. One of the orderlies is a close friend of mine. He warned me Roberta was starting to talk about things she shouldn't. We decided her depression was worsening, and suicide was the only to end her pain."

"I thought you and she shared a genuine passion. It sounds as if arranging her murder barely annoyed you."

A flash of rage tightened her lips and created red blotches on her cheeks. For a second, I feared I'd gone too far. But the flicker of anger disappeared so quickly, I wasn't certain it had been there.

She smiled serenely, her calm pause frightening me as much as her deadly focus.

Her eyes shifted to the box containing my purple vibrator. "I can't believe it's this easy. Lucy, dear, how about you move that closer to me, please?"

"You want my vibrator?"

"When you put it that way, it sounds so dirty. But yes. And I want it now."

I pushed it toward her.

"Wait. It takes two hands to open this. You do it."

My entire body shook as I removed what my friend referred to as the device of desire.

"You need a screwdriver," Bethany offered.

I volunteered there was one in the kitchen drawer, and Janelle ordered her to get it.

"Don't try anything funny, or I'll have to shoot her."

I appreciated how quickly she returned. Then I unscrewed the battery slot.

"That's weird," I said, while shaking the dildo like an awkward maraca. "Something's stuck in there."

"Did you not even check the batteries before you told me it wasn't working?" Bethany scowled at me.

"I was going to, but—"

"Shut up!" I fell back into the sofa in alarm at Janelle's violent shift in tone and volume. I stayed shut as she reached for the vibrator. She sat on the edge of the recliner and held the massive fake penis between her knees.

If our circumstances had been less terrifying, I would have ventured a tasteless remark about the way she looked. But the best I could do was aim a raised eyebrow in Bethany's direction. She flashed me a half-lipped grin. The snarky exchange made me feel oddly better.

"Now ease the screwdriver over to me." She stuck the end of it into the opening and rooted around for a few seconds before dragging out a small rectangular object. A key.

"I hid it in the one place you'd never look because a tight-ass girl like you would never go through the batteries in her dildo."

All the times Lance called me uptight rushed through my brain. Everything from refusing to pose for naked pictures to nixing a threesome earned me the title. I was certain her use of the word was no coincidence. The smirk on her face confirmed my suspicion that my ex-boyfriend and she had shared a laugh about how repressed I was.

"I am not uptight," I screamed before throwing myself across the table into Janelle's lap. Unlike Mrs. Miller, she kept a firm grip on her weapon and backhanded me with it. From a seated position, she failed to garner enough momentum to do more than stun me, cut my forehead, and land me on the floor, where I rolled away from her and rose to my knees. But she was too quick.

"I'd love to stay and play, but people are waiting for me. It's time to say goodbye."

The room spun as I sat on my heels and stared at the gun in her hands. I tried to speak, to tell her she didn't have to do this, but Lance's ex-girlfriend's relationship with logic was shaky at best. She hated losing, and although I lost Lance to her, I had bested her in the game of life. I raised my eyes in time to see a blurred object moving from behind her. The last thing I remember was the thud of the Stallion colliding with the back of Janelle's head.

. . .

Apparently, my assailant hit me harder than I thought because, other than a brief moment of clarity in the ambulance, I was out until waking up alone in a hospital bed.

A thick fog clouded my brain, and a moderately dense one affected my vision. When I opened my eyes, a voice drifted from above.

"Are you awake, honey?"

Please don't be an angel, I begged. I wasn't ready to join the heavenly choir. Or worse, face the humiliation of being tossed into the smoky pit.

My plea must have been an internal one as the fuzzy being leaning over me continued to speak in her other worldly whisper.

"Lucy, wake up, dear."

Definitely not a celestial being. It was my mother demanding I rise and shine the same way she'd done throughout my childhood. Although she didn't use that exact request, her words propelled me to my room with its twin bed and pale pink walls. Tears filled my eyes before tumbling down my cheeks.

"Are you in pain?" Without waiting for a response, Mom raced to me, holding the call button. She pushed it until a woman answered.

She shouted that her daughter was hurting and needed immediate relief. When I grabbed at the arm with the remote, she pushed me away and continued to elaborate on my non-existent agony.

After adjusting into a sitting position, my head began to ache, so I accepted the pain pills. Mom barraged me with questions she didn't give me a chance to answer while I waited for the meds to kick in.

"Baby, did you hear what I said?"

"Sorry, I'm a little woozy."

"Of course you are. I'll just tell your friend to come back later."

I bolted upright, sending a real stab of pain into my eye. "Who's here?"

"That lovely man of yours. The doctors don't want you to have more than one visitor at a time, and he didn't find out you'd been hurt until an hour ago. If I had his contact information, I would have called him as soon as we found out."

If I'd given her Mateo's number, she would have tricked him into religious counseling before enlisting his help with wedding planning

I ignored the passive-aggressive treatment and asked her to tell my visitor I would like to see him. The words didn't come close to expressing my emotions.

"I'll send him in."

"Wait, Mom. Do you have a brush and maybe some makeup?" The woman never went anywhere without her "touch-up kit."

"Here, let me."

Normally, I hate having anyone mess with my face. Today, the way she hummed a nameless tune as she dabbed concealer under my eyes before applying foundation and blush had a ritualistic manner to it. I was a princess being prepared for ascending to a higher level.

When she handed me the hairbrush, I took it as if it were a scepter. She seemed to sense the aura surrounding us. My mother smiled, kissed me on the head, and left without a word. An unfamiliar emotion came over me. For the first time in I don't know how long, I wished she would stay. I closed my eyes, surprised when a lone teardrop escaped. *Get a grip*, I told myself. *It's not like she's never coming back.*

A gentle tapping on the door put an end to further exploration of my sudden fear of mortality. His voice softly calling my name flooded me with joy. Our reunion was a tearful one. No surprise since my second near death encounter in a matter of days rendered me a sobbing fool. He kissed me through the tears and wiped my nose when it turned our romantic interlude into a snotty mess.

"Hugh told me what happened. How Janelle tried to kill you." His voice broke, and he squeezed the hand he'd been holding from the time he sat on the edge of my bed. "My God, Lucy. I don't know what I would do if I lost you. If you want to take things slow—"

A loud knock and the entrance of a bald man in a white coat stopped him from finishing. My muddled mind didn't register the doctor's name when he introduced himself. He began providing elaborate details on how the brain works after a concussion. I started to ask him *what concussion* before it registered with me. I was the concussed one.

After explaining they wanted to keep me another twenty-four hours for observation, he rattled off a list of possible side effects.

"This is a printout of my instructions." He handed it to Mateo. "Your husband can hang onto it. I'll see you tomorrow."

He disappeared so quickly neither of us had the chance to correct his assumption we were married. A nurse barged in to announce it was time to check my vitals. She gave Mateo a piercing look.

"I guess I better go and let these people take care of you." He touched his lips to mine. "But I'll be back for as long as you'll have me."

CHAPTER 36

After lunch, Bethany persuaded my mother to let her keep watch over me for a few hours while Mom rested. Then she confirmed my assumption that she whacked Janelle over the head with the Stallion. Unfortunately, the wild horse had sustained serious damage during the attack. The good news was Sensual Secrets headquarters were thrilled that one of their products had helped take down a murderer. They told her to return the hero free of charge and were working on a marketing angle.

She surprised me with her humble attitude regarding her status as a heroine.

"I did what anyone would if some psycho was about to kill her best friend. Honestly, I don't even remember grabbing the Stallion." She grinned. "But I'll never forget the sound that bad boy up against the side of her head."

Elsie and Hugh arrived within minutes of each other.

"Cody Rae wanted to come, but she and Danny are at his house working on a project." She responded to my skeptical look with a quick disclaimer. "His mother's back home."

My boss told me what happened to Janelle after I zonked out. "The bitch ended up with a concussion, too. Now she's claiming memory loss. Nobody's buying it."

"What about her attorney, Simon Elliot?"

"Mr. Elliot won't be trying cases anywhere. Partly because he wasn't a lawyer in the first place. Mainly because his body washed up on the shore of Lake Lanier. The holes in his head seem to be from the same gun our lady killer planned to use on you."

"Does that mean the police haven't found out who was in charge of the smuggling ring?"

"Oh, they got the top guy. Only it turns out it's the top gal. Our little Miss Janelle was the mastermind of the whole thing. Or should I say mistress-mind to be politically correct?"

I told him there was no reason for him to start now.

"Very funny. I guess you're not interested in what the key was all about."

I apologized and begged him to continue.

"It really was to a security box with a bunch of records in it. Nothing that would send her to prison longer than multiple murder convictions but enough evidence to prove she was the one calling the shots. I think part of the reason for involving you with the hidden key was she loved screwing with your head. Ironic I guess, since that's what got her caught."

I was pondering whether the situation met the definition of irony when Mom called to tell me my father would be taking the night shift. I insisted that wasn't necessary. "It's hard enough sleeping with nurses coming in every two hours to make sure I'm still alive. Then there's all the moaning and groaning seeping in from my neighbors' rooms. If Dad comes, I'll worry about him trying to sleep on that miserable pullout. I promise I will be fine on my own."

Hugh fidgeted in a chair, clearly made for someone with less girth. I gave him permission to leave.

"How are you really doing?" Elsie asked when the room emptied. She had first-hand knowledge of going up against an armed assailant. At the time, my parents wanted me to see a counselor, but I refused. My second encounter with Janelle had been different. Literally, up close and in my face.

"It hasn't hit me yet."

"Let me know when it does, so I can be there for you. On a happier note, Helen Miller is currently residing in the psyche ward at Grady. It's a decent hospital but a far cry from one of the fancy places she's used to."

I shook my head and took a few petty seconds to enjoy the image of Madam High Society in pajamas with no ties.

"Hard to care about a mother who could do such a terrible thing."

Neither could I. Mom might drive me nuts, but she wouldn't think twice about throwing herself in front of an approaching locomotive if it meant protecting me.

"I tell you who I do pity. Big Ron Porter. According to Kanisha, his wife hit the road as soon as she got wind of the moral standards investigation. At least he won't have to worry about her murdering his puppies. He left a message on his machine asking if he could see you tomorrow. Said he had a surprise."

Other than a case of his favorite beer, I had no idea what he might be bringing. The memory of his forlorn face as he slumped against the tree, wondering if Sue Ann would recover from her fury came to me.

"Would you call and tell him it's okay if he wants to stop by after one?"

Elsie volunteered to join us if I was uncomfortable about seeing him alone.

"Are you kidding me? Nothing could be weirder than watching the Stallion take down Janelle. Plus, I promised to let Mom bring me home and fix lunch. She'll be thrilled to hang out."

. . .

My mother and Ron hit it off so well she began matchmaking as soon as he was gone.

"Give the guy a minute to catch his breath. He just broke up with who he thought would be the love of his life. Didn't you hear him say he's headed to the mountains to clear his head?"

"*Love of his life?* She doesn't sound like a prize, and he can't stay there forever. I'm sure when he comes back, he'll be ready for some female companionship."

I couldn't argue with that, so I listened to her prospective candidates, nodding enthusiastically. After a few minutes, she threw up her hands and marched to the door.

"I can tell when someone's humoring me."

"Wait, Mom. I mean it. They all sound good."

She smiled. "I've got to get your father's dinner started. And I don't blame you a bit for not being able to concentrate. Not with that adorable man coming over tonight. Enjoy your surprise together."

. . .

I spent over thirty minutes picking out the perfect outfit, one that said *I'm sorry for being a jerk* and *I want to make it up to you*. Like a penitent sex symbol. I settled on black leggings that weren't quite as tight as they'd been a few weeks ago, and a burgundy silk tunic. At the last minute, I took off my bra, then put it on again. No reason to look like a penitent hooker.

Mateo arrived at seven on the dot. His dark navy jeans hung looser, too. We'd both been on the breakup diet. Suddenly, I was very hungry.

"I didn't know if you liked flowers more than chocolates, so I got both. Oh, and this." He held up a bottle of my favorite white wine, the kind I saved for special occasions,

"Perfect decision. Why don't you take a seat in the den while I put these in a vase and pour us a glass? Hold on to the candy for later."

After taking care of the flowers, I checked the lasagna, not knowing what it was supposed to look like since it was Mom's recipe and I'd never made it before. It wasn't black or smoking, so I turned the oven off and left it to stay warm. Next, I poured the wine.

"I have a surprise for you, too. But first, a toast."

"To us," I said. He repeated it. We clinked our glasses and sipped. Rather, he sipped; I gulped, needing lots of liquid courage.

"There are three parts to my gift, and not all are exactly gifts."

"The suspense is killing me." He put his arm around my shoulder.

"Okay. I hope it wasn't too presumptuous, but I invited your mother and father over for dinner next Sunday."

He set his glass on the end table. "Seriously? My mother's probably calling her family in Mexico right now. Dad will be thrilled, too. But Mom's the one who thought I'd never settle down. Shit! I didn't mean to scare you. We don't have to live together or get married or anything like that. I'm not pushing you."

I shushed him. "You're stepping on part two of my surprise. Nothing would make me happier than having you move back in until we can find a bigger place, one with both our names on thedeed."

"Are you sure, Lucy? Because I can't do this again. Be apart from you, not knowing where I stand."

"I have something to show you that should set your mind at ease about my level of commitment. Sit here and close your eyes. Don't open them until I say."

He obeyed, and I rushed to the sunroom off the back porch, where Big Ron's gift waited for me. She propelled herself onto my legs and slid down to bite my shoe. I scooped her up. Six pounds of fluffy black and white poodle-terrier, the runt of his spoiled litter. She covered my neck and chin with warm, wet kisses.

When we reached the den, I called out to remind him to keep his eyes closed. I sat beside him, holding the squirming bundle inches from his face.

"Okay, open them."

He blinked a few times, then flashed his killer grin before wrapping his hands around the puppy and pressing her to his chest.

"Who is this little sweetheart?"

"Meet the last of Big Ron's Jack Russell terrier offspring. He let Sue Ann have the house in the divorce settlement and is taking a break from breeding. Since the litter was spoiled, he sold the puppies for what he'd spent on shots and stuff. Nobody was interested in her."

"How the hell could anybody resist you? Wait. Does this mean what I think it does?"

"Yep. We've adopted a dog together."

He put the pup on the floor and threw his arms around me. Kissing him was like coming home.

"Does she have a name?"

"Penelope."

"Penelope? Interesting choice." The puppy emitted a series of high-pitched yelps. He picked her up and ran his fingertips across her fuzzy coat.

"It's from the Odyssey. Elsie mentioned it, and I had no idea what she was talking about. So, I looked it up. One of the main characters is Penelope, the loyal wife who waited twenty years for her husband to return. This little girl saw her litter mates disappear one by one until she was all alone. But nothing dampened her spirits because, deep in her heart, she knew we were coming. Like her Greek namesake, she stayed strong."

Our tiny heroine nestled between my breasts. Mateo took her from me and brought her close to his face. "You're trespassing on my territory."

In reply, she bit his nose.

"Oh no. Not another feisty female." She wriggled until he put her down. Then she snatched Mr. Pickle, her loudest squeaky toy, and curled up on the rug.

"Raising a dog is serious business," he said over the bleats of the gherkin in the pup's mouth. "I'd hate for her to grow up in a broken home."

"I have mathematical proof that will never happen."

"As I remember, you and math aren't exactly best friends."

I shushed him before explaining my theory.

"The heroine of the Odyssey stayed faithful to her husband for twenty years. In a dog's life, that translates to one hundred and forty. I think you would agree that equates to a lifetime and then some. Hence, I will spend a lifetime with you."

"I don't have a clue what that was, but it sure as hell wasn't math." He pulled me in for a gentle kiss. "It was much more interesting than geometry or algebra or calculus. And despite your unusual methodology, you landed on the solution to the equation. The only problem is a lifetime of loving you isn't long enough."

He tilted my chin and touched my lips with his fingertip. I closed my eyes, anticipating the warmth of his lips on mine.

Instead, a furry ball of puppy leaped onto my lap. She alternated covering each of our faces with doggy kisses.

"Nobody said family life would be easy." Mateo subdued Penelope in a full body lock and rubbed her belly until she went limp with pleasure. "But I promise you I'll spend all my time making sure every tomorrow will be better than the day before."

ABOUT THE AUTHOR

Katherine Nichols is the award-winning author of Southern suspense with heart and humor. The protagonists in all six of her novels are strong women who don't always recognize their own strength. A vice president of The Atlanta Writers Club, Katherine also serves on the board of Sisters in Crime Atlanta. As a strong proponent of women authors supporting each other, Katherine co-hosts the inspirational *Wild Women Who Write Take Flight* podcast. When she isn't spending time with her children and grandchildren, she loves to read, walk, and travel. She lives in Lilburn, Georgia with her husband, two rescue dogs, and two rescue cats.

KATHERINE
NICHOLS
A LUCY HOWARD MYSTERY
FALSE
CLAIMS
LIES IN LOVE AND INSURANCE

NOTE FROM KATHERINE NICHOLS

Word-of-mouth is crucial for any author to succeed. If you enjoyed *Canceled Policies*, please leave a review online—anywhere you are able. Even if it's just a sentence or two. It would make all the difference and would be very much appreciated.

Thanks!
Katherine Nichols

We hope you enjoyed reading this title from:

www.blackrosewriting.com

Subscribe to our mailing list – *The Rosevine* – and receive **FREE** books, daily
deals, and stay current with news about upcoming
releases and our hottest authors.
Scan the QR code below to sign up.

Already a subscriber? Please accept a sincere thank you for being a fan of
Black Rose Writing authors.

View other Black Rose Writing titles at
www.blackrosewriting.com/books and use promo code
PRINT to receive a **20% discount** when purchasing.